**LIGHTNIN' BUG
PUBLISHING**

Other Books by James L. Fortuna, Jr.

Available now from Lightnin' Bug Publishing:

The Gator and the Holy Ghost
and Other Stories of a Slightly Reconstructed South

Forthcoming novels:

A Rumor of Appomattox

Hell Broke Loose in Georgia

A Burning of Ducks and Other Stories

by

James L. Fortuna, Jr.

a

Lightnin' Bug

Book

Statesville, North Carolina

A Burning of Ducks

First Print Publication, Lightnin' Bug Publishing, 2015

ISBN-13: 978-0-6923629-1-4

A Lightnin' Bug Book

Lightnin' Bug Publishing
Statesville, NC 28625
Lightninbug@att.net

Dedication

For the Folks in Duval County, Florida: Family, Friends, and Foes.

Table of Contents

Introduction

In 1951, to a class of Mississippi high school graduates, William Faulkner said, "Never be afraid to raise your voice for honesty and truth and compassion against injustice and lying and greed." The book you hold in your hand (or which is held for you in the electronic bowels of your e-reading device) contains the fearless, honest, and compassionate voice of my friend James L. Fortuna, Jr. Fortuna's stories illustrate imaginatively, vigorously, and honestly the struggles of his generation to assimilate cultural change. Often alluding to and sometimes wading to the chin in matters of faith, fear, anger, and disorientation, Fortuna's sense of justice permeates these tales and dares his readers to deal honestly with their own secret fears and prejudices. He was not in that room with Faulkner that day in Mississippi, but he heard the challenge all the same. The world is better for it.

I hope you enjoy these stories as much as I have, but more importantly, I hope you accept their challenge to confront injustice and absurdity in our world with the same honesty and compassion as their author.

Christopher Allenby, November 2014

Some Do, Some Don't

The sign outside said "Lola's Quick Eats," but inside the first thing Robin Marvin saw was a good-sized, full-horned Satyr, hooves and hairy legs and all, dancing back near the rest-rooms on what looked to be a solid oak stage, back where the air was smoky and pale yellow and filled with floating puffs of dust. Robin had been in the Quick Eats many times the past half-dozen years, but the Satyr was new. Lola didn't seem to notice anything but her newspaper. A half-gone cigarette was sending up a spiral of smoke from the dented metal ashtray beside her at the counter. Robin worked for Cumberland Trucking, long-haul, heading north to Detroit, and had needed to take a piss for the past half-hour, but there had been nowhere to stop as the shoulders of the highway got narrower and narrower and finally broadened out again just a half-mile from the Quick Eats. He usually only stopped there on his way back down south, but this time he decided it would be best to pull off and piss indoors. Lola turned from her paper and reached for the cigarette, pulling long and hard before putting it out in a coil of near-white smoke that curled up into what seemed to be a faded "NO SMOKING" sign. There were no customers in the place— tables and booths empty—too early (4:00 A.M.) for anyone but the stray trucker and, of course, the Satyr. Its dance was nearly a Celtic clog, but Lola didn't seem to even notice the steady drumming of hooves on solid oak. Robin was about to leave when she finally left off reading and looked up, smiling, and slowly licking her lips.

"Well hello, honey." Her teeth were nearly gone in the front and the streaked red of her hair hung in limp strands atop her over-sized ears. "Ain't seen you in a while."

"Yeah." Robin glanced again at the Satyr and came closer to the counter. The dance was loud and occasionally there seemed to be a kind of flute noise in among it all. "Hey—look—what you got going on back there?" Robin really had to piss, and Lola was making him un-easy.

"Do what?" Lola tried to smile, but her lips seemed slightly stuck together.

"Back there," Robin jerked a thumb in the general direction of the Satyr.

"Oh yeah. Yeah. That's new. Installed it about a month ago now. Been real good for business. Goes on twenty-four/seven. Never runs down. Wait'll you see this place breakfast shift! And, honey, the din-ner crowd is pure tee something else. Yes sir, it is." And the smile finally broke through, jagged front teeth and all and a touch of red-ness out around the upper gums. "Where you headed this time, sug-ar?"

"Detroit."

"De-troit, huh? Cold up there. Need to stay down here where it's warm, baby. You want anything?" She reached for another cigarette and then changed her mind, dropping it back into a dented case. "Coffee?"

"Yeah—gotta go to the gents, but yeah, coffee's ok." He watched as Lola stood up and moved down the counter toward the row of steaming coffee pots. "But what's with the dancer? For real." Robin could see the Satyr slow down a bit and begin to nibble at a bunch of grapes, dancing now more delicately and very close to the edge of the stage.

"Trying to keep up with the times. Y'know? And it works cheap—service contract takes care of most everything 'cept the grapes. It does like its grapes." Lola returned with a full mug of coffee, steam rolling around the rim. "At first it just came whenever it wanted to. Mostly on Mondays."

"But it's Wednesday." Robin saw the Satyr toss the half-eaten bunch of grapes into the nearby wall where they bounced and fell straight down onto the floor.

"Well that was before it settled in. They tell you all about that stuff in the renter's manual—he's a 401K-Model—all kinds of special stuff is in there, buddies—but, bottom line is that it needs to get broke in and then it just stays until it wears out or something. Not real clear on that. Alls I know is that it's been real good for business."

"Where does it sleep?"

"Well, near as I can tell, it don't. It just keeps doin' what it does. Sometimes we have a band in here to help, but it don't need nothing to get it jumping. It just pure tee jumps all by its lonesome." And Lola tried to smile again, thought better of it, and nudged the coffee mug closer to Robin.

"Why does it dance?"

"I dunno, sugar. Ask it yourself."

Robin walked quickly toward the restrooms, passing close by the dancing Satyr, and at one point, just before the door marked "MEN," he looked full into its eyes, beady slits that seemed to pulsate above shrunken cheeks and a chin that came to a shriveled point and a mouth, grape-stained and slightly vicious-looking, teeth all seemingly filed to a point like a shark. Its hooves kept on tapping out a rhythm like some Irish reel gone seriously wrong. Robin felt like it was reaching out for him somehow, while it danced, its fingers hairy and nails long and jagged. And there was a mechanical hum there somewhere down in it all, not strong but just there, a thrumming in a rhythm like the beating of a heart. It finally grinned and almost caught Robin as he crashed into the restroom door. Inside, the Satyr's dancing sounded even louder, but it felt good to finally piss.

The Satyr was sitting on the trashcan when Robin finished washing his hands in a very grimy sink. The Satyr was smiling, a pointed-tooth grin that made its eyes disappear. And then it spoke, a hiss there at first followed by gulping sounds and a kind of gurgling chuckle. "Wanna dance?" The rhythmic thrumming was louder now, an almost proper heartbeat rising up amid the mostly silence of the room.

"What?" Robin moved quickly to the door. The Satyr kept sitting on the trashcan, hooves now drumming on the sides, making a kind of hollow stage boom and rumble in accompaniment to what could still be heard of what might be a living heart.

"Dance. You. Me. Dance?" And the thrumming fell away as did the drumming hooves and in their place a sound of whirring, clicking gears came clear, the Satyr back down on the floor and holding out his hairy arms and reaching for a partner new to hold.

Robin left the restroom almost in a single leap that bumped open the door and made it slam a few times against the wall. And when he finally returned to the counter, Lola was wiping it down with a greasy rag.

"Oh, hon, your coffee's done got cold. But did you like your dance?" She dropped the cloth out of sight.

"Do--do people really—do—do they dance with that damned thing?" Robin glanced over his shoulder and thought he saw a shadow floating around in the smoky darkness near the stage.

"Some do, some don't." Lola lit up another cigarette. "More coffee, honey?"

The Elders at Play

I make no excuses. None. And I want that much understood here and now and over and done with. What I did *was* wrong, of course. And I suppose I knew it to be wrong while I was doing it—when I did it and it was done—when it was finished and past any hope or chance of recall. I make no excuses for that—for the thing I *did* do. It was all a mistake anyway. Simply that. A clear case of the wrong place, wrong time, and me. A mistake, an overreaction to something that (I have been told repeatedly) *normal* people would have either ignored or dealt with in a similarly civilized manner. Would have found a better way of resolving than the one I finally chose. The one that got me in the fix I'm in today. And they, those people—my wife and my doctor and Sergeant of Police Busby in particular—are right, correct, steady on course and true to the core. I *know* that now. Oh boy do I ever know it!

So—I was wrong. I shouldn't have done *it* (the thing I did do) and that much is clear. As for the rest, the things I did *not* do (and no matter how many times I am told I *did* do them), I take no responsibility whatsoever. And I stand on that, so help me God and foursquare against the recent testimony (slander) of certain unnamed members of the Briar Bluffs Community Watch. And, besides, who is in the better position of knowing what *I* did or did not do (and the reasons *why* as well)—me or them? Right.

I think it all started with the building permit. The act of granting the Bide-Awhile Rest Homes, Inc. the right to interject a battalion of senior citizens into the theretofore quiet and undeveloped fastness of the Prescott Woods. The Woods border Briar Bluffs, *my* community, the place where I sleep and eat and make house payments—the neat and gated socio-economically standardized slice of the American Dream I chose (with the full and eager consent of my wife) above all others as fitting ground on which to raise our family (at present two undersized twin boys with very bad skin, and who seemingly are in desperate need of intense tutoring in geometry). Briar Bluffs. Yes. That land was my land. From the Prescott "Forest" to the Okra River. From the Royal Club House to the Glenn Springs Beltway. And then the permit was granted—perhaps on a storm-drenched afternoon, the Town Hall far too cozy and the Zoning Board too full of lunch, cozy and dozing just enough to let the Visigoths get by the outer wall. Awake too late. Too late alert and fixed for combat by the time the chainsaws whined and the bulldozers whomped and popped and cut into the virgin soil—too *too* late when hammers started in to whack-a-whack-a-whack away the morning's peace. Too late, too late by then.

NB: My wife does not agree, of course. *She* somehow blames my lack of patience with our sons. And my job and sleep disorder and the bourbon that she sometimes empties in the kitchen sink. She also told the Magistrate I'd needed help for years.

But that comes later, on the FATAL NIGHT itself, and doesn't shed much light on anything worth seeing. We're after *causes* here and permit-day is still the one for me. It started there and then, the Bide-Awhile, Inc. horde swooped down like locusts on our beauty and our peace, *per-mitted* in like vampires through an open door or window, free to suck away the juices and leave behind a shriveled husk of how things used to be. Oh *yes* it started there! And raised up quick a yellow stuccoed mess that sprawled along the fringes of my cul-de-sac down in what trees were left, a port-holed capsized cement ship aground and clashing with our neo-Tudor theme, in wanton insult to the houses of our dreams as deep as if a trailer park had clattered in to stay.

NB: My wife is not particularly troubled by any of this. And the neighbors didn't seem to mind either. Ignoring both the cement ship and old folks shuffling up and down our lanes. But not a one of *them* (the neighbors and my wife) had seen the things *I* saw. And I want *that* understood.

Enough of this special-pleading. Enough preliminaries. I will tell it straight. Perfectly straight. Without the further cluttering of a stage already jammed and jostled, crammed as tight as it can be by doctors, cops, reporters and a sad-eyed magistrate, a stage full to overflowing with a loving family deep in shock and every precious senior on the Good Ship Bide-Awhile. I'll tell it straight. And *facts* can do this best, I think. Straight facts and given clean—the pertinent players all in order introduced—mixed well inside a narrative-thrust, strong from first to last with special spotlights cast upon beginning and the very end. So just forget the *distant* causes—the Big-Sleep of the Zoning Board, the pens set scraping on the permit page. The computer beeps and clicks to lock it in. Forget the rising up of ugliness out there in the Prescott Woods (the yellow cement-and-stuccoed capsized ship). Forget (although I haven't introduced it yet) my coming trial on charges of assault and other things (tomorrow morning, 9:00 A.M. in Room 5-B of Superior Court of the County of San Cristobel, San Cristobel-by-the-Sea, Florida). And lastly—pay no heed at all to my suspension as department head, the best one Psycho-History *ever* had, a gap they'll never fill at General Gaines, the college *Where the Student Is a Friend.* Clear away all that and try to focus on the *straight* of *it* instead, the thing I *did* do, the mistake I made, the turning that I took and causes near at hand that brought me to the *where* I am today.

Facts: God yes! And how I love them every one.

FACT: *The first morning was hot and muggy and our air-conditioning unit was nearly dead.*

This is important because the day got started wrong and never quite recovered. Breakfast—no—even *before* breakfast there was trouble stirring in the barely moving air. In fact (yes!) the previous night (and never mind the three stiff drinks I had when I got home from work), the night itself, the bedroom part was nightmare-riddled sleeping or awake—the floating faces of the old folks that I passed each day, the shrunken bodies on parade across my dreams just like the ones who used our street. But mostly there was a screech of cats (well, *one* cat then for sure)—a mewing, shrieking, yowl of cat-noise loud enough to cover up the snores my wife put out. And I had slept a naptime close to dawn and then went on to break my favorite shaving mug and cut my little finger on a shard of frosted glass. The Band-Aid box was empty and I came downstairs with toilet paper wrapped around my hand. And bloodstains on my shirt. And Katie Lynn, my wife was burning up the toast again. I'll give you how it sounded then—there in the kitchen-heat with breadsmoke curling everywhere and Katie Lynn nose-deep in what the paper had to say. *I* said the thing most reasonable to say:

"The toast!"

"Oh! Oh—sorry—there—I'll make more—what happened to *you*?"

"I cut my finger."

"I can see that—how did—"

"Never mind. Where are the boys?"

"Finishing up their homework."

"At seven o'clock in the morning? Why haven't—"

"They *tried* to do it last night but the geometry was a problem. They waited up to see *you*. An hour past their bedtime."

"I couldn't help that. Departmental evaluation meetings always—"

"So they're finishing it this morning. Doing the best they can. It's terrible to see them under so much pressure. Childhood should be a time for—"

"Did you say geometry?"

"Yes."

"What's their problem?"

"They don't believe in it."

"What?"

"They don't believe it's real."

"Real? Shit. What in hell are you—"

"James!"

"Real? Geometry, right?"

"Yes."

"Real?"

"Yes."

"Why didn't you handle this one? My God, Katie—why didn't you just take care of it last night?"

"I don't believe in it either. I never have."

"What?"

"It's the *why*, I think. Why it works the way they say it works. In the textbook. There's never enough to go on. I read it several times and it still made no sense."

We're staying here but only for a little way, a necessary side-trip just to *show* the texture of the day: Hot, muggy, air-conditioning nearly gone, kitchen windows open (the breadsmoke, remember?), a night's sleep ruined by Bide-Awhiles and cat-screech, yowl and mew, a broken favorite shaving mug and early morning loss of blood (and just a little taste of bourbon pushing through the toothpaste tingle on my tongue), the toast like coal-chips, and a wife and two sons who don't believe in geometry. The picture is not pretty. The scene is not hopeful. My life seemed teetered on the brink of madness when the boys came in and settled down to eat. They mostly mumbled at first. But I caught enough to hold to.

"You don't have to *shout* at them."

"I'm *not* shouting—I'm simply trying to make myself understood. Axioms. Since you mentioned them, let's just take that much. An Axiom. Do you hear me?"

"The whole street hears you, James. That elderly gentleman out there on the sidewalk just jumped. I think you frightened him."

"Axioms. Do you even know what an axiom *is*? Do you at least know *that*?" They both looked at my wife and almost nothing makes me angrier than that. And they know it does. They all know this. The day was getting worse and worse.

"Don't look at *her*—don't *do* that when I'm talking to you. Dammit—don't you do—"

"More toast, James?"

And here is as good a place as any to stop and take a step backwards—not a side-trip exactly but every bit as necessary here (especially since this *straight fact* approach and *strong narrative-thrust* is becoming more difficult than I had imagined.) So—step back and *look*—the physical description—an oversight, yes, but an easy one to remedy—the *what* we all looked "like"—no—our *physical appearance* or our *pertinent details* perhaps sounds better. *Physical Appearance (and other* pertinent *details) of the Home Team* (after which we will proceed to the *what* all this has to do with the "it" I did and things I did not do):

(1). ME—James Conlon: Age 42; Height—5'11" (or 5'10" or 6' even depending on time of day and footwear); Hair—brown (very short); Eyes—green; Weight—over 200 pounds last year; Skin—mostly clear but tending to blotch in places reddish-pink; Occupation—Chairman of the—but I've told you that already.

(2). MY WIFE—Katie Lynn Conlon (nee Pagliano): Age 38; Height—5'5" (all the time it seems): Hair—black; eyes—brown; Weight—negligible; Skin—what used to be called 'olive' --deep tan all year round; Occupation—physical-therapist-housewife (she insists on the housewife part, and even hyphenates in general conversation).

(3). THE TWINS—Ben and Brad/Or—Brad 'n' Ben—like Chip 'n' Dale, there are only dental differences: Ages—ca. 12; Heights/Weights—undersized to my way of thinking; Hair—brown; Eyes—brown; Skin—mottled; Occupations—students at Peace Market Middle School and God only knows what else. And back to:

"Axioms! Well? Speak!"

"The book says—" Ben or Brad—I think it was *Brad* (the one with the big teeth) who spoke, softly, almost in a whisper.

"I don't care what the *book* says! What do *you* say? What do you think an axiom is?"

"Don't browbeat them, James."

"I'm not browbeating any—"

"A a—ass-summation."

"What?"

"Axiom." Brad again and—no, Ben that time—no teeth in my memory— Ben. "A axiom is a ass-summation—"

"Well—OK—*assumption*—it's an assumption. And what *does that* mean?"

"It starts things."

"What?"

"Starts—it starts things—"

"Well—yes—a beginning. Yes. So what's the problem?"

"But—but where does it come from?"

"That doesn't matter."

"But—but why?"

"Because—because it's just given—dammit you don't need to know *why*—it—it just *is*!"

"But—" A whine of brotherhood with both together now, big teeth and small and wife gone scraping up the latest toast—

"But where did *it* come from?"

"For God's sake—you—you—dammit all—God—"

"James!" And both boys out the door for school. Katie Lynn was *not* pleased. The toast all dropped into the garbage pail piece by crumbled piece before she spoke again.

"*That* was uncalled for."

"I—I can't for the life of me understand why they—"

"You *told* them to question—"

"But—"

"Didn't you? Haven't you always encouraged them to ask questions? To prove things for themselves? Ever since they could talk? Questions—proof—always questions and proof."

"Yes—yes I did. But not—not about—I—I didn't say to be a damn fool, did I?"

"Oh. I see."

And that was over for the day but not forgotten. Oh no. I could see it in her face. Suppressed but barely so. Waiting only for a chance to reappear as something else. Oh yes. Just waiting there to even up the score. This time the wait was short. And here at last is where we have been going all along—the first time that I spoke the fatal words aloud:

"Did you hear that cat last night?"

Looking back and from my present vantage point (a Sunday morning in my study— locked doors and a working air-conditioning unit—one I bought myself for myself—a big solid one humming and clinking in the far window and a truly superior bourbon in my favorite highball glass), it all seems innocent enough, a question much like any other that a man might ask his wife the morning after something ruined his sleep. But—oh and oh again—how surfaces deceive, how nothing ever is the way it seems to be, how very right the clichés are that warn us of the covers of a book and puddings never tasted. She smiled before she answered me, a smile (may God have mercy on me now) near feline in its show of teeth and purring of the words that finally came, a warning clear and bold from *here* (oh yes, so clear so clear from *here*) but lost upon that mug-cut fool back in the toast-smell and the echoes of Euclid, that sleepy fool poised ready set to throw his life away on something that had never needed proving from the first, to bring back the breathing, living proof of what he knew was so was really *truly* so. But Katie Lynn had smiled and sweetly said:

"What cat?"

And here is where we stay, in doubt and nighttime for a setting and a frame—no bourbon for nine nights beyond the one preceding when it first began, each night a building sober and secure on what had come before, a growing up of evidence like Legos locking one on one until the castle or the rocket ship was done, until my eyes saw what my ears had heard, and both together brought me to the doing what I thought (and clearly, clearly so) I *had* to do. But more facts now are needed, three together in the hopes of moving faster on:

FACT: *From the moment I first heard the cat, I was almost continually awake.*

FACT: *During this time period, the Bide-Awhiles began to take more frequent walks through our* neighborhood.

FACT: *The 'San Cristobel Night-Prowler' had been active for at least a month BEFORE my first night out.*

While these three facts might seem unconnected, they eventually (and as you will shortly see) became very closely linked indeed. However, at the beginning, that first night especially, they were for me miles apart with absolutely no possibility of linkage. I *was* awake (and pretty much stayed that way for eight more days). I heard the cat. I personally never even *thought* of the Bide-Awhiles or a prowler. And that was that. My wife, of course, heard nothing. And so it went the first few days. A proper Thurber nightmare come home to stay.

"Cat? I didn't *hear* a cat. Are you sure it was a *cat?*" As well as: "You must have been dreaming. It couldn't have been a cat. Not every night. You know the 'No-Pets Code.'"

And indeed I did. I know it well. I wrote the damned thing and got it passed by the Homeowner's Association: *After 1 January of this year new pets are prohibited within the geographical confines of the Briar Bluffs Community. Cats, dogs, livestock, reptiles, and exotic animals of all kinds are expressly prohibited. An exception is made for the following: guide-dogs, reasonably-sized caged birds and aquarium-life (selected fish and crustaceans). Pets already in place previous to the passage of this Code are to be neutered within thirty (30) days of its full implementation. An exception is made for cats and dogs kept for breeding purposes (show animals)—these pets will need a special license, will pay a special tax, and will be prohibited from roaming free at any time. All strays will be impounded.* And so forth. A sound Code. A fair Code. Five years old and never once contested. But I *had* heard a cat. I *was* awake. And I *had* gone from room to room, window to window, and door to door in an attempt to *see* what my ears so plainly *heard*.

"You've been creeping about in the dark?"

"It wasn't that way at all."

"Then how *was* it, James? Were you drinking again? Is that what—"

"No! No—I—I was just trying to see if I could spot something from the house. That's all."

"Something?"

"The noise—the cat-noise."

"And did you?"

"What?"

"Did you—*spot* something?"

"No—not yet." But that was not quite true. I *had* seen something there all right and seen it early on, through the front window to be exact, the third night I think it was—nearly three o'clock and just a little fog outside, a night mist whirling back and forth from thick to thin, the other houses dark and streetlights not much help at all. But in what light there was, I saw a jogger bobbing on the lawn across the street and heading down toward Prescott Woods, a white-haired jogger, with something like a crowbar close against his chest.

"What? That's pretty hard to believe, James. I know they *walk* through the Development. Twice a day now, I think. In groups. They must have set times when they can exercise. They're adorable in their little sweat suits. All those pretty colors. But—*jogging*? And at *night*? You must be mistaken." And she had paused and licked her lips and then shook her head. "But—but what really bothers me is you creeping about the house when we're asleep."

"I wasn't *creeping*—" A glimpse was all I got and then the man was gone. And nothing else had made a sound that night.

"You might frighten the boys doing that. What if they woke up and saw you?"

"They won't—I'm quiet about it—and it's *not* creeping. I've just been checking out the windows. The doors. Trying to see where the noise is coming from."

"They're already upset enough about that geometry business as it is. Ben's had nightmares—and Brad's been asking to sleep with us again—"

"Well—well he can't. I hope you told him that it's not healthy to—"

"You need to spend more time with them, James. You really need to spend—"

"I already spend all the time I can! I—*quality* time—every chance I get—you know how demanding my job is right now and—"

"Well it just seems to me that if you have all this time to drink and creep about the house, you could at least spend a little more of it with your sons. You could go to ballgames together, fish, hike, help them understand geometry—instead of—of shouting—and—and skulking around in the dark like that—that prowler the police can't catch—"

And so, the linkage had been there from very near the first—the prowler, me, the noises that had yowled up every night—together and all set to spring a trap I never even guessed was there. From *here* (and one more half-glass gone) I see it clear as first light on a cloudless day. The jogger too, oh yes the jogger and then more nights and the walkers there, three old ladies and two wobbly men and more and more come out no doubt from Bide-Awhile to catch the evening cool. And then almost a week had passed and barking dogs turned up as a kind of prelude to the cat-screech and the yowls. But by that time I'd gone outside to get a better look, to hide behind the trees and century plants and boxwood in my yard. Or crouch and hop in shadows on the lawn. And nothing came in warning through it all, no inner voice or prickle on the skin, not one thing there to urge me back inside and safe. The only sound was cat-and-dog and always just beyond where I could see, then cleared off quick and silent, gone away to hide and maybe watch me when I'd scramble to the places where they'd been.

FACT: *The ninth night was positively the first and only time I ever left my own property.*

And this is true—from here most surely truest of the true. And it was also the night I finally *saw*. But other things led to it one by one— the sleep I'd lost began to show upon my face and daylight now a thing too long and drawn out to endure, the clocks a record of a maddening creep and loudly clanking, whirring, buzzing, ringing movement-at-a-crawl toward blessed night and one more chance to find and maybe even touch the proof I knew was there. That day seems now flashed by in whir of insect whines and little stings and whizzing wings across my eyes, a full assault of warnings never really heard or felt, pushed back and nothing left behind but foolish joy to see the setting of the sun. But back inside it—the ninth and final one: Saturday and flowing thick, slow to die from first to last. With many, many steps along the way.

"Did you forget the paper, James?"

"What?"

"The paper—didn't it come today? Or did a dog get it? Or a cat? Or maybe it was one of those old people who jog all night. The ones you like to watch?"

"Shut up,"

"Then where's the paper?"

"What?"

"The paper—remember?"

"Oh. I guess I left it on the front porch. Will Burgess was putting it there when I went out. Have you heard anything about a prowler?"

"Prowler? Yes—everybody has—"

"Around *here*?"

"Well not specifically *here* in—"

"Burgess was pretty upset. Someone stole his lawnmower last night. The new riding one."

"From his garage?"

"No—no, he had it parked beside his garden fence."

"Last night?"

"Yes. But he says it's been going on for weeks. At least five other homes. The Smiths. The Tuckers. The Hedgecoths. Tom Compton lost his tools. The Andersons—hubcaps and gas. It's been going on for weeks. They want to reactivate the Community Watch."

"Really? Well that should please *you*."

"What?"

"Watching. Sneaking about and—"

"Stop it! I'm only trying to find out—"

"Where the cat is?"

"I hear cats. And dogs."

"*Dogs*? When did the dogs arrive?"

"They've been there right along. Several days now anyway. And—and Will thought he heard something last night."

"A dog? A cat?"

"He's not sure. But it might have been."

"But we don't *have* any cats or dogs here, *James*. Not for years. We even have signs prohibiting them. A few signs anyway. Some of them are gone, I noticed yesterday. On my way home from the market. The reflecting ones. *Your* signs."

"The Homeowner's Association put those up! Not me. I never wanted it."

"Has Will called the police?"

"Yes. But there's little they can do. They promised to double their patrols for a while. And the Community Watch can help—I think Will said they'll get it going tonight."

"*They*?"

"I'm turning in early so I begged off. I need sleep. Even Will said I looked rough."

"Cat-hunting getting to you?"

"Go to hell."

And just a little later Sergeant Busby came knocking on the door, a rap-rap-rap of warning clearer than the rest, a Saturday morning whir and whine and sting, whizzed full ahead and telling of the dangers of the night. We stood talking in the doorway for what seemed a solid month.

"So I'd keep things under lock and key. Cars in the garage. Y'know. Until we catch this guy, it's best to play it safe. Gated or no, it's still best to take the extra precautions."

"Is—is he dangerous?" My wife had made her voice go shrill, a little-girl sound there that piped up cute and sweet and special for the brave young man in blue. It made me sick to see the gun belt and the bullets neat within their leather nests, the sparkling handcuffs and the thick black club hung down his leg, the polished hat-brim and the whistle dangling near his tie. The shirt was one size smaller than he should have worn, muscles rippling underneath and every time he moved. But none of it had made me think about my own quest for the truth, not one brass button shining in the light or Busby's teeth all big and white, not the squareness of his jaw or legs that fairly rippled strength and skill in chasing evil down, not even hands that seemed to cry out for a felon's neck had driven home the danger drawing close. I thought of sleep instead and how I wished the boys would run away from home.

"So be alert. And don't hesitate to call us if you hear any strange noises."

"Like cats? And dogs?" The little-girl had smiled and clasped her hands down on her belt, fingers twisting and a smile come out so sweet with just a tiny pout and tremble of her lips.

"Beg pardon, Ma'am?"

"My wife is making a joke, Officer." And Busby tried a smile himself.

"Oh. I see. Yes. Well there aren't any problem animals *here,* Ma'am. And no strays at all. Especially cats and dogs. County Ordinance 245-TV."

"*County* ordinance?"

"Yes, Ma'am. Passed last month. Toughest in the state."

"Did you hear *that*, James?"

I heard I heard. Oh yes I did and yet I hadn't really listened close enough at all. I went to bed right after lunch instead and dreamed of signs with feet that ran away each time a dog had barked or cat screeched in the night.

And then the night itself—a moonlit one and hard to find a place to hide. It took a long time for my wife and sons to go off snoring fast asleep. And all the while I rummaged for my clothes—dark colored pants and tee-shirt (Pogo Possum on its back)—the clothes I'd bought and hidden in the laundry room—all through my preparation time—I felt excitement growing strong, a feeling I now see had stayed behind or gotten lost among the years and years of settling in—the spreading, yawning, crunching thick and sturdy settle-down to stay. *Excitement*! My God! That's *all* I felt. Nothing of fear. Or worry. Or even mild concern. No thought of what I'd say if I got caught. Nothing there of family, hearth and safe-dreams by the flicker of the TV in my den. *Excitement* only. Only that and nothing more.

And so I went outside. And followed shadows for a while and listened, listened hard and close and nearly laughed out loud when that first wail and purr, that hesitating spit-and-screech of cat came tumbling from the Burgess's garden on a rich, sweet-scented breeze. My God, my heart felt like it wanted out up through my throat, and my temples tightened in a pounding rush of blood when I took off low to the ground, a crouching run and quick across a patch of moonlit boxwood dark between our yards. And then I saw it—them—four, five—six old ladies on their knees and up and down and up again and screeching the whole time, spitting, yowling in a back-and-forth dance among the squash and pole-beans. And dogs—old long-

haired men come out to bark and growl from somewhere toward the
pool, I guess, and crouch down in a loping trot across the shadow-
speckled lawn. And everbody running then, and me there too, faster
and faster toward the Prescott Woods.

It seemed like something in a dream, especially now when everything has settled mostly into place: the sting of bugs across my
cheeks, the smell of flowers strong and stronger in the air and out
into the moonlight at the very last, the cats a constant screeching,
yowl and spit, the dogs a bay and howling near at hand, a riding-
mower's pop and roar off to the right, driven by some ancient dog
that seemed the closest kin of death itself, turning wide and with a
little cart bobbling out behind and clanking some and showing just the
tops of two reflecting signs. And then the mower stopped just inside
the woods and turned around and blinked its headlights once or twice
while each old face (cats and dogs together then) came smiling by,
pale arms a flap and flutter in the shallow light, waving as they
passed and laughing at a sudden siren-sound and me. Then gone
away, dropped down quick like they had stepped off into open holes,
the pathway up to Bide-Awhile an empty white and well-lit curve
among the pine trees and palmetto thickets there. And me in blinding
spotlight then and one last cat swept almost by—a female with a
bushy mane and pointy ears that tumbled off her head and slid away
and into darkness solid gone right when I caught her low about the
legs and brought her hard down on the ground. Voices soon were all
around and close and proof, my only proof now turned back into skin
and bones and wispy hair pushed down within a sweat suit covered
up in little shiny stars. She twisted and she rolled and wiggled while a
gakking noise came out with every roll and push and shove, a sound
like some great bird brought up too soon from sleep. On one last roll,
I caught a glimpse of mower gliding to a clanking stop and near
enough to touch. Dust rose up quick from both sides as it sat and
pop-pop-popped almost a greeting to my friends and neighbors gathering round.

"My God—it's Jim Conlon!"

"*Jim!*"

"*Gakgak*"

"Easy Ma'am, easy—let me help you—"

"Hold him hold him—hey—"

"He's always hated those old people—we all know that—but—*attacking* them?"

"And my mower—it's—it's—"

"*Gakgak*"—spake the cat-bird shrill and loud!

"Easy Ma'am—there—are you hurt?"

"I never would have thought he'd *attack* them."

"Anybody seen any tools?"

"What's happening here?"

"It's the prowler—it's—"

"The *prowler*? Hey—you got *him*?"

"*Gakgak*" And Sergeant Busby's jaw was much harder than it looked, and my neighbors came in fast in a shoving rush of hands and fingers and kicking feet—and down I went, cuffs tight and pressing deep into my wrists, rough tumbled finally onto the floorboard of some foul-smelling car.

And questions—questions—papers—fingerprints and photos—papers everywhere—my lawyer out of town and Katie Lynn a whimper over bail. The little-girl, co-owner and afraid.

"But—will—will we lose our home? If—if I do this—if—if I sign this? Will we lose our home?"

"No, Ma'am—no—we've gone all through that and like I've already said—there's no problem if he shows up for trial—no problem at—"

"But—but he—he drinks and creeps about at night—prowls—they say he even prowls, you know—outside—and—what if he runs away—while he's creeping—and prowling—what if he runs?"

"Sign dammit!"

"Easy, Sir—easy now—"

And back home slow, a smooth crawl in the car, near dawn and a breeze come in the window tinged with gasoline and tar, the empty streets and well-kept lawns a dreamscape in the misty gray, and something like a cat, not far away at all but purring soft and waiting, just beyond the headlights then and now outside my study door.

An Undiscovered Hypocrite

The Reverend Lail Pergnum was enjoying his new car. He especially liked the tinted windows and the textured seats, the CD player and the leather-covered steering wheel, the new-car smell, and the way it all felt as he pressed on the accelerator and turned out of the parsonage driveway and onto the road toward town. But even as he settled back in his seat, he could see the smoke curling up through the pines, far off to the right of the tip of the Seacrest Marshes, evidence that Fishbait Johnson was at home, unknowingly serving as a mild irritation or momentary smudge on the otherwise almost crystalline perfection of a proper North Florida autumn day. The Reverend Lail Pergnum sighed and gripped the soft leather of the steering wheel and tried to ignore the feeling of disgust which had begun to form somewhere near the center of his stomach from the moment he had first noticed the smoke. He didn't want to see the shack or mounds of rotting fishnets or the various ruined boats which lay scattered about on the edge of the marsh like the remains of so many undersized beached whales. He pushed in a disc and let Bach ride with him past the dunes and San Marcos Lighthouse and hoped that the notes intricately linking and flowing their way in some miraculous circuit within the sealed car would be enough to keep his eyes from even once glancing toward the chaos of Fishbait's land. The man had seemed a personal reproach to Mr. Pergnum from the first moment they had met, an accidental confrontation on the backside of the parsonage's well-tended grounds one afternoon in late summer. Swarms of yellow flies and the dry buzz of tree frogs and a warm breeze thick with the smell of the sea had washed over the scene, giving it even in memory the feel of the last moments of a dissolving dream. The man had been shuffling through the palmetto thickets, a strange-looking sack slung over one shoulder and a long and thick stick swishing through the fronds before him and one arm angled out and up as if invisible wires were guiding it beside his body toward a stand of stunted palms. Mr. Pergnum had been birding that afternoon but had found nothing more interesting than a gull with a crooked bill. Johnson had stopped near the edge of the lawn and seemed to be sniffing the air.

"Good afternoon." For some reason, Mr. Pergnum had used his warmest tone, the one which had won him the frequent praise of his Pastoral Mechanics professor at seminary. But Johnson seemed not to have heard him and instead began to poke with the stick at a particularly thick clump of palmetto. "Good afternoon." This time the tone was sharper, touched slightly with impatience, and Johnson had pulled the stick free and turned his face toward the sound. "H'yar. Heard any rattlers?" His mouth had looked peculiar, only two teeth showing, upper and lower, giving him an expression almost feral as he rested his weight on the long stick, its tip forked and hooked with fishing line. "No. But, I'm birding."

Looking back on it, the car moving ever closer to the fringes of Johnson's acre, Mr. Pergnum winced, remembering particularly the way the man had smacked his lips and smiled, the two teeth clicking dully together. Johnson had made him feel both foolish and uneasy.

&

"Birds? Ain't bird season. Where's your gun?" He had straight-ened up and rested the stick on one shoulder like a rifle.

"No. I don't hunt."

"Then what you do with 'em?" His head had seemed too large for his body, looking vaguely oval-shaped, melon-like and topped with a tangle of reddish hair. Mr. Pergnum had wanted to turn back toward the safety of the parsonage, to walk quickly through the springy grass and regain the feeling which had surrounded him as he left supper and picked up his expensive binoculars and went out in search of beauty. Johnson had revolted him, had made his skin feel as if a thin layer of oil were being applied to it by unseen fingers. And then he had come closer, head cocked like an inquisitive puppy and the fork-tipped pole now looking like a spear some child had made and bro-ken.

"I watch them." The words, even in memory, sounded foolish and he wished now as well as then that he had left them unsaid, had not gone on in conversation with a man whose very physical form in-creasingly made the cold meat and soup he had eaten begin to churn and bubble in his stomach. Up close, Johnson's face seemed a mass of wrinkles and purplish splotches.

"Watch 'em?" He had seemed genuinely puzzled, reminding Mr. Pergnum of a school child presented for the first time with an idea alien to the patterns of his family and friends. At first he stared blank-ly to one side, watery eyes blinking and squinting into the edge of the setting sun as if trying to decide if anything were worth noticing. And then his eyes focused and he grinned, lips cracked and peeling and the two teeth looking like dented fangs. "I'd rather eat 'em. Why you wearin' that hat?"

"Hat?"

&

Again Mr. Pergnum winced, the memory making him wish he had destroyed the pith helmet long before that afternoon when he finally freed himself from Johnson and regained the safety of the parsonage.

"Y'know what I thought when I first seen you? Seen you come out of th'preacher's house 'bout an hour ago. Know what I thought?"

"No."

"Thought you was th'mailman. What kind a hat you call that thing?" His mangled left arm had looked curiously wing-like, sunlight causing the bushy white hairs to appear almost golden and feathery.

"Pith helmet." A gift from his wife, a Christmastide joke which had lain beneath the tree like a pregnant gray pie and made him think of cartoon bird-watchers and television actors in short pants stepping gingerly through borrowed fields, binoculars at the ready, poised to catch the first glimpse of some seldom-seen and misplaced blur of blue or gold or red.

"You in th'army?" Johnson's grin had become smirk-like, the two teeth nearly invisible behind his thin lips.

"No." He remembered wishing that the helmet would dissolve or disappear from his head in a blinding light or be whirled away by a sudden gale which would also take Johnson and deposit him somewhere beyond the scrub oak, pine and palmetto forest, anywhere but standing arm's distance from him staring and smirking at a helmet he himself now despised. "I'm Mr. Pergnum. I live here." He had jerked a thumb over his shoulder in the direction of the parsonage.

"You th'new preacher?" The spear-stick had bobbed a bit as Johnson stepped even closer, an odor of rotting fish washing over Mr. Pergnum and making him grip his binoculars and try to will his now churning stomach into submission.

"Yes."

"Why you in a hat like that?"

Gripping the wheel even tighter, Mr. Pergnum braked for a small dog that suddenly darted out from beneath one of the palmettos which lined the road like the once well-tended ornamental shrubbery of an aging estate. Johnson's acre was just ahead and even Bach was unable to keep him from glancing sideways and seeing briefly the thin, stooped figure there whose arm seemed always to be waving. And then he had safely passed it all and could settle back and enjoy the rest of his drive toward Seacrest City and the luncheon with the United Daughters of the Sea. But that afternoon with Johnson would not leave him, would not stay behind with the rotting nets and ruined boats but continued to ride with him, making even the passing dunes and the rippling sea-oats seem less beautiful than they had seemed to be even a few seconds earlier. It was as if he could not truly leave their meeting, as if he and Johnson had become melded or at least linked in a way perhaps not capable of articulation but as real and true as the sea-oats and dunes and glinting, dented beer cans littering the side of the road.

He couldn't now remember how long they had talked, but it must have been for hours because the sun had set by the time he reached the back door and tossed the helmet into the trash and went inside to take a long, hot shower. His wife knew nothing of the incident or of the superficially friendly but increasingly sinister-seeming waves or head nods or cap raisings which Johnson threw his way whenever he saw Mr. Pergnum's car. He tried to direct his mind to Bach and the occasional glimpses of the ocean between dips in the dunes but the talk with Johnson kept returning like the dull spasms of a chronic toothache. The talk gradually had shifted from birds and the helmet to things Mr. Pergnum had difficulty holding to, slippery bursts of words which made his unease grow almost as fast as the odor from Johnson's mouth, at times several inches away, lips pulling back with each sound and face moving from side to side as if trying to physically punctuate the sentences.

"Ain't got much use for church, Preacher." And with each fresh burst the odor of rotten fish and shrimp would pass over Mr. Pergnum and raise even higher his disgust and cause his legs to feel as if tiny rappellers were bouncing down them from thigh to toes.

"You been a preacher long?" He had gripped the forked stick with his good hand and squinted down at Mr. Pergnum with eyes that seemed to catch and hold the dying rays of the sun.

"Fifteen years." Again he had regretted answering, giving anything to a man who seemed to delight in watching what must have been an obvious and growing discomfort building even on the surface of Mr. Pergnum's skin. He could feel the red blotches begin to break out on his neck and cheeks as he watched Johnson's mouth, teeth tapping together, moving like some tongue-less ancient snake that had learned to stand upon its tail and speak.

"Long time. Most as long as I been huntin' rattlers. I sell 'em to that place over at Ponta Gorda. Moccasins too. Before that a'course, I shrimped. Like everbody else."

Mr. Pergnum could not remember the precise moment when the panic had hit, when he knew he must turn and run if necessary back to the safety of the parsonage. It had something to do with the way Johnson seemed to nod him into agreement with positions and insights clichéd or ludicrous and yet somehow touched with a child-like reasonableness that invited acceptance and trust. He had listened and grown ever more frightened and inwardly cursed himself for not reaching out and grasping the man's sweat-stained shirt and shaking him until the two front teeth popped out and sank down and out of sight into the hot sand. He had remembered trying to bring back the face of his Pastoral Mechanics professor or the way the ivy clung to the deep red walls of the library during those long past afternoons at Wakefield Seminary, to put anything in the place of what he was seeing and hearing and smelling. But Johnson's slippery and clattering words would let nothing form except what they themselves brought up. And then one image came to stay awhile.

"You think this crap music th'kids lissen to is of the Devil?"

"I never really—"

"They even play it over at th'Cafe. Took out all the good music an' put in this crap that sounds like tin cans bein' beat. Words you can't unnerstand. Not one Elvis song in th'whole pile. Nothin' but crap. Heard a preacher on the radio say it was all of the Devil. Not the King though. Not Elvis. You ever hear Elvis?"

"Yes."

Mr. Pergnum turned up Bach and tried to blot out the rest of Johnson's words, but they kept pushing against the swelling notes inside the car until he had been jerked back once more into a consideration of things he never wanted near him.

"What you think of th'King?" Johnson had pushed up his chin and seemed to be sighting one watery eye down an invisible barrel.

"Nothing. I think nothing." From somewhere toward the sea, behind him and beyond the parsonage, Mr. Pergnum had heard the sounding of a freighter, the short and long blasts seeming to blend into each other until becoming almost a wail—long, undulating and deep. Johnson had paused before speaking, looking down his nose as if trying to find something only he could see or knew was there at all. The odor of the man was overpowering, a stench it had taken Mr. Pergnum hours to no longer smell as he tried scent after scent from the bottles on his wife's dresser, spraying the air and greedily sucking the particles inside his nose and later standing in the shower for close to twenty minutes.

"Well y'ought think somethin'. Nobody don't think *nothing* of th'King. You ever see him on TV?" Johnson's voice had become softer, a modulation which suggested the drowsy muttering of a child just before sleep.

"No. Yes. Yes, I think so."

"'Course y'have. Everybody has. An' them movies. All them mov-ies. I seen ever one. You know my favorite?" His eyes had seemed on the point of glazing over as he began to sway slightly, his bad arm jerking upward each time the torso moved and the forked stick jig-gling above his head like a broken wand.

"No."

"'Blue Hawaii.' All that blue water. An' them girls." He had frowned, thin eyebrows bunching together above the nose like tooth-brushes being pressed into each other tip to tip. "An' that damned wife of his run out like that. Leavin' th'King an' takin' his lil' girl. Th' King loved her though—right down th'line he did. An' all that good he done—givin' away all them cars. That made me feel real fine. You think he'll come back, Preacher?"

"What?" Looking into the momentarily wide eyes of Johnson, Mr. Pergnum had felt something inside him explode, tiny fragments of seminars and group studies and Sunday sermons ripping through him like shrapnel, and he had hated with an intensity he had never known before. He remembered feeling like he had when he was young and preached for the first time to a room full of sweltering derelicts, hating the sin but forced to love the sinner, on those Sun-days and holidays before he escaped to Florida and discovered Bach and the company of reasonable men and the feel of deeply polished pulpits. And there before him, in the dying sunlight, Johnson had seemed the sum of all the rheum-eyed bums and trembling junkies and hollow-cheeked hookers who had passed before his rickety podium in a seemingly endless parade of what he had later decided was demonic manipulation disguised as desperate need. It took years, but in the end he had given them all over to their own and varied saviors whether in bottles or needles or Halloween-like costumes and took the first Call south.

"What you think, Preacher?"

"What?" He had wanted Johnson's mouth to stop moving much as he had prayed for the stench to lessen and the moaning to quiet down back there in the boringly similar chapels of, until then, almost forgotten missions, crowded places where all movement was painful and the roadside clotted with debris.

"About th'King? You think he'll come back?"

"I don't know." And he had realized even as he spoke that Johnson was pulling him back to the urine-soaked hallways and the now meaningless words which had passed for therapy in all the cramped and drafty conference rooms of all the soon-to-be-condemned buildings in all the cities of his early ministry, calling him without even using the right and proper words or striking the proper posture of feigned supplication or sorrow, without even a grudging acknowledgment that there might indeed be something out beyond the limits of a fix or drink. But the man had been hunting snakes. "I don't think so."

"Well, " Johnson had grinned and stepped closer, raising himself up to his full height, breath hot and steady across Mr. Pergnum's forehead, eyes becoming deep wells, rifled pits into which a clear fluid had been poured as they came down even with the preacher's own, "you can't never tell about th'King."

&

Bach stopped as the first tourist shops and motels of Seacrest City came into view. Mr. Pergnum wiped his forehead and gripped the wheel as he crafted the prayer he would shortly deliver to the United Daughters of the Sea.

In a Dugout

It was a "don't dress-out day" on a cold and wet December morning. 1960. Crows did their bobbing walk on the muddy baseball infield, and the faint cackle of indistinct migratory birds was audible even inside the relative shelter of the visitor's dugout. Three students, coat collars pulled up on their necks, kicked at clay clods and watched a slender and slightly stooped man skirt the mud of the infield and interrupt the ever-increasing crow-dance.

"Is it Coach? Damn, I never even saw him come up—I'm getting out of here."

"Wait a minute, Bill—it ain't Coach," pulling his collar tightly about his neck and stamping his feet. "Hey—look—it's old man Skully."

"Papa Skully? Shit, I ain't seen him since sixth grade."

"Hidy boys—lemme see now—Billy Jenkins? Right? Billy Jenkins an' Ralph Carter an'—an'—I don't know you, son," to a squat boy in a red hunting jacket sitting on the bench.

"Hey Papa, what you doing over here at the high school?"

"I don't know this one here, Billy—what's your name, son?" Resting a hand on the roof, dividing the infield in half, the man squinted into the dugout at the boy in the red hunting jacket.

"Ricky—Ricky Poretta."

"Ricky, huh? Well I'm right pleased to meet you. I'm Edwin Skully—Papa Skully to my friends. Shake on that how's about ?" The man's flesh appeared cracked into tiny gullies and whirling craters and Ricky's hand retreated almost upon contact into the security of his own coat pocket.

"Ricky didn't go to Arlington, Papa. He was in a Catholic school."

"Well now. Catholic school, huh? Well now. Then he ain't been one of Papa's boys for sure. How you boys been doin'?"

"Fine, Papa," Billy scratched his fingers through his hair and looked toward the infield and the returning crows. "You still over at Arlington?"

"Well now, boys, maybe so. Maybe so. You know ol' man Evans couldn't run that school without Papa, right? You know that for sure, right?"

"Sure thing, Papa. Hey Ralph, you remember how Papa hid us out in the john that time ol' lady Boss was after us—in that summer session thing?"

"I guess so."

"Yessir, Papa treats his boys right. Always have, ain't that so, Ralphie?"

"Yeah."

"Yessir. Boys'll smoke and boys'll cuss an' ol' Papa knows that—say, you boys got a smoke on you right now, I bet."

"No we don't. We're just hiding out from Coach Black and the clean-up detail. We don't have to dress-out today."

"Now c'mon, boys—I bet you got a smoke on you for sure. Hows about loaning ol' Papa a smoke—remember how he always done right by you boys?"

"I ain't got one, Papa."

"How about you, Ralphie? Ol' Papa always give you a drag when you needed one, hey?"

"I left mine in my locker, Papa."

"You letting ol' Papa down, boys—you hurting his feelings bad. Say there, you, Ricky—you wanta be one of Papa's boys I know so hows 'bout a smoke to seal the bargain? What say?"

"I don't smoke."

"The Lord you say—my my my what is this world coming to? Catholic school musta taught you that. No smoke at all, boys?"

"Sorry, Papa."

"Well well, big high school boys now and no smokes. How about girls, though? Huh? Bet you getting all you want there, huh? Right? Hey Billy, tell ol' Papa 'bout your girl."

"I got one, Papa, don't worry about that."

"Well I know that, Billy—ol' Papa knows that—why, you remember how I used let you look through that hole in the wall in the storage room? The one that let you see all them little asses in the girl's john—remember that? You ain't forgot that, have you now?"

Billy kicked at the bench and pushed his hands deeper into his pockets. "Yeah, Papa, I remember that sure."

"An' you, Ralphie—you remember too, don't you? Remember that one—that lil' Reg—Reg—whatever in hell her name was—that lil' blond one you was so sweet on? Why you and me used watch her in there every chanct we got, hey? Remember that lil' red place on her ass, hey?"

"Yeah, Papa. Hey, we got to get on back to the gym."

"So tell me about your girls, boys—you doin' ok there? Hey Billy, who you goin' with now?"

"I'm doing ok, Papa. I'm getting mine."

"I know it, Billy. Yessir, I sure knew that. Tell me about it—you got in her pants yet? You ate her yet?"

Ricky stood up. "Wasn't that the bell?"

"Might be—good seeing you, Papa, but we got to get on back now." Billy stepped out from the dugout and stared toward the gym, indefinite in contour, a gray bulge above the tall grass in centerfield.

"Hey, boys, wait now—wait—look at what ol' Papa got here," fumbling in his jacket pocket and producing a kitchen match box. "Just look here now what I got—look inside here. What you see?"

"Hell, Papa, that's a toad frog."

"Right, Billy, but it ain't just any ol' toad frog—nosir, ol' Papa wouldn't have just any ol' toad frog—you boys know that, hey? Nosir, this here's a trained toad frog. See this here bubble-blowing hoop here? See it?"

"Yeah, Papa, yeah—we can see it," Billy looked at Ralph and winked.

"Know what this toad frog can do?"

"No, Papa, what?"

"He can squeeze hisself through this hoop. Yes, by damn he can, and for a quarter each I'll show you—just a quarter, boys. What say?"

"Papa, that big toad can't squeeze through that hoop."

"Yes he can, Billy—a quarter says he can. Here's my quarter right here—put yours up an' I'll show you he can do it clean. What say there, boys?"

"Ralph?"

"Hell, how can you divide a quarter if we win?"

"Ricky?"

"I'm going back to the gym—period's about up anyway."

"Don't you want to see it, Ricky? Don't you want see ol' Papa's trained frog?"

"Well—"

"C'mon, boys—Billy, Ralphie?"

"Ralph?"

"Ok, Billy. Here's my quarter—this I got to see."

"Here's mine, Papa."

Just the eyes of the frog were visible in the opening, but it some-how seemed as if the box itself was quivering slightly in Papa's hand—sides and top steadily breathing.

"How 'bout you, Ricky?"

"Well—I'd like to see it but it just ain't worth a quarter to me."

"Have you ever seen a frog squeeze hisself through a hoop be-fore, son? Have you now?"

"No—but, it just ain't worth a quarter is all."

"Well now, boys, it's all or none. If you don't pay you can't see the show—all or none, boys. That's Papa's way, y'know? That's always been Papa's way."

"Hey Ricky, why not?"

"I'm going on back to the gym."

"Let him go, Papa, we're paying."

"Ok, boys—you're Papa's real boys anyways—let him go—go on now, son, an' leave us to this here bidness."

Taking flight suddenly, three crows flapped toward the stand of pine trees near the home team's dugout as Ricky walked through the tall grass of the outfield with the sound of laughter behind him.

Dead Dog, Live Hogs

It was a mile-and-a-half from Bobby's front porch to the front gate of the school house. A mile-and-a-half though the piney woods and palmetto thickets, along the sink-hole ponds and ground sometimes more liquid than solid beneath a cover of pine needles and fallen moss. He would be alone this morning. Last day of school—fifth grade—North Florida, 1952—and his friend, Harry, sick in bed and nobody else any good at scaring off the wild hogs.

Nobody much even lived nearby anyways, not like Harry did—Bobby on the riverbank in a houseboat that never quite stopped moving, and Harry in a cracker-shack about a half-mile away on the old postal road. Harry and him were called river-rats by the other children, the ones who lived in the houses that had started popping up like toad-stools on that long, thick stretch of woods old man Ponsell sold. He'd heard his daddy talk about all that. About the way everything was changing. About all the city folks moving in and taking the best land. His daddy had lived on the river forever and drove a big truck for the Jax Overland Company and was nothing like the fathers of the other boys and girls in the school. He was gone most of the time and left Bobby and his mom to take care of things at home. Harry's dad was dead. In the War. Some Jap had killed him. His mom cooked at Pappy's Oyster Bar. Harry was the best. He wasn't never scared of hogs. But today Harry was sick (his mom had called a half-hour ago) so Bobby stuffed his lunch bag and his books in a croaker sack, kissed his Ma, and took off right as the sun was coming up.

Down the trail toward the school. Barefoot and alone and trying not to worry about the hogs.

The first little bit was smooth-going, straight on through the pines and never a hog that close in, just coons and possum and squirrels and such. Quiet and easy footing, nothing much on the way to slow him down. He tied the croaker sack around his waist, the books and lunch now bobbing on his right hip. He liked his hands free. The next part was harder, the trail dipping and twisting through cypress and pine, down near the ponds and the swampy ground his Pa had warned him to keep free of. It was getting hotter by the minute and he wiped at his eyes a few times and swatted at a swarm of mosquitos and slid a bit when the trail dropped off into a palmetto thicket. He found a long stick and pushed it out in front, swishing it side to side, trying to follow the trail as it zigged and zagged its way toward the deep woods where the hogs lived, where the hogs ran free. Suddenly he heard what he thought was the dry buzz of a good-sized rattler off somewhere deeper in the fronds. He pushed through the last of the palmetto as fast as he could go. It was noisy everywhere at once it seemed. Tree frogs the loudest of all. Mosquito whine mixed in. And hot.

The deep woods were on the other side of a little ravine, a vine-choked gash of stunted brush just on the border of the oaks and camphors and big pines all pushed together and making a black shade that jumped and flickered in the occasional light from the still rising sun. He hated the darkness there. And the last half-mile was the worst. The hogs were everywhere nearly. He could hear their grunts as he came up from the ravine and pushed on down the trail.

It was even hotter by the time he reached the "resting place"—a massive oak stump, wide and mostly in the sunshine—just a few yards before the trail began to snake down another ravine and along-side the biggest pond, Ponselle's Lake, a place where the hogs liked to drink and wallow in the thick mud. Bobby wished Harry was with him. Harry wasn't afraid of nothing. But not today. Harry's Mom had said he might be in bed the rest of the week even. Wiping at his fore-head, Bobby sat down on the big stump, legs dangling over the side, and watched some dragon-flies glide and dive above the scrub grass and dog-weed. It was getting even hotter. Time to get going.

Something was moving up ahead as Bobby started down the ra-vine. Off to one side and down deep in the brush, a crash-rattling sound that seemed to pull into itself other similar sounds, coming to-gether and making him feel a deep stab of fear, deep in his belly and cold and reaching out to touch his arms and legs, making them feel light and useless—a hog sound now clear—as he began to slide quickly down the rest of the ravine and onto the spongy ground near the lake. Bullfrogs there and gators too and the sound gone louder and closer and Bobby was running now, fast as he could, croaker sack untied and thrown away back in the last of the ravine some-where (when the books began to beat hard against his hips) and run-ning on the trail by sight when it was clear and by memory when it wound down into the palmetto and scrub, hoping then no buzzing came up quick or nothing else came slithering or waddling or snap-ping up to catch his bare feet and bring him down. Hogs were back behind, he now knew clearly, and there was a long way yet out ahead before the woods let go and the Chaseville Road came clear. Hogs. And it seemed like more than he had ever heard before.

And then he saw it there. Right in the middle of the trail, right at the place it forked and pointed straight to where the woods ended and the road began, out where the cars and trucks could help to keep the hogs away. It was a mound of something dark, flies in a buzzing swarm above and to its sides, a mound that, the closer he got, was maybe a dog, a dead dog that had crawled right onto the trail, right at the fork, and died with front legs stretched out and paws dug into the hard sand, with hind legs splayed and torso bloat-caught and alive with flies. Bobby edged around the mound, slowly, not wanting to look but looking anyway, standing still to better see, staring at the snout nearly gone and eyes lost and a few teeth visible in a way that made it seem that it was just about to snarl and snap and bite. And

Bobby kept standing there, hog noises getting closer and closer, but his legs not able much to move, his belly cold now and his face so hot and tight he felt the skin might crack. And then he noticed the stench, on a whirl of breeze jumped up from somewhere back toward the deep woods and the pond. Standing there, the dog face-on and nearly touching his toes, Bobby felt sick, like he was going to throw up what was left of his breakfast. The dog seemed alive, the flies a swarm there and worms there too, moving back and forth and up and down, all else blocked out and gone away down in the nothing it had turned into when it dropped down to die. Nothing really left—he saw now clearly and at once—nothing really left of anything it might have been or done before it fell down dead.

And then Bobby heard the hogs again. Closer now and many of them he was sure, come closer to the buzz of flies and stench that rose up from the worms and made him so afraid that nothing would be right again, that nothing ever would be like it was just yesterday or when he first woke up today. The dog head was moving, worms thick along its snout and where the gums should be, moving its ears up-right and all together seeming to be eager for a run much further than the trail. But not today. Not any day. Not never.

The hogs came out from the trees. Bobby saw one. Back toward the ravine. A big one with tusks. And others back behind, little and slightly bigger ones. Coming slowly, almost shyly into the light speck-led shade, rooting down in the darker soil close by the big oaks and the camphor trees, not knowing that anything was wrong

Christmas Island

Jim Canaan left the boat tied to a charred stump on the south shore of Lake Lucina and pushed his way through a tangle of razor reeds that grew chest-high along the bank. Underfoot, the ground went quickly from moist and spongy to a coquina-layered sand, cement-hard in places and at times squeaking beneath his heavy boots. Although it was Christmas Day, it was humid—the morning sky hazy and heavy with what later might be rain. But as he walked the last few feet to the Stone Crab Beach road, he ignored the squawks of seagulls and the sky and thought about last night and Sally and her promise to go with him that afternoon across the lake and down a rutted logging trail to Carson Bluffs. As the outskirts of the Strip came in to view, a van passed by, coming up behind him as if it had simply materialized out of the haze back toward Seacrest City, its metallic blue sides seeming to blur and the music which followed with the wind it left behind making his chest feel hollow. He wanted to reach the lake by mid-afternoon so that they could cross it and drive the few miles to the bluffs well before sundown. He had left the truck on the other side.

Sally's apartment was not far from the Seahorse Café at the dead-end of a narrow street which began at McCoy's Point jetty. Jim looked up in time to see a pickup slowly pull out onto the highway a few yards ahead, its dust-covered cab dented and the driver seeming to fight to get its tires to respond to the wheel. A load of trees obscured the back window as it finally settled into the right lane— Christmas trees, spruce or fir improbably bouncing down the road through a heat better suited to June than late December, a strip of white cloth fluttering down weakly from one of the deep green tips, dust trailing behind to flatten out and wash over the road as Jim reached the outskirts of Stone Crab Beach. The truck made him feel cold, as if a stream of true winter air had managed to survive with the trees from whatever northern forest they had been cut, shipped along with them free of cost only to spin off behind the truck in its turn toward the city and sink down behind on the low shoulder of the road. It was a feeling from another Christmas, a Christmas of little disasters and slippery dreams and weather so cold that even the oldest farmers could not remember having faced its like.

He had been eight or nine, and it seemed now, as he pushed on through the sand and moist air down the road beside the sea, that it must have been a dream, that no such winter and no such Christmas had ever come to him or to anyone else in Seacrest County, that memory had created what he needed to believe to help him make his way alone through all the other Christmases until this present one. But he knew that the cold had come, early and without warning from the sea, with ice needles in the wind and the bawl of stranded cattle cutting through the night like the cries of giant babies left to suffer colic untended in an understaffed nursery. He had been sleeping at first, an undersized lump bunched beneath a knot of quilts, when his grandmother's long fingers found his shoulders and pushed and pulled him into the dim light of his room. He could hear his father's voice outside, shouting down the hallway to the two Negro hands whose answers came improbably from the direction of the front door, their words mixing and tumbling over each other and lost finally amid the whining roar of the wind and the undulating and sometimes almost human bawling of the cattle.

"Cows got out in this. C'mon Jim." And the smooth plank floor felt so cold that he thought it was wet, that his grandmother had decided to mop it before she woke him up and started him tugging himself into his clothes. Dogwood limbs beat on the shutters of his window, popping and scratching sounds which made him think of the crackle of the fire he had left surely only moments ago for the at first slab-like chill of the sheets. But it was hours later and dirty light was coming in through cracks in his bedroom door and then he was being pushed and prodded from behind by fingers as hard as the dogwood limbs whipping about in the air outside.

"Your Pa wants you." It was then that he remembered the day, the small pine in the parlor blurring as he passed by and stepped into an arc of weak light thrown through the front door from the raised lanterns of the black men.

"Been goin' like that for most of an hour now, Mista Can'in. Can't see nothin' out there. Can't tell where they's got to. Ma'am." Noticing Jim's grandmother, they tried to step back into the wind, lanterns bobbing in their hands.

"Close the door." His grandmother had let go and now stood beside his father. "Close it."

"Just be open again." It seemed in memory that his father had nodded the Negroes into the house, the door partially shutting off a clatter of ice against the screen. Jim had stood there shivering while his grandmother snorted and turned toward the kitchen.

The truck passed out of sight and Jim stopped a moment in front of an abandoned service station to wipe his face with a large blue bandana and watch two seagulls tumble through the sodden sky out toward the dunes. Near the ruined entrance to what once had been the garage, he noticed a boat resting among rusted car hoods and mounds of old tires, its flat bottom caved in and part of one side splintered as if by an ax blow. The gulls were squawking behind him, the sound at times tinny and distant, a piping not unlike the higher notes of a calliope.

&

On that other Christmas, the men had spent what seemed to be hours trying to find the boats, the wind driving them backwards each time they neared what should have been the shoreline of a tidal pool but which instead had turned into a lake, distended with a water that flew up and whirled about and over the palmetto thickets and saw-grass like some giant hand were stirring a boiling pot. The dawn had been near as he tried to keep pace with his father and the hands, trusting to the rope about his waist and the dim lights they carried and straining to hear their voices among the clatter of ice and slosh-ing roar of the lake. He had closed his eyes between gusts and thought of the warmth of the fire and the glitter of the Christmas tree before he had fallen asleep. Back there at the house, his grandmoth-er had tried to keep him from going with his father, holding to his arm and at times shouting to be heard above the rattle of the shutters. His mother had stood in the hallway outside her bedroom, her eyes re-minding Jim of a treed coon as she buttoned and unbuttoned the top of her faded housecoat. And then his father had tied a rope to him and pushed out into the wind securing the other end to his own hunt-ing belt. Jim had fallen down four times before they found the boats.

"Won't do in this, Mistah Can'in! Best try around by Carson Bluffs!"

"Can't hear 'em now! Can you?"

" Naw suh--they done got in behind them bluffs, most likely!"

"What's out there? Can you see anything?" But the dawn brought only a gray confusion of water and sky and bending sawgrass with ice passing over it all like a quilt being pulled forward on a bed. He had wanted to shut his eyes and lie down on the grayish grass and dream of the tree and his presents and let the wind go away. But his father had yanked on the rope and they all had pushed on toward the higher ground of the bluffs somewhere further ahead of them in the blur of ice and water.

Jim turned away from the service station and headed toward the Seahorse Café, its net-covered façade visible beyond a trio of palms that angled almost tentatively out over the shoulder of the road. He had dated Sally now for almost a year, their first real meeting taking place at Christmastime a year before when a nor'easter had played upon the café and the sea like a child with outgrown toys. For weeks afterward, she had seemed to enjoy his infrequent visits to the café, times when he would ignore the stares of people he had never really gotten to know in all the years he had lived among them on his grandmother's and now his own farm, moving through them much like his father and the other men had tramped on through the pelting ice of a nearly forgotten storm and pulling after them a boy wishing only to be anywhere the wind was not. He had told Sally of the storm and the island he had seen being born in the driving surf and shifting sand below bluffs finally reached by touch and bump and feel and not by sight at all. The first time, she had sat most of an evening in his pickup and listened, nodding at times as if his words were enough to join her with him during his brief stumble along a frond-littered ridge of wind-blasted coquina to stand at last beside the men and look with them, eyes burning and watering, down through the ice needles at an island seeming to be raising itself up like a whale breaking the surface of the sea all at once from fore-flippers to flukes. She had nodded and at times smiled at his description of the descent from the ridge, down the eroded side of the bluff, with palm fronds whipping above as the rope broke and tangled itself and wrapped around the men, bringing them to their knees to bumble over each other all the way to the crashing waves themselves and leaving only Jim up among the bending trees and whirling sand and pinpricks of airborne ice.

"Stay there, Jim! Don't move!" His father's voice had sounded delicate among the wind roar and sudden bawling of unseen cattle, and Jim had sat down behind a twisted and ripped palm trunk and lowered his head against the cold. It had felt good to be free of the rope. He tried to press himself into the ice-encrusted sand, clinging to the trunk and hoping that someone would turn off the wind.

It had seemed like hours before he gathered the courage to peer over the rough trunk and look down at where his father's voice had been and focus his burning eyes on a moving landscape over which a glowing web of ice reflected the yellowish tint of a sky trying to throw off its cover of boiling clouds and let the sun come through to make everything below fresh and dance on the vines and bended trees and sand and deep gray water like dew on blades of grass bending in the morning breeze of a summer's dawn. It could not have lasted more than a few minutes, but while the island flashed and danced, it blotted out all memory of the glittering pine tree in his grandmother's parlor and the presents beneath it and even the sounds of the bawling cattle, now closer and mixed with the shouts of his father and the men. It was as if the floating ice had gained a pow-er able to touch him not just on the skin or through his eyes but deeper in a part of him not tied to touch or sight at all. He felt as if the wind and trees below had turned to fire, like the night sky above Bethlehem in the stories his grandmother had told him, with stars there burning coldly brighter and brighter till the One they waited for had been put safely down to sleep beside his mother on the straw. It made Jim happy, warm and filled with what the years ahead had taught him was the first faint touch of peace, a thought to help him smile his way through slippery times and dark.

Passing the Seahorse Café, he noted briefly the almost deserted parking lot, its few cars and trucks, most likely the leavings of last night's party, sitting there into a Saturday sure to turn to rain and a steamy darkness better suited to mid-summer. But last night there had been stars. He had walked Sally home after it all ended and the last caroling drunk had staggered off into the night, and they had sat on a dune near the jetty and watched the red blinking lights on

McCoy's Point. Later she had kissed and patted his face and laughed when he tripped over her doormat.

"Hey Canaan." A face suddenly peered out at him from around the tail-end of a battered Pontiac, cheeks sunken and two lone teeth showing as it smacked its lips. Fishbait Johnson. Jim half-turned as he passed, eyes not resting long on the shriveled form that stepped free of the car. "Canaan—hey, where you headin'?"

"Christmas Island." Jim looked away toward the jetty and noticed a lone fisherman approaching the gray boulders and the spit of white sand which flared from beneath the tallest of them like a dry river entering the sea. A shrimp boat labored against the incoming tide and narrowly missed the McCoy's Point buoy.

"Say again?" But he left Fishbait at the car and stepped around the edge of a wind-smoothed fence that ran the distance of Sally's street. He could see her there sitting on the front steps of her apartment.

The clouds seemed closer now and the piping of birds from the direction of the Café made him wish he could fly with Sally over the greenish water of Lake Lucina and into the battered truck which would carry them down a rutted and overgrown logging road to a sandy trail up through the palmetto and stunted pine and finally to a place high on the bluffs where they could see at a glance the sweep of coast and sea. He had told the story to her more than once, parts of it last night on the dunes, and again the bluffs and the newborn island in memory had blocked out all the other things they had talked about the past year. But last night she had helped him notice what he never thought was there at all, had gotten him to laugh with her in seeing through her eyes three men and one small boy, rope-tied and off in search of half-crazed cows inside a storm as hard to hold to as a palm tree made of ice.

"Why did you go in the first place?"

"I don't know." From the open door of the kitchen, his grandmother had shouted something, the meaning of her words lost to him as his father had pushed at his shoulders and made him join the two men with the lanterns. His mother hadn't budged from the hallway, still fumbling at her housecoat and watching the men leave and her mother-in-law shake her head and mutter herself back into the kitchen. "The cows got lost in the storm."

"And the rope? Whose idea was that?" She would return to that part of the story, smiling as if unable to find in her own past anything to help her keep in memory or imagination something which his words alone made real.

"Daddy's. To help keep me from getting lost."

"Like the cows?"

"No. They'd already done that." She had upset him, her words come up like stabs of light within a smoke that darkened why in memory he was with the men at all. "I mean, he didn't want to lose *me* out there." And then her brown eyes seemed to lighten, reflecting his own image as he moved in close to rearrange a curl and touch her face.

"Then why were you out there?"

"To help with the cows." And Sally laughed; and he had fought to stop from joining her, had clenched his teeth and tried to push back at the dark and let his father's purpose start to clear. But then the smoke had simply whirled itself away and left behind a light he couldn't help but use. "I was a damned fool. And so was Daddy." The laughter had felt good.

"Did you ever get to the cows? You never have told me that part of it."

"The cows?"

"Yes. What all that tramping through the ice and wind was about. The cows?"

"I don't know. Yes. Yes, we got the cows."

"And the island is still there."

"I think so. Yes."

"Have you ever been back?"

"No. Not to the top of the bluffs."

"My God, Jim. And you want me to go?"

"Yes. Tomorrow. Today. Christmas."

"That's a pretty cheap gift."

"You should have seen it that one day."

"But there's no ice this year. What do you think you'll see?"

"Will you come?"

"What time? " And she had held to his arm as they walked through a deepening fog toward her apartment.

Ahead, Sally stood up and smoothed down her skirt. Jim felt the bulge of the box in his shirt pocket and wondered if the ring would fit.

Altar Call

Jim Canaan sat on the crest of a dune and stared out to sea. It was late and already the buoy lights were blinking off the Point. He had lost the dog an hour before and decided to rest awhile before heading home. It had been a long afternoon and he hoped the dog hadn't doubled back and made for the pasture. The Meeting already had been camped there for three days when the preacher drove out to the Canaan place in a dented Buick, yesterday afternoon, dust trailing out behind and the brakes sounding rat-like as he made a quick stop near where Jim was feeding the dogs. It was a smaller Meeting this year, but Jim had noticed that the tent had gotten larger, a three-poster now with a white-and-blue striped canvas cover that stood near a line of Winnebagos and one tractor-trailer in the middle of the north pasture. The preacher had been dressed in a green, three-piece suit and his face looked deep red in the late afternoon sunlight. He had seemed to be clucking to himself as he stepped free of the car and started toward Jim and the growling dogs.

"Mister Can'in," the preacher's voice had seemed irritated and for some reason Jim wished he had gotten the hired hand to feed. "Mister Can'in, can I please talk to you, Sir?" He had stopped several yards from the dogs and patted at the front of his vest. Jim turned toward him and kept mixing the feed. The dogs had almost danced around the plates as he started dishing out dinner.

"Stay there, Pastor Robbins. Let me finish up." The last of the scrap and meal mixture plopped down on one of the tins, and Jim let go the can and wiped his hands on his pants. One of the younger dogs had begun to growl, and Jim smacked his nose. "Eat it, Dandy, before I take it away. Dogs're hungry today, Pastor. What can I do for you?" Coming closer, he had noticed that the man was sweating heavily, dark splotches fanning out from his armpits and around his belt. In front, the vest had worked itself up, revealing an oval of pink shirt and a massive belt-buckle, deeply polished and looking for a moment like some kind of catfish. "You want to come on up to the house? Sal might have some chicken left."

"No." He had seemed to wince, eyes fluttering and then looking straight into Jim's. They were different colors. "I don't have time. Service's about to begin. I need you to come and get that dog of yours. That brown-and-gray?"

"Stone Crab?" Jim had thought he was still in the swamp. "He's down there?"

"Yes sir. Yes—two days now. He howls, Mister Can'in. Did you know that?"

And Jim had followed in his truck behind the preacher, down the gravel road to the place in the fence where a week before he and the hired hand had made an opening large enough to let in the cars. Bright red flags were fluttering on each of the three tent poles and already a few rows of the congregation had taken their places in the wooden folding chairs. The tent flaps were up and even before Jim had stepped down from the cab he heard Stone Crab, a broken series of growls seeming to come from beyond the makeshift altar and the row of speakers that had been pushed together and pressed into the canvas at the far end of the tent like a wall started by a child and abandoned before the last pieces were in place. The preacher had come clucking over to the truck, his head angled slightly to one side and his face even redder than before.

"Hear that, Mister Can'in? Can you hear it? He's growling now. Out back there. He stays out behind the altar all through the service.

He won't move. And he acts like he'll eat you when you come too near."

"I'll get him home." And Jim had walked around the tent, the growls growing louder with each step until he could see the dog, head lowered toward the striped canvas and his fur all ruffled like someone had stuck his tail into a wall socket and turned on the juice. Several young men in choir robes had tried to pass by, but with every growl they stepped backwards, pulling up the hems of their robes and looking over at the preacher for direction. Jim stopped and called the dog. The preacher had stayed well back at the edge of the tent.

"He won't come, Mister Can'in. Better watch yourself—look how flat his ears are."

"C'mere boy. Here Stone Crab. Easy now." The dog had turned his head slowly toward Jim and seemed about to growl. His teeth showed briefly, making it look almost like he was smiling and then his ears had raised up and he dropped down on his belly and began to pant, snout aimed at the back of the tent and his tongue dropping down out of the middle of his teeth. Kneeling beside him, Jim had brushed at the rough back hair and watched the choir boys flutter over to the tent and the preacher wipe at his face with a blue cloth and for some reason it had all made him think about his grandmother and the change which would come over her on Saturday nights after the supper dishes were washed and it occurred to her that the next day was Sunday.

"Be sure you wash everywhere, boy. Everywhere."

"I did—before supper."

"No—in the tub. Soak. Visiting preacher tomorrow."

And it had seemed in memory that all the preachers of his childhood were visitors and that only the small gatherings they shouted at and pleaded with, only the farmers and shrimpers and trappers and their well-scrubbed families were somehow permanent, belonging there in the white-washed meeting hall in a way that reminded him of cypress knees poking through the greenish-black water of the deep swamp.

"And make sure the elbows get scrubbed."

"But nobody'll even see them."

"Don't backtalk me, boy. Do it. You're goin' to church."

And he had, until she died, and he began to avoid the churches, mostly Baptist, which seemed to him at times to have been planted seed-like among the pine forests and palmetto of the county and left to grow unnoticed until perhaps enough rain and sun and money brought them to a time of towers and steeples and parking lots big enough to hold even a football crowd on championship Saturday. The preacher was saying something.

"What you going to do with him, Mister Can'in?" The preacher had glanced at his watch and wiped again at his forehead with the blue cloth. It was deserted in back of the tent and the band was tuning up inside, amid the congregation noises and the sound of an occasional car engine out toward the gravel road.

"I'll take him on home." As he pulled out the leash, Jim had watched the preacher visibly relax, in stages from his face on down his arms and chest. And at that moment, his suit all sparkly green in the sunlight with a thick gold chain drooping from his vest pocket, the man looked nothing like the ragged version of five years ago who begged to use a field unfit for cattle and made Jim think of dwarfs and Colonel Waller and the way the pasture looked one time before, with lanterns there that seemed to push away the blackness of the night and put down in its place a multicolored glow that carried in it strength enough to pull him from his bedroom window like a candle calling in some giant moth. And when the Colonel left, Jim's parents had gone with him, to tell fortunes and take dimes and quarters from the farmers and shop girls and the others who gave them up in hopes that even briefly in a darkened tent they might get near a promise brighter than the one they daily lived without and mostly didn't miss. He had thought of all that and had said yes to the preacher but the Meeting had brought less light than noise to the pasture, returning year after year with bigger tents and better singers and yet somehow for all it tried to do not coming even close to what he felt that one night as a child who wanted to go sleep among the Colonel's lanterns in the joy he knew was there. He had never felt that way in church.

"I've got to get going, Mister Can'in. You hear?"

"Yes. He's fine now, Mr. Robbins. You go to Meeting." A sea-breeze had ruffled Stone Crab's fur as Jim hooked on the leash and fought back a sad and strengthening memory of the Colonel's camp next day.

"You're always welcome inside, y'know. You can come back any time." The congregation had begun to sing "Jesus Is A Rock" by the time Jim got the dog to the truck.

As he stood up and brushed sand from his pants, Jim heard the dog, howling somewhere beyond the nearby pines in the general direction of home, short wavering bugle-like sounds that mixed badly with the steady crash of surf behind and made it difficult to tell exactly where to follow. He side-stepped down the dune and found the trail that bypassed the marshes and dead-ended on the eastern boundary of his farm. He was glad he had brought the big flashlight with him and he clicked it on and let the oval of light sweep across the semi-darkened trail before him, the sound of the surf gradually lessening as he followed the howls and tried to gauge their direction in the intervals when the sea-breeze slackened and the clattering of the palmetto underbrush grew still. He knew where he would find the dog. He would be crouched in the darkness behind the big tent trying to catch the band and match the people whoop for whoop.

A Burning of Ducks

Once, in his teens and long after he knew his parents were not coming back to the farm, his grandmother had taken him to a brush-arbor meeting on the other side of the county. They had arrived late, the old truck cutting out on them twice before they managed to make it to the palmetto-and-moss-roofed pavilion and the rows of shouting people and a preacher so drenched in sweat that every movement of his arms sent large drops spraying out in all directions. They had sat on the last row, and Jim had watched the old woman's face, wrinkles and furrows in the skin catching and holding the soft light from the lanterns that hung from stakes ringing the inside of the tent. And then everything had changed, and he felt her somehow begin to leave the splintered chair, her hand gripping his arm with a force that she had never used before, trying to pull him with her, to make them maybe soar together up above it all and right into the music and the shouting and beyond both to a place that only she knew how to find. But he had not gone with her, drawing back before they cleared the ground and leaving her to fly alone and let his legs push free to stumble him away and full into the cooler air outside. And that was his last memory of church.

The flashlight caught the eyes of some animal hunched at the edge of the trail, reddish dots that seemed to hang suspended for a long moment before disappearing amid the crunch of broken under-brush and the shriek of an owl. He passed the seaward rim of Sutter's Swamp, the scimitar-shaped series of canals and grass and cypress that ringed his farm from east to west, and the clatter from it helped ease him away from the brush-arbor and his grandmother's visiting preachers and the Saturday nights when he would lie awake in bed and try to understand where it was she wanted him to go and what it was she wanted him to see.

He was close to home, the dog's howls able to cut into even the swamp noise and ahead he could see the searchlights of the Meeting, still a full mile away. He pushed through a tangle of saplings, the trail abruptly ending, and stepped into a field, tall grass parting as he moved and the occasional whir and clack of a startled locust becoming a kind of counterpoint, dull and mechanical-sounding, to the steadily increasing thump and whine of the Meeting's band of robed musicians and the now piercing yelp-howls of the dog. The searchlights seemed to be wavering at times, stabbing out stutter-like through the early evening mist at the starry sky above like stubby fingers flexing and un-flexing in swamp water. He knew his wife would be worried, most likely already cooking supper and trying to decide how long to wait before setting the table. He skirted the house, moving wide to the right of the front yard, and cut off the flashlight. He could walk by sound and feel from here, and he let his thoughts go and tried to bring back Colonel Waller's voice as he stood near the barn, flanked by dwarfs and talking to a father Jim had never really known, his words long since grafted onto memories of church that somehow never grew beyond the size they reached the night he almost soared up toward a roof of moss and fronds. Earlier that one morning he had been taken to the center of the carnival, his father moving easily among the dwarfs and mismatched others who did whatever Colonel told them to and never seemed to notice how things looked by daylight. And he had tried to run away, but the dwarfs had caught and juggled him, passing him with their feet until he felt his stomach nearly leave its proper place.

"The boy will grow, Colonel. Be too big in a year."

"But he'll do for now, Jothua. Manny and Thandy can uthe him."

"Road's no place for him, Colonel."

"He fith their shoes, Jothua. He ith the right weight to fly."

"Wait a season."

"Like you thaid, Jothua. Be too late then. Their legth won't hold him in a year. He'll be too big for their shoes."

The tent was just ahead, a dust-choked blur of lighted movement and the people there inside, arms raised up toward the canvas and their bodies looking from a distance puppet-like, dancing dolls who jerked and kicked and followed every urging of the unseen pressure on their strings. And the dog was in the music, sometimes muffled or near lost but still there strong and clean, a part of everything most clearly in the moments when the band or people paused, filling in the empty spaces with a sound to make Jim's father or the Colonel stop their talking and his grandmother swoop down and stay awhile to hear. And the music stopped and as the people settled down among the glare of lights and whirling dust, the preacher's voice came out to touch them and to move beyond, a rush of words that reached into the nighttime. Jim stood near a fence post and listened, the voice now pleading and soon joined in jagged counterpoint by howls and yelps, together sending out a chant-like call, echoic and for him alone.

Freedom Road

Randy Canavan sat under a thick, heavy-limbed camphor tree watching the chain-gang shuffle slowly along the side of the road. He was up a little hill—the tree was there—and he was mostly hiding out from his job at the paint store. He hated his boss, Jeffrey Melton. Every day the same. Over and over the same:

"Hey Canavan—the ol' lady keep you up last night?"

He hated the other workers too, especially the part-time high school punks, the bums who knew the boss, and the boss's own son who was the worst among them all—Junior. Every day just like his dad. The same every single day. At least once and sometimes twice:

"Hey Canavan—you still eat boogers, man?"

But he hated the customers the most of all. Their voices always like a whine in his ear. Like a mosquito in a dark room, nearly but never close enough to swat. Just there. Always there:

"Do you have vanilla paint?"

"White?"

"No—vanilla."

"We have all kinds of white."

"But I want vanilla."

So Randy left at lunch and kept on going—not stopping until he walked right out of town a good ways on a seldom-used two-lane that branched left from the State Highway just past the city limits sign. And then he had found the little hill and the tree and sat for awhile just thinking and finally watched the chain-gang pull up in state-issue trucks.

The convicts were in traditional black-and-white stripes and their ankles made a clanking sound against the long chain every time they moved. They all seemed to be waiting on something, or someone, having climbed down from the trucks finally and been herded to the opposite side of the road like a same-suited parade and then made to come to a stop below Randy's tree. A couple of them looked up at him and spat and a few others just laughed. The guards had long-barreled shotguns and a rifle or two and watched from beside the trucks as all the men finally sat down. There were no tools in sight. It was hot now. No clouds. Full sun. The only shade was Randy's tree.

There were ten guards. Randy counted them twice to be sure. Ten guards all in state-issue uniforms and Stetson hats and yellow tinted sunglasses and faces all alike. And then the chain-gang went quiet. Quiet all around. No cars even on the road. None for the past hour. Randy could hear the big guard clearly. He had clambered up (minus his shotgun) onto the roof of the middle truck. It all happened real fast.

"Now boys—you know it's time. Right?"

The convicts looked at each other, clanking sounds up and down the line as their heads moved side to side.

"Right?" The other guards all yelled it out. "Right?"

"Right, Boss!" The convicts sounded out nearly together with a few late-comers sticking out strong.

"Yes sir—yes sir." The big guard took off his Stetson and rubbed his face a few times with a blue handkerchief. "It's sure enough time—yessir it is. Time." The hat went on strong and the handkerchief disappeared into his back pocket. From where Randy sat, the chain-gang looked like a giant wounded caterpillar, its parts sliced through in places and not really let come together again. "You boys ready to go?" He nodded and a few of the guards began to free the men from their chains, an almost rhythmic clanking that carried clearly to Randy's tree, all of it mixing in with the pumping of shotguns and the chambering of rounds in rifles. The men stood very still, looking straight ahead.

"Cap'n?" One of the convicts, a tall black man with a shiny bald raised his hand.

"You got somethin' to say to me?"

"Yeah, Boss. I don't think it's time."

"You what?"

The other guards laughed.

"Time, Boss. I ain't ready."

Even some of the convicts laughed. The big guard was not even smiling. Several guards aimed their weapons at the line. Randy stood up.

"Well now, boy—I can't help none of that. You've had long enough, I reckon, to get yourself all ready. You other boys have, right?"

"Right, Boss!" The voices were now almost totally together, late ones more like the barest hint of an echo.

"What about it, boy?" The big guard nodded toward the tall black convict and almost smiled. "State says today. An' today it is."

"Well, Boss—I just don't know."

"Too bad then. Too bad."

Randy felt bile rising up in his throat, and a pain in his belly like he was just about to shit in his pants. Clouds were building now toward the north, toward the town, and the big guard's hat bobbed a bit on his head. The other guards all fanned out along the line of convicts, shotguns and rifles at the ready. The big guard stepped down from the truck and began to walk back and forth, slowly, his own shotgun now resting on his right shoulder. Randy's mouth was dry. He tried to swallow but a taste of bile seemed stuck down in his breathing in and breathing out. The clouds were filled with lightning now and a distant rumbling was in them too, and Randy watched the guns and the guards and the convicts dropping their black-and-whites down onto a growing pile near the rear of the middle truck. Most were dressed in what looked to be jeans and tee shirts and a few of them had produced baseball caps and were snugging them down on their heads. The thunder was sounding stronger.

For some reason, Randy thought about the paint store. Ten years there as a clerk. Ten years with only two raises. Ten years also with a wife and kids who never even seemed to know the difference between when he was there and when he was not. Ten years of back and forth and back and forth and nothing of his own to show for none of it no matter how hard he tried. Ten years and the years before all that nothing much to even think about beyond knowing that it added up to 45 and counting—and then the guards began pushing the prisoners toward the south—on down the road away from town—on toward the county line. The big guard's voice was clear even in the gathering flash and rumble of the coming storm.

"Move it on out, boys. Time. So get on down the line. On down the road. Time's up. An' don't come back now, y'hear?"

And the laughter of the other guards was loud and sustained and the thunder seemed to be so close that no time was given up between flash and noise and Randy got away from his tree and ran through the tall grass down the little hill, faster and faster and in behind the slowest of the free men heading south.

Purgatory: a novelette

Chapter One: First Steps of the Penitent

It was late. And hot. Ninety degrees and after midnight for sure. Matthew Clawson had left Rebarb's Bar hours ago. Drunk again. And now lost as well. Trying to find his car had been more difficult this time. The car was not where he left it, and after a few minutes of walking around in circles, stumbling through the gravel of the front and side parking lots, he had gotten mad and began for some reason to run in a direction that he somehow thought the car should be, off into the shadows and deeper darkness beyond the weak lights out around the bar. He ended up somewhere nothing like where he expected, and looking nothing like what he had ever seen before. The place had to be near the bar, he thought, had to be, since his legs had given out and his wind nearly caved in after what seemed to be only a few yards run out back of the parking lot. Down a side street and into what might have been an alley or playground. He was covered in sweat, and he threw up twice on some bushes and stumbled into a bare place on the ground and went down hard, legs buckling and body pitching to the left and head snapping forward as he hit the hard-packed sand.

After what seemed to be a very long time, he raised up on an elbow and tried to focus his eyes on anything he could find, trying to stop the spinning in his head, trying to keep the ground steady and not whirling back and forth and jumping up into the sky and back again. But it was too dark to find anything steady enough to hold to, the moon gone behind some low-hanging clouds and even the stars overhead not quite there. He could hear crickets. At least they might have been crickets—or tree-frogs—or something else off in the deeper darkness further on down into what looked to be a patch of piney woods with clumps of what might have been briars pushed thickly down among the trees. He shook his head a few times, and rubbed his eyes, and threw up again, almost gently, aiming it all to one side, nothing much left in his stomach beyond bile. It had been a miserable week so far, and it was only Wednesday, a hot August night in Duval County, Florida, 1965.

He had been fired earlier that day from the City job his wife's brother had gotten him, a real cake-job too, driving some fat commissioner around town, nothing to it, and good money there for the taking. He had done it for almost a year now—four months longer than the last job, the one at the zoo that had ended in fourteen chimps getting loose and attacking some Jap tourist and his ugly wife. And nearly six months longer than the street cleaning one and the busted front of some damned car wash or something, with several people being nearly run over by the big sweeper right after he took a nice long toke of some good stuff one of the colored clean-up boys gave him. This time he drove the car over the feet of the commissioner, over his toes really, as he was waiting to be picked up out behind that fat whore's house he visited every Wednesday. The trip to the hospital was real loud.

Matthew had been at it for years and nothing seemed to work, no job seemed to stay with him long enough for him to really feel it was his. It was always the same, always. Year after year. Job after job. This time, though, the wife had thrown him out. That was new. After ten years and four states. Threw him out and called her brother, the city cop, to make sure it stuck. And so he went to Rebarb's and drank up most of his pay. Rebarb at least was friendly. And his bar was pushed back into this little dead-end road not far from the Arlington River. Real private-like.

"Over his toes, huh?" Rebarb was very tall. And always wore a baseball cap with JAX TARS printed on it in big red letters. He had been in the Navy or something, and ran a pretty safe joint. No real trouble there. No bums or beatniks or college kids. Plenty of booths and a long curved bar and nice pictures everywhere of ships and seagulls. And Jax Beer on tap. "Bet he squalled, huh?" Rebarb had been rubbing down the bar with some sweet-smelling oil. Matthew had already lost count of the beers by the time he began to tell about his day.

"He did, for a fact. Yes sir, he did. Crushed 'em, I think." The place was nearly empty, too early for the shipyard crowd and too late for the shrimpers. The beer was cold. The wife had thrown a big glass ashtray at him just as he made it to the door, missing his head by inches and smashing into the wall where it stuck. He slammed the screen door behind him and didn't look back. He still had plenty of gas in that wreck of a car his brother-in-law had loaned him. That was a good thing, he had thought, as he finished off number who-knows and asked for a refill.

And there had been many more refills and then the lost car and the run into the darkness and the heat and the here-and-now and the approach of something-like-a-man coming from the direction of the piney woods—along a pathway that was now clearly there, a white-ness that curved into the dark—a crunching sound rising up amidst the cricket chirr as the figure came closer and closer—taking long strides and seeming to be holding to a tall, curved wooden staff. The moon came out from behind the clouds, and the figure now seemed to be gliding toward Matthew, smoothly and silently, and suddenly coming to a full stop just a few feet away.

"Good evening." The voice was familiar somehow, but with a trace of something not quite safe. An edge to it. A little something that caused while not exactly fear, at least carried a memory of it down deep inside. The staff he held in his right hand was thick and carved in long swirls that resembled rising smoke.

"I—uh—I was just—" Matthew tried to stand up, but his legs buckled, causing him to drop sideways back onto the hard-packed sand. The something-like-a-man dropped the staff to one side and reached out and mostly patted Matthew into place, into a kneeling position, dusting him off and giving his shoulders a light squeeze before stepping back and beginning to hum a tune almost familiar, something that Matthew thought he remembered from back before all the fuzziness and the pain. Way back. In South Dakota. Near Mobridge and helping with the cattle. Watching his Ma bake bread. The something-like-a man seemed to be smiling, although it wasn't clear at all, not in the darkness come in strong from the hiding of the moon behind a stout bank of clouds. Mobridge and the ranch and his parents and the rest seemed to flicker a bit and then drop away with the dying of the tune. The next words were nearly friendly, but again sharp edges poked through, giving them a harsh feel in the silence that fell into place out behind. But at least the spinning and the belly-roll and the taste of vomit all seemed to be slowly but steadily going away.

"Why are you out here?" The something-like-a-man was squatting down now, close by the kneeling Matthew, the staff again held in one hand and his face nearly clear and somehow familiar, like the faces of people long dead, family, friends, a lover somewhere back west and lost without a proper word. Matthew thought the face was peaceful looking, kindly, but not weak in any way. "Why did you come here?"

"Well, shit—y'see, I--" and he had intended to state the obvious, thinking through the litany of words that should make it all as clear as day: he was drunk—unemployed— homeless—wifeless—friendless—lost—drunk (but he had already thought that—the very first thing)—broke—sick—nowhere to go—drunk (it kept coming back, and now he was belching up a taste of beer and lunchmeat)—

"I—I just don't know where my car is, y'see—an' if I could find it, I think I could—"

"Do what? What could you do?" The voice, the timbre was not unkindly, but the words came out sharp-lined and clipped. The face, however, remained familiar, a softness to it that now reminded Matthew of all the faces that had looked out at him from their boxes, their coffins, in the old days when he was still part of a family. The grandparents and parents and uncles and aunts and cousins and all the rest who had died before him in various disasters and accidents and meannesses back in those High Plains days. Peaceful-looking in death. Even if the dying was anything but peacefully done. The something-like-a-man now was leaning on the staff, both hands clutching it, and the voice came with a sadness there deep within, an unspoken pain that struck hard at the memories that kept flooding in—making them group together and then line up one by one—from Mobridge to Jacksonville and most especially the times before his wife had shut the marriage down—and all together touching Matthew in a way that made him feel that never in his life had he done one thing right or true. Nearly forty years of nothing worth a memory fit to share. "You need to get going now. You need to go find your way. You need to get it right."

"But I can't find my car, buddy-row—I done told you that. I don't know where it is."

"You don't need a car. But you do need to go find what it is you want. What you want the most. You need to do that." And the voice made it all seem perfectly reasonable. Perfectly right and straight-on to get up (and he did—with some help) and begin to move with the something-like-a-man, trustingly, as if he had never wanted to do anything else, as if everything gone before had been waiting for just such a fuzzy-minded shuffle toward some piney woods, on what was clearly now a trail packed deep with oyster shells, a crunch and crack with every step they took, both moving well into the darker shadows all alone and toward what might have been a light far up ahead.

Chapter Two: Run to Ground

He had been walking down the railroad tracks for at least two hours, mostly heading due west by the sun until the tracks curved and began to point who knows where. It was a cold north Florida day and the wind that whipped up occasionally from the direction of the river had a hint of ice down in it. January 2, 1966, and an overcast day, big clouds boiling around overhead and Matthew Clawson's near-dead blue jeans and frayed pea-jacket not nearly enough to keep away the shivers.

The past few days were a blur—like most of them since his wife threw him out—since everything went spinning around. Nothing was right. The nearest messes began back in August. Last year. 1965. He pulled the collar of his jacket close about his neck and tried to keep from stumbling on the ties. Over to the right was the river and to the left some marshy-looking stretch of palmetto and cypress and up ahead more track and with some smoke off in the distance that seemed to be floating down through a good-sized stand of pines. Back behind was nothing but pain: No more wife. No more job—the third one he had lost since August came just yesterday—or two days ago—or whenever New Year's Eve turned into the biggest drunk he had ever pitched and kept him from delivering those damn chickens or pigs or whatever it was that he had been hired to deliver over in Bryceville. He never did find the truck, but the owner sure did find him.

"You go'damn piece a shit—I oughta just kill your sorry ass right here!" And the shotgun the man had started to pull out of his car seemed five times bigger than it needed to be and Matthew had run so hard that it seemed his feet gave off even bothering to try and touch the ground. All that had been yesterday, he suddenly remembered clear, and he had kept running for a good while. Out into the country. Out along the river until he found the railroad tracks and some bullet-pocked sign that said: BAKER COUNTY. The whole thing had begun in Maxville, he thought, in Duval County. But it hurt to think.

Up ahead, the smoke was getting thicker and a bit darker off in the piney woods. The tracks began to curve again, and he stepped over and off and down a pretty steep embankment and sat on a wide oak stump to rest. There was a smell of frying bacon in the drifting smoke, and it made his stomach flutter a bit and growl. He had been lucky, he thought, to have been wearing the jacket when pig-or-chicken-man showed up in that bar's parking lot in Maxville. Feeling in his pockets, he finally pulled out a crumpled ten-dollar bill and a few ones and some pretty banged-up change—all that was left from the odd jobs he had been collecting since everything went bust, wife and all the rest back there in August. He divided the money and stuffed it into his two front jeans pockets and looked slowly around: Pines and palmetto and clumps of bulldozed timber in a few places and a strengthening smell of bacon. He decided to follow it.

The fire was about a yard or so in front of a crudely-built cabin and neatly contained by what looked to be uneven paving stones, piled onto each other with a grill of some sort placed on top. Bacon was frying in one skillet, eggs in another, and a good-sized, thickly bearded man in overalls and a khaki jacket stood over it all and gently dropped a handful of chopped potatoes into a smallish pot and began to hum some tune that Matthew almost remembered. The man looked up and frowned, smoke whirling around his long, nearly gray beard and the sun coming in strong just then to give his face a bronzed look with cheeks deeply red and a full head of curly blond hair that seemed to glisten in the sudden burst of sunlight.

"Who th'hell are you?" His voice was rough-sounding, deep and frayed around the edges, the words husky and pushed out slow and careful and not at all friendly. "I said, who th'hell are you? You deaf?"

"No—no—I'm Matthew Clawson—I—"

"Larson? Jack Larson?" The words continued slow as the voice came up a notch with a kind of growl beginning to show down among the pauses. "You did say, Larson? Right?" And he reached behind him, pushing away his jacket and showing the handle of a good-sized pistol. "Larson?'

"No no no—" Matthew's stomach felt all cold and he stepped back a few feet and tried to smile. "No—not Larson—no—"

"Then who th'hell are you?" He looked quickly to both sides and in back, as if searching for some unseen something out in the vines and deep brush, out in the jungle that seemed near ready to consume the little circle of bare ground, the hard-packed sand that held both cabin and campfire.

"I'm—I'm Clawson. Claw-son. Matthew."

"Clawson?"

"Right. And I'm just passing through and saw the smoke and smelled the—"

"Clawson, huh? I don't know no Clawson. Never even heard of one. Why you here?"

"The fire—smoke—bacon?"

"An' that's it f'you—yeah? That it?"

"Well—I—" Matthew thought back just a blink or two, seeing the shotgun and the chicken-pig-whatever's face and felt his own stomach begin to roil, a taste of rust come up strong in his mouth. "I—I'm just passing through—I—" .

"Nobody just does that, son. No damn body. Guess you're hungry though, right?"

"Yes—I—yes—" The rust-taste was lost down in the sudden growling of his stomach. Nothing else mattered. He couldn't remember when he last ate anything of value. "Yes."

The meal was eaten in silence. Inside the cabin. At a table of sorts that had SEABOARD burned into the dark wood across its nearly even top. The chairs were peach-crates and the plates were tin. A kerosene stove hummed in the corner. The room had one window—a flap of leather was pulled down almost to the rough-hewn sill and a steady, but weak stream of cold air mixed with the kerosene fumes and the smell of the quickly vanishing food. The room was very hot and both men were in their shirtsleeves. The food had been good. Just-right eggs and the potatoes juicy from the bacon grease. The bacon itself was the best he had ever eaten. Matthew felt better.

"Where y'from?" The voice was low again, husky, almost a whisper. "Y'hear? Where?"

"Uh—I—I'm –South Dakota—originally, that is. I'm from all over, really." And he suddenly remembered a woman, Maggie Knox, a young woman he had known for years before he drifted further south, someone who'd be sure to give him a place to come in for a while and rest. Maggie Knox. Red-headed and big-chested and always up for a good time. And that's where he was going all along, he thought—it must be—that had to be it—all along—all through the bad times—never quite clear until now—someplace safe. Maggie Knox. It was clear as day. "I'm heading up to Atlanta, I think."

"Atlanta, huh? Why you heading there?" He wiped what was left on his plate with his thumb and sucked on it a second or two. His face had very little expression, nearly rigid from cheeks to forehead, eyes a deep and cold-looking blue.

"I dunno—some place north, I guess."

"North." The man made a snorting sound and shook his head. "North, huh? Sure you are. F'sure—everthing better up north." He shook his head again and seemed to be studying his plate. A train whistle began to blow. Off in the distance. A nearly patterned sound that seemed to be gaining strength the closer it came. "Noon run to Folkston. You riding the train?"

"No—no, I'm walking—walking—"

"Walking? To where?"

"Atlanta—I already said that I am—" And Maggie would be glad to take him in and hear his stories and make him glad to see another day. He could almost see her face and taste her lips. "Atlanta. I'm going to Atlanta."

"Yeah yeah. Atlanta. Right. Going to Hell is more like it." The man dabbed at a crumb of bacon and brought it up quickly to his lips.

"What'd you say?" Matthew's stomach began to cramp a bit, spasm-like, like he needed to shit. And then Maggie's face dissolved into a fear that seemed to rise up and put down roots with every word the man let free.

"I said, you goin' to Hell from what I can see. And I seen plenty." And he smiled, eyes lost in wrinkles and teeth showing even and mostly white. "Hell? You heard of it maybe?"

"Yes—but—but I'm just passing through—"

"Here? Passing through here? Right?"

"Well—yes—yes—and—and thank you for the food, but I need to—" He tried to stand up , but his legs had gone to sleep and he felt something drop down around him in the now stuffy and too-small cabin, something that seemed just before touching him with a smothering feel of pain and fear. The man's voice was now very strong and nothing like before.

"Here? It's all around here—and coming in sure one day. Been hiding out one place or another. Been lucky so far. Been here over a year now. Waiting. On my way to someplace else. Any place but here. But here I sit. Train or no trains. Highways or no highways. Since 1963. Since the summer of 1963. Waiting. Thinking. Even praying. I got gone back then. I got away. But only just as far as here."

"Look, Mister—I thank you for your food—I really do—but, look now, I need to go—I—"

"To Hell? You in a hurry to get there? Well then—go on—I can't stop you." He nearly laughed and seemed to be nodding at some un-seen something out around him in the cabin and beyond it in the piney woods and swamp, a something that might be coming closer with each breath he took—as if he were bringing in whatever was about to come by simply breathing in and breathing out. "You just go right on, son. They coming for me and not you. You got you a ways to go yet. Atlanta, right?" And off in the distance—in between the train sounds coming closer, Matthew thought he heard the baying of hounds. "I done most everything myself, son. Not to that nigger den-tist, though. I wasn't no part of that. He got away. Clean away. No—I done it to plenty others—to that nigger boy over in St. John's County. I did that one all alone. Ruint him first. Field-dressed him and burned him up near Hastings. I did that. You heard of that one, sure—right? You heard of all that—1963—right?" And the face went neutral—skin tight-looking and the eyes now only slits of blue. It seemed more like a mask than real.

"I don't think—I—don't remember." Matthew finally got his legs and feet to work. The baying sounded nearer now—many dogs were coming.

"Well, that's right—that's right. You got your own, son. Got your own bidness. Me? I done my bidness. Ever bit of it. But no more. I left 'em all. That last nigger called out to Jesus and all he got was me. No more, son. No more. I walked out on the boys. I run hard but only got to here." He tried to smile, but the mask held firm. "I got money. You want it?" And the face again tried to come alive, nearly there for a second or two before collapsing into the slit-eyed mask. He pulled out his pistol and laid it on the table near his plate.

"No—no—"

"Take the money, son—it's in that little bag over there—the canvas one—see it? Take it. I got paid good for it all. Years of it. But not no more. I'm through. And tired of hiding. Finished with all that. I'm waiting now. Praying—hoping—this side of Hell." And the face softened and seemed to be pleading with Matthew to do something no one else could do. But then the mask returned for good and all.

Matthew nearly dove into the vine-choked woods just as the hounds reached the cabin. The shouts and gunfire echoed back behind him as he pushed through the thickness of the woods and found a logging trail and headed where he hoped a train would pass again—the canvas bag held tightly in one hand.

Chapter Three: When I Reach Atlanta

The past few days had been messy and loud. Riding the rails might have seemed romantic at some point way back in his younger days, way back when he was still supple enough to actually make it on board a fast freight without help. But not anymore. Not since he left Florida and began to point himself in the general direction of Atlanta. Matthew Clawson was thirty-six years old, and tired beyond any hope of easy rescue. Tired and hungry and riding some ACL freight car that clattered and banged so loud at times that he almost wanted to take a running jump out into the Georgia countryside, out into what must be better than the bump and roll of wood and steel and the muttering voice of the one other human on board—somebody who seemed to be eighty and whiskered and never quite shutting up long enough for Matthew to even hope for sleep. He was on his way to Atlanta and a woman who was sure to make everything right again. He had nearly gone down for good in Florida and going north seemed the best thing left to do. The only thing left to do.

The freight was a slow one, moving through South Georgia as if it had no care for schedules or deadlines. Starting and stopping and moving up and then back and stretching for miles the last time Matthew looked, with the engine too far up ahead to see. There had been no sign of railroad bulls, even in the small towns they passed through or stopped only long enough to attach yet another boxcar. He never did get straight what the main load was, but there were many empty cars and he had snuck into one of them when the train was stopped deep in some piney woods. The old man was already there.

"Sonny—who th'go'damn hell died an' made you king, huh? Jus' you tell me that—

Jus' tell me who—you hear me?" The old man was red-faced and sent quite a healthy spray of spit out around his words. He hadn't really even paused much since Matthew swung on board just north of Folkston. "I ain't asted you to come in my home—I'm getting pretty sick of all your bellyaching too—I ain't going tell you agin to wipe them damn shoes before you set down to supper—you hear me, sonny?" And then he began to walk up and down in the far corner of the boxcar, every so often looking over at Matthew as if to keep him from moving any closer.

In his own corner, Matthew sat down, opened his pea-jacket and patted at the canvas bag he had pushed in snug against his chest. He had snatched the bag (and on the run) as he got away just ahead of the dogs and the rest. Back down in north Florida. Back down in that crazy man's cabin. Nearly fifty thousand dollars in the bag. Counted quick just before he found the train. A day or so ago maybe. Maybe longer. And here he was with another crazy one, older but just as crazy, and loud this time, louder than anybody he had ever met before.

"You don't know shit, sonny—don't know shit, you hear?" The old man sometimes skipped around back at the other end of the boxcar, skipped and shuffled and then kicked at something in the air that only he could see. "I seen your kind, bub. I seen many a man like you— you crazy sum-bitch. I seen one like you just last week—just like you. Wouldn't lissen no better'n you neither. I tried to tell him what was up ahead too—just like now—tried to get him to lissen—but he wouldn't. They's things up ahead, sonny-boy—they's bad things up ahead—"

Matthew kept his legs raised up a little bit. The shake of the wood behind him, rough against his back, mixing in with the clatter-hum of the rails outside, and the sway and bump of the car itself seemed to be coming all together in a way that offered a rough harmony with the old man's ravings, some kind of linked rhythm that almost floated up into the dusty air to hang suspended and gently float back down to begin again. He rubbed at the bag, snug against his chest, warm under the heavy fabric of his pea-jacket, filled with neat stacks of hundred-dollar bills it seemed, making him smile at the thought of what they could do. A new day coming, he almost spoke the words, a new day coming and finally someplace free from all the darkness and the pain. But in the here-and-now, the old man was running full-speed ahead, his words mostly untethered to anything even resembling sense or reason, but for all that still flying out toward Matthew's end of the car with a power that made him think of the preachers in his youth, the old-timers who traveled the high plains in old beat-up trucks town to town with tents that barely held off the sun and meetings filled with shouts and songs all there to bring the farmers and Indians home to Jesus in the quickest, surest way. Matthew wondered where all that had gone.

"You don't know nothin' about what's up there, sonny boy! It's waiting for you sure enough an' you don't even know what it is!" And he jumped a bit and skipped with the words, dust billowing up around him and the sunlight suddenly come in and strong from various busted out places in the walls. "You don't know, sonny boy—nosir, you don't know—but I do, bub—I know—I been to Alabama, you hear me? I been to Mississippi—I been all around—you hear me?" And then he sat down, hard against the far wall of the car, legs stretched out in front and arms folded on his chest. His head drooped a few times, jerking back up each time as if in protest to what was about to come, and then staying down, mostly still among the loud snores and grunts and little whimpers that came in clear even in the clatter and bang of the moving car.

Matthew thought of Maggie again. Big-chested and red-haired and always up for a good time. She lived in Atlanta. He had met her years ago when he was still single. Roaming around and working when it suited him. He was with a road construction crew that time. Maybe fifteen years ago. Maybe more. Sometime back in the mostly blur of towns and faces and bottles always empty far too soon. Before he got married and all the rest of it. He was sure of that. Maggie. Her teeth were a little lopsided, but the smile was still straight on and her lips large and warm and those tits—big and firm and colored like cream—and that red hair that just kept tumbling down all thick and soft when she climbed on to ride. It had lasted nearly a year. She lived on some street near Georgia Tech. Toombs Court, he thought. No. Not Toombs. Something. It wouldn't come clear. But in a big old, two-storied house anyways, a big old place with high ceilings and a wide front porch that had a hammock strung out on it and magnolia trees in the front and back yards. He had liked to sit on the porch, sometimes sleeping in the hammock, on rainy days especially, listening to the tapping on the tin roof and the water dripping off the trees and making everything cool in the early summertime. They had talked a lot. And made promises. She had wanted him to stay. But he left with a crew heading to Alabama and lost touch after a few months and then drifted through several long binges until he found himself married to a flat-chested Floridian with a cop brother and friends in the Jacksonville City Hall.

He thought briefly of the money and what they could do with it, him and Maggie, all the good times and long days and nights and listening to the rain and talking and making promises and never thinking again of all the craziness out around and the meanness and the pain. Just spending the money careful, slow and easy and watching close where it went. But a car would be necessary, he suddenly thought. A car since he lost the old one, the borrowed one, the one he never could find back there in Jacksonville. And maybe some new clothes—especially for Maggie—maybe some rings and a watch or two and some fancy meals in a big hotel and trips on the train, long trips, living in a fancy compartment and eating all high and mighty in the dining car. Watching the world go by. A new day. A new way to go. It was all clear now. All of it. He was glad he had decided to take the money. It was the best thing he had ever done in his whole life. He couldn't wait to see Maggie's eyes when he opened the bag and laid all those bills down in front of her. A new day for sure.

"So you're on your way?"

Matthew stood up quickly, the voice a different one, nothing like the old man's, a vaguely familiar one from down where the old man clearly was sleeping in a noisy mix of snores, grunts, whimpers and little cries for help. There was it seemed a fog come in, the outside now darker and smelling like rain. No light could be seen through the cracks and in a place halfway between the old man and Matthew stood something-like-a-man—a long, thick staff clutched before him and a face that seemed to fade in and out of focus. Matthew tried to remember where he had heard the voice before.

"On your way?"

"I—yes, yes I'm going to Atlanta."

"That the best you can do?"

"What? I'm just going to see if I can find—"

"Atlanta?"

"Yes. Y'see there's this—when did you get on, mister? I never saw—"

"And after that?"

"After Atlanta?"

"Yes."

"Well if I hit pay-dirt, pal, there ain't going to be no after."

"And that's what you want? Atlanta."

"What I want? Yeah, I think it is. I think I've always wanted what's there. Yeah. That's it. Say, do I know you? Meet you somewhere?"

"I see you, sonny boy—I see you—you ain't comin' no closter nei-ther—I see you clear, you crazy sum-bitch—I see you—" The old man was awake and the something-like-a-man was gone, but the fog was lingering and outside it seemed like a proper rain storm was set to come in strong. "Sodomites and fornicators and adulterers and sneak-thieving sum-bitches and back stabbing bastards—and fire, sonny boy! Fire this time. No more water, but a fire this time! You crazy sum-bitch! I see you clear an' I see what's waiting. I see the bad things coming—coming quick, sonny boy—coming quick and sure!"

Matthew left the boxcar just as it stopped on the edge of the Atlanta yard. The old man was sleeping again, and the rain was now a light drizzle that seemed to have flecks of ice floating down in it from time to time. He turned up his collar, made sure the bag was safe against his chest, and saw some dim lights up ahead and to the right of a tangle of empty rails. It felt like daybreak was almost near enough to see, but still held off by a darkness that seemed to be moving in waves that bulged and dropped back almost in time to the beating of his heart. He started moving slowly toward the dim lights, just beginning to cross the rails as a particularly dark wave washed over him, something moving down in the blackness, forms there that seemed to be coming closer and closer and then to be standing near enough to touch. And then a splinter of light flashed out from the forms, and another and another until they were all around him, back and front and side, with voices there and a smell of whiskey and laughter down in it that sounded dry and then cough-choked and finally one voice broke free.

"Don't do nothing stupid, boy. You hear? Jus' stay right there."

The voice was almost friendly, quiet and calm and just loud enough to be heard without straining. The forms came in closer, lights now focusing on his face, blinding him, making him try to take a step back but there was no place to go.

"I—I'm trying to get to," and he suddenly remembered the street's name, and the number, and how it all looked in the early springtime. The porch was lit with early morning sunshine and the hammock was waiting for him to climb onto and rest, "—to Peach Orchard Lane. 568 Peach Orchard Lane."

"Peach Orchard?" The voice seemed to dissolve into a snorting sound, and a kind of laughter began all around, a snarling wheeze clearly there that died down almost as soon as it began. The others were coming in even closer. He thought he could feel their breath. "Shit. Peach Orchard. Ain't no peach orchard 'round here, boy. Nothing but us." And the laughter returned, lasting longer this time, the forms clear in outline but in little else, the darkness still holding them mostly close within the moving waves and the dim lights out beyond now gone away and lost. "Peach Orchard. Shit."

"Look, all I'm trying to do is get to Atlanta, and—" He crossed his arms and pressed the bag tighter against his chest and tried to see the faces of the men, to see something there that might give him a clue as to the right reaction, to the right way to go. But the darkness held firm.

"You made it, son. Atlanta. What you got for us? Somethin', I bet. Gift? You got somethin' to give us, I know. Right? So—give it—then you can get on gone to that orchard a yours."

"Look—I—I'm just trying to—" And the words stopped there, a few thoughts left to flicker awhile before a stab of pain came down to stay and grow deeper and wider and hotter as he fell to the ground and felt the bag go and the darkness strong behind his eyes and the wheezing laughter floating off away and gone.

Chapter Four: Pallet on the Floor

Dawn hurt his eyes. Matthew Clawson's face was bloody, and the bright light seemed to make the various cuts and bruises he knew were there feel even more painful. He was partially under a shed of some sort, fifty feet or more from the first line of track, somewhere in the brush alongside what looked to be (when he wiped his face with his sleeve and blinked his eyes) some sort of water tower. When he first woke up, he had frantically felt for the bag, almost tearing the buttons off his pea-jacket and nearly pulling his pants apart. But it was gone. All he had left were the clothes on his back, his shoes, and a throbbing pain that seemed to have put down deep roots all over his body. And an address there in among it all: 568 Peach Orchard Lane. Somewhere north of the city, he thought.

"Hey—hey you—hey what you doin' out there—hey—" The voice was a deep one, coming from a tall man dressed in blue, a police-type hat on his head, and what looked like a good-sized club in his hand. He was fast-stepping from the rail yard, jumping over piles of gravel and busted ties, and jabbing with the club in front of him as if he were cutting through some sort of barrier only he could see. "Hey—yeah you—what th'hell you doin' there, bub? Hey—"

Matthew began to run toward some trees beyond the water tower, a scrawny patch of nearly dead pines that seemed to offer at least some promise of cover, or at least a way out of the rail yard, a way toward the tall buildings he could clearly see in the distance. The tall man in blue was yelling louder now and trying to run faster. So Matthew did the same, the pain clutching him as he went, legs feeling like hundreds of tiny needles were poking him at once, chest and belly and shoulders all seeming to converge into one massive crash of scalding agony that throbbed and melded with the needles and the rest. But he ran hard in spite of it all. The man in blue was left far behind as Matthew pushed through an opening in a tallish chain-link fence and sprinted toward the trees and then kept on going. Down a red-clay path that veered a sharp right toward a giant culvert with a busy road up above it. He slid down a grassy bank and into the culvert and waited in the shadows for his breathing to begin to slow and his heart to stop racing. He couldn't hear the man in blue, hadn't heard him since the fence, seeming to have been stopped by it, not even trying to follow Matthew through the opening. And now there was traffic noise overhead, rumbling and echoing in the culvert, and he leaned back against one of the slick metal sides and slumped down into the soft clay and raised his knees to his chest, holding them there for a while with shaking hands. And he thought of Maggie. Almost seeing her in the near-darkness of the culvert. Almost hearing her words and feeling the warmth of her skin against his own, healing the pain and soothing away all trouble and care. He thought he could see her face, for just a second or two, and then longer, back in the deeper darkness of the culvert, floating there and smiling and making him welcome, bringing him home. And other faces there too. And other voices. And then the something-like-a-man came drifting in, slowly down among the others who all seemed now dancing around the place he finally stood.

"Maggie!" And the word echoed down in the darkness, mixing with the traffic sounds, and a train whistle that seemed very close at hand. "Maggie!" But the something-like-a-man was all that he could see, the darkness taking everything away, a voice there deep within and raising up a feeling like none that he had ever felt before, perhaps not coming from his life at all, perhaps come seeping in from someone else's story being told.

&

I-Man was the first one to see the falling-down man. I-Man was home sick with his Ma and had been sitting in the front parlor, on the little couch and looking every once and awhile out the big window. He saw the man stumbling along the sidewalk, come up from the big road, from the place that I-Man was never, never to go. Ma was in the kitchen with the dog, Pea-patch, and Uncle Daddy. She was fixing food to eat. It smelled good. I-Man watched him fall down and rest some, head down in the tall grass of Mr. Vosickle's yard, feet pushed out onto the sidewalk and his arms wrapped around his middle. I-Man wondered when the man would wake up. Maybe he could come play when he woke up. Maybe he could sleep in I-Man's room. Uncle Daddy was yelling at Ma again. Bad words in it. Loud. Outside, the man tried to roll over but only made it half-way. The wind was blowing hard. Nighttime soon. The sky looked like rain. Cold out today and I-Man was glad he was home. School was no good. Bad boys there. And bad girls too. Something went pop-pop-pop back in the kitchen. Pop-pop-pop. And a funny smell came with it quick. The falling-down man was standing up and stumbling again on the sidewalk. Getting closer and closer to the house. I-Man heard Ma crying. Uncle Daddy never made a sound.

It wasn't easy leaving the other story, leaving its words behind, the something-like-a–man gone too, taking it away for a time, pushing Matthew from the darkness and finally to the front door of a house. 568 Peach Orchard Lane. It had taken him most of the day to get there. Catching a ride with some Marines. Up above the culvert, he had stood for quite a while trying to get somebody to notice him enough to even think about stopping. But the two Marines had stopped, almost the moment they spotted Matthew swaying a bit in a wind come up from the south. The Marines were drunk. And going overseas, they said. In two weeks, they said. The driver looked like he was twelve and his friend all of thirteen. Matthew got in slowly and settled into what there was of the back seat of a rolling puzzle of pieced together junk, door panels not matching the front or back either one, multi-colors everywhere and no sign of how the car started out, looking like everything had been made up as the owner went along, the chassis welded together enough to provide a place to sit and keep out of the sun and rain. But the engine sounded new, a rumbling-roar coming out in time to the screech of tires and bump and jump and clatter of the chassis as the driver slammed on the gas-pedal and pointed the whole mess toward the tall buildings of Atlanta. The Marines were passing a bottle back and forth. They offered some to Matthew and he took a long pull. Bourbon. It felt good.

"Wha' happen to you there, man?" The driver had turned around to ask the question. Matthew noticed that traffic seemed to be staying away from the rolling junk-yard. "You look like hell." He turned back to the highway and shook his head. His friend seemed to be singing some song, his voice low and phlegm-choked amid all the clatter and screeches out around.

"I—I got robbed—beat up and robbed—" Matthew had thought of Maggie, of how disappointed she would be to hear of the loss of the money. But he was sure she would welcome him anyway. Find a place for him to sleep and heal. The money was no good anyway. No good. The devil's pay. "I—I need to get to Peach Orchard Lane—568."

"What you say?" The driver took back the bottle and took several quick pulls before handing it to his friend. "Peace what? You ain't some commie or something? Peace? Hell, son, we're in a go'damn war. Ain't you heard?" His friend laughed and pushed the bottle down between his legs, closing his thighs to hold it, bottle bottom resting on the threadbare seat. "We going back over there, son. Peace, you say? No damn peace there, right? Right, Bobby—right?"

"No damn peace, Jerry. No damn peace." And the friend's head began to nod and droop until he seemed asleep, a few mumbling words coming out every so often, but mostly just heavy breathing in among the rest of the car noise.

"Peach—Peach—not peace—Peach. Peach Orchard Lane. It's up past Georgia Tech, I think. Up toward Gainesville. Somewhere."

"Peach, huh. Hell, everything's got peach in it around here—shit—peach. Yeah sure—you going home?" And the car lurched and shook and Matthew grabbed for the edge of the seat to steady himself.

"Friend lives there. A good friend." And Maggie, he was sure, would hug him long and hard and make him sit down in some comfortable chair while she took care of his wounds, while she took care of the healing, while she helped him begin to live again. "I'm going to see a good friend."

"Well we goin' to Charlotte—tha's in North Car'lina—we goin' there." And he gunned the car, forcing Matthew to fall back hard into a pain that seemed to be everywhere now, from head to feet, arms and legs throbbing, vision at times blurred and his ears ringing and hot. "I see Peach an' I'll stop, ok? Peach, huh? Like up there?" And he nodded toward a battered road-sign, bullet-pocked and faded, but clearly stating "Peach Orchard," a smiling peach-face there dead center and some sort of arrow pointing to an exit that looked seldom used, patches of grass clumped at places along where it met the highway, and in a few spots further on showing what looked to be vines. "Peach Orchard—see? That might be Lane there—see? Beside that whatever it is near the peach head. See it?"

"Yes—yes—" And it was a miracle, he thought. The car shuddered as it slowed and nearly stopped and let Matthew find his way free and hard onto a patch of grass. He rolled a bit as he hit. Elbows taking the brunt of it although his hands and some of his face got into the mix. It was getting dark and it looked like rain coming in. And out around him once again, especially when he shut his eyes, the other story, closer then, came in to finally mix in strongly with his own—and stay.

&

Ma had put a bunch of clothes in a funny-looking bag. And had made I-Man put on his heavy coat and boots. And fed him some grits and eggs. The funny smell was not as big as it had been. Uncle Daddy was staying in the kitchen, Ma said. And she and I-Man was going up north. In the old truck. Uncle Daddy's truck. Ma did not see the falling-down man at all. But he was on the porch when they started to go. He was there. All beat up. Ma pushed I-Man behind her and closed the door. She and the man were on the porch. The wind was blowing hard. It was getting dark. The funny smell was all gone, but another one was coming in. Another funny smell. It made I-Man cough and rub his eyes. Ma was on the porch with the man.

"Look, Mister—I ain't got no time for—"

"Maggie," The man's voice was barely a whisper. "Maggie," his face was bloody and his clothes looked like he had rolled around in briars and then got wet down and made to roll some more. "I—I've been trying to—Maggie—"

"I ain't Maggie, mister. I ain't her."

Matthew sat on some sort of a couch. It smelled like wood-smoke in the room. Like something burning. A boy was staring at him from across the room. He seemed familiar. Something. The other voices and the faces floating in the wood-smoke and settling down to rest. The woman was trying to clean up Matthew's face. She had helped him inside, finally, and let him sit down. Maggie no longer lived there. She had died, the woman said. She had been her mother and she had died years ago. And now the woman was leaving. Today. Just as Matthew came up on the porch. She had to leave. The boy was making gurgling sounds and coughing and rubbing his eyes. There were suitcases and bags there by the door. The woman did not seem happy about Matthew being there. The smoke-smell was getting stronger.

"Look, mister—I'll help a bit here—but—you need to go on, now. You hear? I got to get on the road my own self—and now. You hear?"

"Yeah," It hurt for Matthew to speak, his face swollen and his lips all cut up and the right side of his head feeling like something was stabbing needles down in it every half inch or so. "Yeah, I can see that—I can—but, you see, I knew your Mama. I knew her way back. I knew her and used to live here—and—I ain't got nowhere else to go, and I—" And something about the way the woman cocked her head, like a puppy trying to puzzle out a strange sight or sound, made him think of Maggie, made him think of those long afternoons and nights, with the rain dripping outside and the comfort of her arms around him, and the rest of the world far, far away. And he felt drawn to the young woman as well, to the sound of her voice, to her hair and the way she pouted up her lips while she wiped at his face. The strange boy was smiling in the corner of the room, his back resting on the peeling wall, and his arms folded across his chest. There was now smoke visible in the room, lazily drifting in from some place behind a closed door to the side of the boy.

"Well, we're going, Mister. We got to go. You feel strong enough to travel?"

"I—I—yes—I think so—I had money, but—"

"Not interested in that. Can you drive stick?"

"Yes. But—but I got no license—no ID—I was robbed back there in—"

"We'll make do. I got extra. C'mon—we got to go. North. We're headin' north. To Jerusalem Hill. Pennsylvania."

The strange-looking boy began nodding his head and for a moment, just a blink of an eye's worth, Matthew thought he saw his own face there, flickering out in the smoky light like a shadow turning real.

Chapter Five: The Road to Jerusalem

The truck was a Ford of some sort—with an oversized cab that looked to have been home-made and a bed covered up by a tightly tied-down tarp. They had pried up one side of the tarp and pushed the suitcases underneath, and the woman had given Matthew a driver's license and other papers and some cash (she said it was "near fifty dollars") and then they all piled inside the cab. The house was now blazing—flames wind-caught and whipping around the front porch and rising up to the eaves on the stronger gusts. Matthew put it in gear and rolled down the driveway. The boy was humming and the woman, sitting shotgun, hugged him to her and shook her head.

"You need to climb on in back, I-Man. Get on back there and try to sleep. Ok?"

"You got blankie? Blankie back there?"

"It's always back there, I-Man. Get on back and sleep now, ok?"

The woman helped the boy climb over the front seat and helped settle him down and then wrapped some kind of shawl around herself. Her voice sounded tired.

"Keep going straight up here for about a mile or so—until we hit Old State Road 432. 432--that's the one we got take on up through to Virginia. It'll keep us off the main roads for a while."

"What about the house?" Matthew felt like he was somehow dream-caught—that all this was simply some sort of elaborate nightmare—that he was still in the culvert or back in the boxcar with the old man cursing and stomping in the darkness and yelling about nothing good waiting out ahead. And right now, nothing felt good for sure. Nothing was good. The whole thing seemed wrong from the boxcar to here. Maybe from the time he left the Dakotas to here. Maybe even before that.

"Don't worry about the house. I ain't left nothing there I need." And she pulled the shawl even tighter about her shoulders and coughed. "Just keep your eyes on the road. We'll get to 432 pretty quick now. It's a right-hand turn mind. You got that?"

"Yeah." And Matthew tried to focus on the road ahead, the mostly darkness to either side showing nothing in it but the occasional glint of something distant, a porch light maybe or maybe some kind of store or gas station sign. There was fog coming in which made the darkness seem to be moving at times, puffs of shadows that drifted across the road and flattened against the windshield. He turned briefly to glance at the woman, her head now leaning against the window, bobbing a bit as the truck bounced over something in the road. The boy was snoring. Ahead was a sign that read "Old North Georgia 432"—seeming to be new, and leaning just a bit to the right—seeming to point to a two-lane that was lost in darkness.

The Georgia Boy Quick Stop was almost deserted when Matthew rolled into the parking lot and aimed for the closest gas pump. They were nearly on empty. It was almost dawn and somewhere ahead was South Carolina—if they hadn't already crossed over in the fog. There hadn't been any road-signs for hours. Not since he found the road and started to follow it as best he could. The woman and boy were both sleeping. He left them in the truck and walked toward the office. An old man was already at the door. A familiar old man.

"Mornin', son. What you need?" The office behind him was well-lighted and there was a small television screen pushed in amongst some boxes near a battered desk in one corner. The tiny screen seemed mostly dark with a bright oval in the center that flickered out nothing much beyond wavy lines and an occasional buzzing sound. The old man was not smiling.

"What? I—I just want some—some gas, is all."

"Gas? That's all you want this time? Gas? Where you going, son?" The voice was tired-sounding, like someone nearing sleep but fighting it. He was dressed in a faded, blue jumpsuit—sleeves tattered and front stained with what looked to be oil.

"Look—can we just get some gas and go on down—"

"Sure. I'll pump the gas, son. Glad to. But—what else do you need?" The man's face, streaked by the light coming from the office, was covered in wrinkles, his eyes seeming to move in and out of the darkness to either side of the door.

"Just the gas. Just the gas. That's all." Matthew thought he saw the woman wave at him from the truck, but when he looked again, she still seemed to be sleeping, her head resting against the smudged glass of the window. He wondered when it all would end.

"Soon as you decide, son. No sooner than that." And the old man smiled and patted Matthew on the shoulder. "Then it'll be clear. Right and clear and straight ahead." And his fingers felt warm and then hot as Matthew frowned and shook his head.

"What will? Where? I just can't see nothing no more. Nothing."

"Fill 'er up, bub?" The old man was gone and a short, fat red-faced man in a baseball cap was there in his place, in the office door, the television screen now brightly lit with some kind of test-pattern. "Filler'up?"

"Uh—yeah—yeah, I guess. Yeah." And he reached in his back pocket for the money the woman had given him. The bills felt old and frayed. The dawn was trying to break free of the fog, bright streaks out toward the road and all around. The road looked freshly washed, slick and black and waiting for the sun. The woman woke up and stared out at him. And behind her, the strange boy was reaching for her hair.

They had entered Pennsylvania sometime past midnight. Hours ago now. Moving slowly along beside the Susquehanna, the two-lane highway nearly free of other headlights for at least the past half-hour, the river itself just a promise that showed up occasionally in signs that pointed to where it must have been. Matthew was sleepy, but kept sipping at the thermos of coffee the woman had filled at the last gas station. The coffee was helping but the snoring of the boy and the droning on of the woman made him want to pull off the road and sleep forever. Days had passed since Atlanta—maybe a week—it was difficult to remember. All the little towns. At times seeming to double back each time they made forward progress. Following the woman's directions. The back roads and the gas stations and the burger stands and the incessant chatter, the nearly monotonic mumbling of the woman all through the Carolinas, and Virginia, and some of West Virginia and Maryland and finally Pennsylvania—finally within, he guessed, striking distance of their destination, of her destination at least—Jerusalem Hill. He took another sip of coffee and noticed that the road was steeper now, just a little but steadily winding upward into what he guessed was the higher ground above the river.

"How long you know my Mama?"

"What?" The question startled him, not anything like the other rambling series of stories and observations and whatever it was she did to calm the boy when he had a bad dream or forgot where he was. It came out of nothing that had gone before.

"Mama? Maggie. How long you know her?" She was resting against the door with her knees drawn up under her, arms around them and fingers tapping sometimes on the rough cloth of her pants.

"I—I knew her a long time ago. Way back in the early fifties, I think. Way back." He tried to remember how Maggie looked, tried to remember the house, the springtime and summer, the long afternoons and evenings in bed with the rain a gentle tapping on the tin roof, how she made love, her scent, her voice, but nothing would come clear but the face of the woman and her boy. Especially the boy. His face seemed a close thing to Matthew's own. Especially at the same age. From the old photos Mama had kept and shown him sometimes in a South Dakota that seemed as far away as a clear memory of anything before the first steps he had taken away from Jacksonville. The boy looked very much like Matthew.

"Well she never said nothing about no Yankee." Her voice sounded sleepy, low and with a bit of a lisp there that made it seem child-like. The boy continued to snore from his place directly behind the driver's seat.

"What?"

"You. Nothing about no Yankee. An' she told me near about everthing—'specially there towards the end—when she was dying. Told me just about everthing she ever done, I think. Everybody she ever knew. Talk talk talk—that's all she did—all she wanted to do—talk and talk and talk until I thought I'd go plumb crazy from it. An' then she just died. Just died one morning at dawn. Just stopped breathing and died. No more talking. It was real sad, y'know? I-Man kept poking at her arms—trying to get her to get up an' play, y'know? Real sad. Took me near a month to quiet him down. But—no Yankee nowhere in none of it. No sir. You sure it was Mama you knew?" And she had released her legs and stretched them out in front of her. Her hair was long and draped over her shoulders. The boy kept on snoring.

"Why is his name, 'I-Man'?" The words were a surprise as they came out. He had intended to say he wasn't a Yankee, that he was from South Dakota, that he had known her mother better than anyone else in his life, that he had come to find her and be healed and go on and live for a long, long time. But that wasn't what came out. 'I-Man' instead.

"He named his own self, I guess. Couldn't change his mind. His real name is Carter. Carter Knox. But when he was about three or so, he used to dress up in my boyfriend's clothes and stomp around the house. "I need a smoke. Bad. Been stopped for a year, but all this stuff's gotten my nerves just all shot—smoke might help. I don't know. Maybe not." And she smiled over at Matthew and reached behind him to tug at a blanket that was covering the boy. "Man, wish I could sleep like that."

"The name? 'I-Man'?" And it had been like that all along, the whole trip, except when she slept or ate or did whatever she did in the various garage restrooms. Never staying on target. Never finishing up much of nothing. But just talk and talk and talk. Maggie had been quiet—a listener—someone who made others feel like telling their stories and sharing their lives. "'I-Man'? Remember?"

"Oh yeah. He named his own self. Used to try to dress up in some of my boyfriend's clothes—like I said—big boots and shirts. Looked like halloween sometimes. Stomping around yelling 'I-Man—I-Man—I-Man.' Couldn't get him to answer to nothing but that after awhile—so we just all started to call him 'I-Man'—'cause of him wanting it, I guess—wanting to be called that. So he named his own self. Y'see?" And she smiled brightly and twisted a bit in the seat.

"Yes." And ahead the sun was rising, and to the right, as they rolled into a little curve, the river was suddenly there—wide and filled with rocks and little houses out along its bank, down in the trees all bare and bending just a bit in a wind come up from somewhere in the lingering darkness, little houses of various colors with smoke curling from their chimneys and twinkling lights there too and up ahead a deer alone and grazing near a boulder painted red.

&

The truck—picking up speed for about a mile or more had suddenly begun to make a clunking sound and smoke came curling up along the front hood just as they neared the bottom of a rocky hill. Matthew turned sharply to avoid a dog that seemed to be dragging something from the shoulder toward the center line, causing the truck to skid a bit onto a nearby graveled road and finally coast to a clanking-clattering stop beside a hand-carved wooden sign proclaiming: ST. GADARENE'S MONESTARY. CONVENTUAL FRIARS OF THE HOLY SPIRIT. 1 MILE. The woman had screamed at some point during it all, waking up the boy who kept yelling "I-Man I-Man I-Man" even after the truck stopped and the woman had reached back to pull him forward into the front seat. Matthew got out and tried to open the hood, but it was too hot.

"Damn—God—that thing must be about to flame—damn—"

"I-Man Man Man Man—"

"What you going do, Mister? You know how to fix it?" The woman had moved to the driver's side and rolled down the window. She then began holding the boy, trying to calm him.

"No. No, I don't."

"Well what th'hell, Mister? I thought you knew all about—"

"No. Not me. Stick, remember? I drive stick?" And he pushed his fingers through his hair and looked over at the sign. "Y'know—we—we ain't never talked none about all that back there. The fire? I mean—I wasn't in no kind of shape to be picky—still ain't—but I never did understand why all the damn rush—leaving everything like you did?"

"What you going do now, Mister? Now? We can't just sit here. I got to get to Jerusalem Hill."

"Yeah? Why? You never have said why you need to go there—or even where exactly it is, for that matter. Just these strange roads—back behind everything—never no main highway—"

"I know the way we need to go, Mister. Don't you worry about that—"

"I-Man Man Man Man—" The boy was rocking back and forth in the front seat, held tightly against his mother, almost chanting his name—now loud, now soft. The woman was trying to rub his head and face. "I Manny Manny Manny Manny Man Man—"

"Ok Ok—look—I'll walk on down to whatever it is down there—the sign says a mile—I'll go see if we can luck out on some help—maybe a mechanic—who knows?" The sign had stirred something in Matthew—a memory—South Dakota surely—and brown-robed men—something too far back, however, to do more besides nag and make him feel uneasy. "You ok with that? I'll just go see what's down there. Maybe get some help."

"And maybe something else—I don't even understand that damn sign—it don't make no sense at all." The boy was still rocking, but slower now, his head resting longer and longer against the woman's shoulder. "I don't know what it is down there—I don't understand—"

"Like I do?" Matthew was beginning to feel scared, not quite panic but something close to it seeming to rise up and wash over him each time he looked back at the woman. "Like I understand any of this—any damn thing that's been happening—right from Rebarb's Bar—last thing that made any sense was Jax Beer and some whiskey." He swallowed hard a few times, his breath getting short and his heart racing. "I mean—who just leaves their damn house to burn—who does that? Maggie would never—" And for a moment, he thought it was Maggie in the truck, smiling out at him and welcoming him home. But the woman came back strong instead.

"None of your damn business, Mister. None of it. My Mama'd do the same damn thing—'cept sooner'n I done it—"

"I-Man Man Man—" The boy was slowing down, way down and the woman helped him down gently onto the seat. Her coat was under his head. "Mama?" His voice was calm now, soft, near sleep. Matthew walked away.

"Yes, baby—yes?"

"Where is Uncle Daddy?"

"Granny came and got him, baby. Granny took him away."

The friars were mostly silent, but the Abbot talked enough for all of them. His name was Gerard, Father Gerard, and Matthew had been brought to him by several friars dressed in rough burlap and wearing sandals that looked to have been put together from used tires and scraps of cast-away leather. They were standing in the Abbot's office, a high-ceilinged room that was windowed on three sides with a wall-to-ceiling bookcase behind his ornate desk. The Abbot smiled often and finally came around the desk to offer Matthew a seat on a plush-looking couch.

"Rest awhile, brother. Rest. You look like you have seen some hard times." Indicating Matthew's face with a slow, circular movement of his finger in the air, he frowned a bit and shook his head. "Were you in an accident, my son?"

"No—no—just fell down—y'know—fell down."

"I see. Well, Friar Edward and Friar Mark say you are also broken down, yes?" And he smiled and immediately began to talk again. "Down our road. Broken down? Your vehicle? We can help, of course. Our order is an imminently practical one. Friar Mark there is a master mechanic. And Friar Edward makes the best soufflé this side of New York City. We pray, of course. Pray quite a bit actually." And he smiled again, but not for long, seeming unable to keep the words from tumbling out. "Pray and work. Work and pray. We have been here for a long, long time, brother—brother? I'm not sure I heard your name, brother—did you give it? I sometimes don't hear everything that's said. A failing of mine. Yes indeed, a definite failing. Do you have failings, brother? Do you?" And he smiled again, keeping it going a bit longer this time, and the silent friars coughed a bit and shifted their weight, sandal to sandal.

"I—I—well, yes—I have—failings—my—the truck is right at your sign back there. I don't know what's wrong with it—it just won't do nothing but clank and smoke and—"

"Splendid—then, it's decided, yes?" The Abbot nodded toward the friars and put a hand on Matthew's shoulder. "You will stay here until we fix your vehicle—we have a guest house—and you are most welcome to stay as long as it takes." The smile up close was filled with very straight and very white teeth. "As long as it takes."

"There's more people back there, sir. More people."

"People? Back at the truck? People there?" The smile dissolved into a near-frown. The friars coughed again and a bell began to toll from somewhere close at hand. "Mid-day prayer in thirty. Time enough, I suspect. How many people, eh?"

"A—a woman and a child—a little boy—they're waiting back at the truck."

"A family then! Splendid! A family—did you hear, Friar Edward—Friar Mark? A family. We pay special attention to families here, brother—brother—again, my son, I'm afraid I don't know your official name." And he laughed a bit, and raised his eyebrows, and nodded to the friars. They both left the room, almost without any sound at all, just a slight squish of sandal and rustle of burlap and the faint click of the door. "What shall I call you, brother?"

"Uh—Matthew—Matthew Clawson—"

"Excellent! Matthew, it is. Matthew. Let's go find your family."

The guest house was a three bedroom cabin with a sizable bathroom and kitchen. The Abbott had made a fuss over the woman and the boy and had left them finally in the care of an elderly friar named Rudolpho. He was more round than tall and insisted on taking in the luggage piece by piece all by himself. The Abbott said Rudolpho was the oldest friar at St. Gadarene's—and was ready to help in any way he could.

"Just ring the bell here—on the wall here—see? And help will be on its way." And the Abbott had walked quickly toward the other friars, moving almost in unison amid the now steady tolling of the bells.

"Mid-Day prayer," Friar Rudolpho had said brightly, and then he said, aiming the words directly at Matthew, "Do you pray?"

"I—I—" The woman and the boy had disappeared into one of the bedrooms and the bells were now louder and more insistent. "I—no—no, I guess I don't—not anymore, that is." And he thought quickly of South Dakota and his mother and the rest all sweating in the little church, all shouting out their praise or need or fear, the preacher red-faced and dancing before the little choir, and jumping almost high enough to seem to float on air.

"No prayer?" His eyes seemed teary, glazed a bit and wide. "None? Sad. Very sad, brother Matthew." And a familiar figure had stepped into Rudolpho's place, into him it seemed, top to bottom and without much fuss at all. A tall, familiar figure. "And now you're here? Is this what you want? Have you found it here?" And the figure seemed to be puzzling out something that perhaps only it could fully appreciate, cocking its head a bit, face not quite clear, but the eyes sharp-looking, bright and staring, it seemed, deep into the places

Matthew seldom bothered with, the places that he never looked at long enough to see.

"I—y'see—I—I don't know what you want—I don't know—"

"It's not what I want. It's what *you* want. *You.* All this moving around. All this searching. What have you lost?"

"Lost? I ain-t—I ain't lost nothing—I just been having a run a bad luck is all. I just can't seem to get things in line long enough to make 'em work out—see? That's all there is to it. So—you don't need to keep on coming into things and asking—"

"What do you want?" And the figure seemed to float a bit, side to side, robes fluttering and scraping against the rough wood of the cabin wall.

"I—I just want to get along is all. Just get along—I mean—how th'hell do I know? I don't want nothin' but to get along. That's it. Just get along."

"That's all. And so you're here to get along. Here? In this place?"

"Hell—th' truck broke down—the damn truck broke down—"

"Going where?"

"What?"

"Going where? Where was the truck going?"

"Truck was—we—we was going to Jerusalem Hill. That's where. You'd have to ask her for the rest of it," and he nodded toward the bedroom, "go on an' ask her. I don't know no more."

"Jerusalem Hill? That's it? That's the place?"

"Hell, mister, hell—I don't know nothing no more—nothing—I'm just so go'damn tired I could sleep for a month. I been banged around and messed with so much that I don't know a damned thing—nothing."

"Nothing?"

"Yeah—nothing. I don't even have an idea no more. It's all just a whole shit-bucket full of nothing." And nothing it surely had been, he thought, from Rebarb to here and back again to South Dakota to everything since he could remember anything at all. Nothing.

"Good place to be." And Friar Rudolpho returned, suddenly there and smiling at Matthew and nodding toward the bells. "Want to go to chapel, Brother Matthew?"

"I don't know."

Matthew had returned from the chapel confused by what he saw and heard, confused and even more exhausted. The woman and the boy were in the kitchen cooking something that smelled like onions and some kind of meat. The boy was at a little table near one of the windows, playing with egg shells. The Abbott had led a long chant in some kind of foreign language, and the friars had all finally lit candles and milled around in the middle of the main aisle and then filed out one by one. There was a huge Crucifix over the altar, and the side windows were rose-colored, and the chanting had nearly put Matthew to sleep. And none of it had made any sense at all. None of it. The Abbott had stopped him outside. The temperature had fallen, and the sky was heavy with clouds.

"Glad you could come, brother Matthew. Evening prayer is next. Wait for the bell."

"Well—thanks—but, I might not make it, y'see—I'm pretty sleepy."

And the Abbott had smiled and walked quickly after the retreating Friars, moving in the direction of a long row of cabins that seemed to jut out of the nearby woods.

The smell in the kitchen was a good one. Taken all together. And the woman smiled when he came into the room. And the boy had smiled as well. And Matthew had sat down in a rocking chair and watched the woman cook. A decent fire was crackling and popping in the fireplace over in one corner of the room. It was very nice.

"Fridge was full up with all kinds of stuff. Good stuff too." The woman's hair was long and reddish-colored in the indirect light from lamps placed in opposite corners of the room. She was wearing a long red apron that came down almost to her knees. "I think this is some kind of steak. An' I found onions an' po'taters an' big ol' loaves of bread." She was almost dancing around the stove, prodding and poking at the steaming food, and humming sometimes a tune like he suddenly remembered Maggie used to hum, something like a lullaby. The boy had found more egg shells and was trying to pile them on top of each other. It sounded like a wind was coming up strong outside. And through the curtained window nearest the boy, Matthew saw snow begin to fall. "I like it here." And she smiled over at Matthew, a kindly smile, a gentle smile, and for just a second or two, it was Maggie again, Maggie looking to see him come home to stay. "Bet you're hungry. We are. Right, I-Man?"

"Mama?" He pushed at the eggshells gently, slowly twirling them around on the table.

"Yes." She stepped back from the stove and wiped at her forehead. "What is it?"

"Will Granny bring Uncle Daddy back?"

"No, baby. They ain't comin' back."

"Never?"

"Never."

"You sure?"

"Yes. Yes, I am."

"Is this your Daddy?"

"Who, baby?"

"This man—the man who falls down—this man here—this man—"

"No." And she frowned toward Matthew, watching him turn slowly toward the boy. "I don't think so, baby. No."

"Did he know my Granny?"

"He says so."

"I think he's your Daddy." And the boy smiled over at Matthew and pushed the eggshells off the table.

Outside, the snow began to fall faster and faster, a slanting and whirling mess of white in the play of the wind. The night would be a long one.

Matthew fell asleep to the tolling of the bells, to the sound of the call to evening prayer, to the beating of ice on the window of the bedroom and the murmuring voices of the woman and the boy. The meal had been delicious. Steak and potatoes and green beans and a bread like nothing he had ever tasted. They had sat at the larger table in the kitchen, the fire nearby and the smell of the wood seeming to be layering itself throughout the room. They ate in silence, mostly in silence, a few words here and there from the boy, an "I-Man Man Man" coming out from time to time, and the woman sometimes speaking to him and to Matthew about nothing much in particular. It was nice to sit there. To eat and feel the warmth of the fire and think about nothing much at all but the next bite of food. Matthew had never had anything like this. Not in his whole life. Not even when he had been a boy back in South Dakota. No matter how hard Mama tried, peace never came home to stay.

The dream was a short one. Or at least later it had seemed short. Matthew and the woman and the boy all together in the Abbot's office. It had started out that way at least. The three of them listening to the Abbot talk about family and how important it was to have one and how important it was to make it stay together. And then the woman began talking about how her Mama had died and how she kept wanting somebody named Matthew there and how she kept praying for him to come home and the Abbot had cried some and some other Friars had come in—maybe ten or so—and they all were playing electric guitars and singing Elvis tunes and dancing some kind of bebop and a few were flying around the room and John Kennedy was suddenly there—still with a full head of hair—and several flamingos began a little bobbing dance around him and then they all flew off into the whirling snow outside and then Matthew woke up. He was alone. No sounds were there. Deep darkness all around. It was cold and he was on some sort of hard bed and there were moving shadows out beyond him on all sides and he was afraid and trembling and cried out—but his voice was too faint a thing to make it much past his own ears (and even they were not quite sure what he said)—and then a deeper kind of darkness came down over him and he felt warm and quiet inside and sleepy and then asleep and drifting, almost wind-caught and spiraling deep down into a place without sound and without the feel of anything to stop his fall.

Matthew Clawson awoke lying on a bare place somewhere on a very hot night, the moon above going in and out of low-hanging clouds and only a very few stars visible and a sound of tree-frogs and crickets there too and off in the direction of some piney woods, something-like-a-man came closer and closer, taking long strides along a shining pathway and seeming to hold to a tall, curved wooden staff. He seemed familiar somehow, something round about him that seemed old and trustworthy and tested hard in all the places needing to be strong. Matthew knew what the man would say. And Matthew also knew how hard and bleak the way back home.

Georgie Porgie

George E. ("Jaybird") Donovan, Director of Institutional Effective-
ness and permanent Chair of the Tenure Committee at Pee Dee River Technical University had planned to sleep late. Yesterday's series
of meetings had been very stressful, so he decided to treat himself to
an extra hour or two before tomorrow's Board of Trustee's Retreat at
noon. He told his wife as much last night when he finally made it
home. Late again. The smell of his current girlfriend only minimally
subdued by a few spritzes of cologne and a cigar he had smoked
outside on the University Quad. The sunset had been magnificent.
His wife had been angry. As usual. But he had passed through her
words quickly, not answering. As usual. "Late again, Jay? That's
three this week. This one like to talk afterwards?" After carefully
showering, he slipped into bed and set the clock for nine instead of
seven. His wife slowly shook her head and then plumped up her pil-
lows.

"I'm sleeping in tomorrow," he said. It was always best not to answer her questions, and he had stopped paying serious attention to
her years ago, after the last of the three kids had finally graduated
from college. She mostly bored him. "Did you hear? I'm sleeping in."

"Yes. I'm sure you will." She sounded full awake, words clipped
and crisp as she gathered the quilt about her shoulders so that only
the top of her head pushed free.

And he slept. Soundly at first. But then around two (he had
looked at the clock) a dream awakened him and didn't let go. To-

night's girlfriend, Anita something, long black hair and a rack truly first-rate, sitting on him, riding slowly, face nearly obscured by her hair but lips full and pouting, until, improbably and only there as he came mostly awake, the young Professor's face rising up strong amid the general grogginess—the last of the dream not wanting to leave, but the young man's face unmistakably there, a man he had been fighting with for months, a man he had been working behind the scenes to fire, and finally a man he had mauled at today's— yesterday's—Divisional meeting, cutting him short publically in a way that neutralized his puny objections to the oncoming array of cost- cutting initiatives that would save the University thousands of dollars a month. Big changes all around and President Broome himself in attendance and frowning as the young Professor stood and asked:

"So—no more paper at all? None?" The young Professor was from the Traditional English Department—a dime-a-dozen bunch that never agreed on anything and kept shrinking year by year.

"That's the plan—yes." And Jaybird had smiled over at President Broome who had begun talking on his cell-phone.

"Handouts? Tests? Even diplomas?"

"All on-line. Yes." Jaybird had noticed Anita whatever on the back row. A graduate student in English, he had guessed. He never could remember their majors. They had been dating for a few months now, and she never talked much until tonight. But back at the meeting, she had sat like a proper school girl, hands clasped in her lap and a smile there each time that Jaybird looked her way. She had seemed to be impressed with his presentation. But then they always were. Over ten years now. Secretaries (his and others), faculty (fourteen at last count)—all after something—some help or edge he could give them in their careers—and, most recently—students (always carefully se- lected—age first and most important, of course). Anita, he suddenly remembered, had wanted him to put in a good word with President Broome concerning a post-graduate internship. Back at the meeting, however, the young English Professor had become more and more frustrated and looked it. Change always made people antsy. Always.

"Then—then why have face-to-face classes at all?'

"Exactly. Well put! We're with you on that. Yes, we are. Would you like to be part of the first major conversion?" Jaybird had smiled his best smile as the last word came out.

"What?"

"We're going to go live in the Fall. Fourteen face-to-face classes at first—literature, I think. A—D, at first. Would you like to be part of that first group? What do you teach?"

"Literature. Chaucer. I..."

"Excellent. Chaucer is in the top ten. Among the traditionals, of course. I'm told he's made for online. So—you're in, yes? Welcome, sir, welcome!" And Jaybird clapped his hands together and smiled again a lesser version of his best.

"What?" And the young man had simply turned a strange shade of red and choked a few times and left the meeting, stumbling at the top of the aisle and finally making it through the big doors in back. President Broome and a few Trustees had laughed and then the whole room joined in—Anita the loudest and longest of them all. He had met her at her apartment later. In a neighboring town. They often met there the past few months. When he could break free from the others. She always had drinks ready and a symphony of some sort playing low. He never was exactly clear on what sort of internship she was after.

Waking up even more, he wondered why women were so pre-dictable. Like Anita. Drawn to power. Pulled to it again and again whenever it suited them. Power. He almost trembled with pleasure thinking of how many lives he could derail by a single phone call or memo—something he had done over and over again when he discovered even the least bit of disloyalty or contradiction or ingratitude. He loved his job. Anita had pouted even more than usual as he finished his first drink and then the riding and the rest and afterwards a disjointed attempt at conversation about her internship chances and hopes for a distant future. He had nearly fallen asleep twice. And finally home to bed and a dream ending once and for all when all faces dropped off into that of a gold-toothed, bald-headed man with a massive neck and eyes that seemed far too big for his face. The gun looked huge and was pointed right at Jaybird's nose.

"You bastid! You filthy bastid sum-bitch!"

"What?" Jaybird's wife was no longer in the bed, and the man shifted the gun to his left hand and yanked down the covers. Jaybird was naked.

"Good god-a-mighty—you sleep that way with my Bonnie? Lookit you—I bet you ain't even five foot even—pinched face and hair most gone in front! Bonnie let you in lookin' like that? Did she, you sum-bitch?"

"Who are…"

"I'm the Angel a Goddamned Death." And he smiled broadly, a crooked mouth mostly and showing at least eight gold teeth—uppers and lowers both—glinting dully in the weak light thrown by the lamp on the wife's bedside table.

"What?"

"Yes sir, I am. Angel a Death. Your time done come." And he laughed—a gurgling sound there and bits of something floating out into the air each time he moved his head.

"Where's my wife?" And Jaybird scrunched against the headboard and pulled the covers up to his chin. The gun barrel looked enormous.

"Lose a little there, did you, bud?" He pointed the gun barrel a few times toward Jaybird's lap. It was wet there, a big circle that seemed to be growing. And then the man snorted and sucked in some breath and shook his head slowly side to side. "Time to go, bud—time to go."

"Why are you—where's my wife?"

"Never you mind about no wives no more, bud. That's no never mind to me anyways. Not no more. No sir. Jus' you this time. Jus' you." And for a moment, the face looked sad—but quickly gone away into the crooked gold-caught smile. "Jus' you."

"But—why—why me—why now? Why?" And for some reason, Jaybird tried to remember his wife's face, and those of his children one by one—but failed. Only Anita Something's face would come clear—seeming to be floating free over by the bedroom door and laughing, without making any sound at all. And then the others were there—all the women stretching back as far as he could see—as if the room no longer had walls at all but somehow had become simply four dark corridors from which face after face showed itself—three sides clear and no way to see what loomed behind his bed. All the women—there from, it seemed, the very moment power fell upon him full and sweet and steady onward through the years. And others too—mixed among the women—among their silly sighs and moans and painted faces—among their smiles and gentle touches of his shoulders and his arms as he went through his day. Other faces. Not clear in focus but throbbing out behind the man like some monstrous film gone free to click and whir and tumble by with no regard for time or space. And all together finally turned a face too fearsome for a steady looking-at, too painful to be studied long enough to recognize or take inside. The betrayed. The man was frowning— the gun now still. Barrel full pointed at what Jaybird guessed would be his mouth.

"You know why, you sum-bitch. You know why. An' Bonnie's only one—only one. She told me all about them others—told me what you done."

"Who? But—listen—listen—I don't know any Bonnie—I—"

"Yeah?" And he pulled back the hammer and flexed his fingers a few times beside the trigger. "Well, she told me everthing—everthing. Tonight. Yeah. And then I heard from God."

"What?"

"God. Heard Him clear. An' you know what He said?"

"What—no—no, I—" And, improbably, one of the women was rising up, out somewhere in his fear or memory or for real perhaps, rising up behind the angel-a-death—long legs and long blond hair and green eyes and a rack that—and he felt hot and cold together and began to shake all over. He wanted her. Right now. Right here.

"God said to set it right. Said that clear: Set It Right!"

"But—look—I don't know any Bonnie—I—"

"An' it don't matter none to me anyways. I think that's why He chose me, y'know?" He waved the gun back and forth, barrel coming again to rest mid-face. "That's it, y'know? Yeah that's it sure." And he smiled the crooked smile again, gold nearly lost to sight this time as he quickly closed his mouth and seemed to be running his tongue over his front teeth, slowly, deliberately, a slight clucking sound there from time to time. "Chose me because of it, I think—because of it." And he blinked his eyes several times as the gold came back in a half-smile.

"Because of what?" Jaybird couldn't feel his feet. They seemed to be asleep, toes not reacting even when he tried to flex them.

"I'm a three-time loser this time, y'see. I busted out yes'day and robbed a gun shop. Yeah. And a couple of old people and some little grocery store, I think. So—I go away forever this time. Them other two times back ten year ago, no. But this time, yeah." He began waving the gun again, barrel going up and down now just an inch or so from Jaybird's nose.

"Where's my wife?" Jaybird had suddenly missed her closeness in the bed, her tiny sighs during the night as she moved in her sleep, and her smile in the morning. He missed her deeply, achingly, in his chest and stomach, a longing to touch her and hear her voice, all of it growing stronger and stronger the longer the gun barrel moved before his face.

"Don't you worry none about no wife. Ain't no wife to worry about anyways. I know that much. It's all better now. Yes sir. Now, my Bonnie—well that's too damn bad about her, y'know?" He tried to smile but nothing seemed to work. His face had become mask-like, rigid-looking, almost porcelain smooth in its immobility, the skin a shade of gray Jaybird had never seen before. The gun was steady now, barrel seeming to grow wider and darker. The mask began to speak again, lips barely moving but the sound loud and clear: "But—hell—I might just be a busted trucker—town-raised and a damned jailbird too, y'know? Not one a you smart-ass college kids, but I won't have no damn body getting away with what you done. You got be stopped, bud. Stopped right now." The mask smiled a bit, a quick glint of gold visible as the lips let free a few more words, a slight tremble in them at first and then a growling there full on and somehow out around: "Bonnie told me who you was and sure enough here you are. President or no damned President—you hear me? Don't matter none at all. Angel-a-Death done come on down to bidness, boy—done come on down—"

"President? But—but, I'm not the President—I'm—" The explosion of light and sound brought in the darkness quick and woke up Jaybird's wife off sleeping in the downstairs den

Joe Hill among the Oranges

Joe Hill was seen at a Farm Workers' strike in south central Florida. 1950. He was spotted on the picket line at the outskirts of the Talbot Citrus Company's biggest orange grove, and some of the workers claimed he sang "The Preacher and the Slave" and a few verses of "Casey Jones" and then vanished. He was there one minute—singing and playing an ancient concertina—and then gone—smiling as he went—tall and proud. Gone it seemed forever. And the strike was busted. Scab workers bused in and National Guard troops assigned for their protection—and then came the dispersal of the strikers and, with the help of the Morgan County Sheriff's Department, the arrest of the ring leaders. And no more problems for the Talbots until 1960. Until two years after Jesus O'Brien opened a bar near the Talbot #3 groves. Until two years after Florida Landgrant University established a satellite campus in the nearby town of Cowford.

O'Brien's bar was called "Viva Zapata" and was almost immediately successful. A must-stop on the college folk-singing circuit—and a favorite of the sorority and fraternity girls and boys at Florida Landgrant South. Jesus raked in the money—two years of solid profit and great write-ups in the Florida Chamber of Commerce magazine, Good Times Florida! And then a serious-faced stranger showed up.

"What you call that thing?" Jesus was wiping down the bar and keeping an eye on the fruit pickers that had just come in for their afternoon foosball and beer.

"Concertina. It's a concertina." The man smiled and patted at the top of the instrument.

"Looks like an accordion to me." Jesus was on the Talbot payroll (a kind of spy and recruiter both) and was worried about the fruit pickers. The ones he had helped hire. After they busted the last strike and the scabs played out, pickers were hard to come by until the college boys and girls stepped up. Nobody knew why. There they were, though, at the hiring gates, only a few at times, looking out of place in among the leftover Mexicans, but there they were leaving school and getting hired and working a full day, working a full season, who knows why. And more and more had showed up, sent out by that time from Jesus's bar and with the help of Talbot recruiters and straw-bosses, every one turned into a passable picker. Not a few of them even settling into the little cracker-shacks the Talbots built and sold on the cheap. When the oranges were through, a good number of them even volunteered to ride off daily in company trucks to other counties to pick beans and tomatoes and whatever else the Talbots had growing. It was crazy to Jesus, but the bar kept on profiting which gave him the money to keep hiring folksingers and country music bands and the beer was cold and the sandwiches mostly edible and it all added up to a pretty good life.

The college boys and girls seemed to be in endless supply. Way back when it all began, most had been horticulture majors, with only a few in liberal arts and one or two business majors hired to fill out the crews. The business majors turned out to be the worst. Too sneaky and too quiet, especially the accountants. The liberal arts workers were the best. Never questioning anything. Beer-lovers every one and mostly single and free with a dollar. Looking at the stranger at the bar, however, Jesus felt a pain in his stomach, a sharp one, like he used to get before the bar opened. Back when he worked only as a spy and a full-time union-buster. The stranger was smiling, but something seemed wrong about how he looked, his face too white and his hair too dark and slick, and the accordion seeming to be somehow breathing, moving slightly on its own. Something wasn't right. Something wasn't right out in the groves as well. Jesus had been told just this morning to keep his ears open and his mouth shut. The stranger put the accordion down gently on the bar. "You play that thing?" Jesus swallowed a few times, a taste of bile caught just behind his tongue.

"Yes. Yes, I do. I've been playing for a long, long time now." And he smiled an even bigger smile, showing strong-looking white teeth. "I've played most everywhere."

"You got an agent?" Jesus scratched at his stomach and shut his eyes for a few seconds and tried to see the stranger on the stage, tried to see how he might look to the boys and girls on payday night, how he might help sell beer and sandwiches and loosen everybody up enough to talk freely. To find out what was going on in the groves. Just yesterday Joshua Talbot himself had called. Before the bar even opened up. To tell him to keep on top of things. To find out what was stirring out in the groves, out in the bean fields too, out on the land from Miami to Micanopy. Something wasn't right, he said. Something didn't feel right. Something was in the air.

"What's that? Agent?" The stranger pulled himself up on one of the barstools and frowned.

"Somebody to represent you. If you play that thing. Y'know, get you bookings. All that kind of stuff. Handle the money."

"Represent? No. No, I don't have nobody like that."

"They come in handy sometimes. Keeping things going smooth. We get lots of acts in here, bub. Big names too. Kingston Trio a year ago. Brothers Four. Pat Boone. You got a name?" Jesus watched the face of the stranger. Nothing there at all. No frown. No smile. Just a wide-eyed stare. His eyes were nearly glassy. But the voice was steady and sure.

"Can I get a beer?"

"Sure thing. Imported or domestic?"

It was payday and the bar was packed. Jesus had hired two extra bartenders and three waitresses. It was spring break at the university, and it seemed as if most of the students had decided to stay in town. Parties were going on everywhere. The local cops had busted up three fraternity messes and at least one burning roadblock before noon, and more and more students kept rolling into town. By late afternoon, Viva Zapata was full up with beer-soaked college boys and girls, most of them newly-hired field hands, and most of them spending money faster than Jesus had ever seen it go. The first acts were barely heard over all the noise. A male and female duet, playing matching mandolins and singing sad songs in some foreign language had not caught the attention of anybody past the first row of tables (and that only by accident when the microphone stand fell over and caused a reverb that was truly painful). The next act was a muscular-looking, bearded man in a tight-fitting tee-shirt (with a scowling monkey on the front). The man seemed to be chanting something, but it was difficult to tell. Words not clear except for an occasional and loudly shouted "Bastard" that was immediately lost in the drunken near-chaos of an audience that—in various places—seemed just before coalescing into a kind of ragged conga line. The bluegrass quartet was a bit better, at least causing some drunken dancing to break out, mostly female and mostly nowhere near the beat the band was putting down.

And then Mr. No Name took the stage. He stepped slowly into the spotlight, a mix of blue and red and green washing over him, and the concertina held up chest-high and ready to begin. The microphone buzzed once but everything settled down by the first notes and words. Later, Jesus had said there was something in the voice, something, a strong something, a soothing something, a something that made you want to remember things you didn't even know you had forgotten.

"Long-haired preachers come out after night,
        and they tell you what's wrong and what's right..."

The crowd at first kept going on as it had been since noon, but a few had heard the notes and words, a few on the front row and at the tables on the sides; a few began to listen.

"until asked about something to eat..."

Someone up front yelled "shut up" at the drunken bawling behind him and several others took up the cry and added to it "let him sing— let him sing"—and a few others began to chant "shutupshutupshup" and No Name smiled and started the song over—this time to an ever lessening level of noise—until it was quiet all over the bar.

Jesus came in from the back room when the silence came finally down all around, his face mostly frowning, just as No Name began to sing.

"Long-haired preachers come out after night,
and they tell you what's wrong and what's right.
until asked about something to eat,
they reply in voices so sweet:
You will eat by and by,
in that beautiful land above the sky;
Work and pray—live on hay—
You'll eat pie in the sky when you die—"

And the noise started to come back, to rise up again, to take over just as it had done to the other acts, but No Name stopped playing the concertina, pressed it against his chest, and finally said—in a low and gravelly voice—loud enough to be heard without the microphone: "That's a dirty lie!" And the place suddenly exploded in applause and whooping and someone toward the rest-rooms came in strong with an air horn. Jesus had never seen anything like it before, not in all the years of scraggly folksingers and out-of-tune country bands and rock-a-billy pretenders, nothing like it at all. But No Name wasn't finished. The song started up again and the crowd got quiet.

> "And the Starvation Army they play,
> and they clap and they sing and they pray,
> until they get all your coin on the drum,
> then they tell you when you're on the bum:
> You will eat by and by
> in that glorious land above the sky;
> Work and pray, live on hay,
> You'll eat pie in the sky when you die—"

And this time a dozen or so were singing along by the time he got into the chorus, and everybody was ready when he shut down the concertina, pressed it to his chest, and said—along with everybody else: "That's a dirty lie!"

Jesus looked at his senior bartender, Jake, and they both shook their heads. The crowd was now entirely quiet, many of them pressed in as close to the stage as they could get, waiting while No Name got the concertina back to the place he wanted it to be. And then he began to sing again.

> "Holy rollers and jumpers come out,
> and they scream and they pray and they shout,
> bring your troubles to Jesus they say,
> He will cure all your problems today."

The crowd was ready even before he said the expected "But"—some already into the chorus before No Name jumped in himself:

> "You will eat by and by—"

The song went on as before, a few more verses, and the crowd by turns loud and quiet and finally letting No Name finish up and step back toward the dressing rooms. And then, as if nothing had happened, everything got loud again, real loud, even louder than before, several fights breaking out and the bouncers having to bust some heads to get it all back under control. But, before that—before the song ended—on about the fourth verse or so—the one about "working men of all countries unite"—Jesus had thought he saw something behind No Name, something hovering in the shafts of red and blue and green light, faces there, faces he had seen before, farm workers, Mexicans he had known from many years ago, field workers, fruit pickers mostly, their faces all sad and weepy and every one already surely dead.

Looking back on it years later, Jesus wondered when it had all changed beyond hope of ever returning to how things used to be. Those gone-away days now lost, just a sometimes memory that worked its way in when he was trying to fall asleep. The happy time sometimes there then, flickering behind his eyes as he waited on the pills to kick in, seeing in flashes those good old days when the college kids had worked in the fields and the oranges and beans got picked with no trouble coming to the bosses or to him. Back when Viva Zapata was the most profitable folk club in the southeast. Back when he could still sleep at night.

The only thing he could make work as a cause was No Name and those songs of his. Those union songs and all that laughing at God in the lyrics and poking fun at the bankers and the cops. The college kids ate it up, but soon there were fewer and fewer of them and more and more Mexicans. Everywhere. Mexicans. No longer weepy-eyed but most assuredly dead (the stench was there and the dissolving cloth and graveyard hair and the sometimes greenish tint to the skin) and speaking English every one. English. Faces familiar to Jesus— faces he had seen before—people that had worked for him, for the Talbots, years ago—people who he thought were long dead or in prison or gone away for good. But there they were. At the bar. On the dance floor. Singing along with No Name. And finally—after months of this—after months of No Name seeming to call them down out of the stage-lights and the smoke and the lyrics of those songs—with others joining in the singing—scruffy-looking travelers smelling like empty boxcars and diesel fuel and mixing in with the Mexicans like they all were part of the same club—after all that had happened, the bar filling up with people who never left and never got quiet, the groves and fields by then empty of local workers, and the Talbots busing in Canadians, Jesus shut everything down and began drinking more and more until he couldn't really tell at first who it was that had sent the ambulance that carried him away to the small hospital in Maxville and the daily visits of some priest who thought Jesus was a Jew all prime for conversion.

No Name was the cause of it all, he finally decided. No Name and those songs. But one afternoon when the Priest, Father O'Rama, had stomped off in a huff after an argument about infant baptism, Jesus suddenly remembered that No Name had disappeared even before the ambulance ride to Maxville, had been somehow lost down in the Mexicans, vanished, songs and concertina and all—just gone away clean. Nothing left but Mexicans and more Mexicans who finally, after months of gathering together and dancing and whooping had begun to pray—all together and sometimes in unison— and to sing hymns and praise a God Who they said was just about to come back and take them all to glory.

And that was how he had left it. That was how it was when the ambulance arrived and three big Canadians had snugged him down into a tight cloth jacket and strapped him on a stretcher and shot him up with something stout and packed him away for the long ride to Maxville, a Talbot Company town just south of Jacksonville. But, right at the first, the ride had taken him through some beautiful orange groves filled with happy Canadians, everyone it seemed singing along to concertina music (roving bands of Nova Scotians there on both sides of the road) with No Name there as well, a Bishop's miter on his head, waving hard at Jesus passing by and singing "Power in the Blood" full tenor-sweet and loud just as the drugs hit home.

The Union Forever

Woody Guthrie stood staring at the crowd. Most were ignoring him, and each other, and had been doing so ever since the rally began, ear buds and wires separating them into distinct units, caught up in their own peculiar musical taste or motivational speaker or maybe even the political huckster du jour. Nobody seemed interested in his songs, nor that he had been dead for well over a half-century and was here in the People's Park by special dispensation. As a messenger of sorts. Or maybe as a bargain-basement prophet sent to stir the pot before it was too late. Before the final curtain came down. To see if anybody listened any more. But, so far, he wasn't having any success at all. And this was supposed to be a political rally set up by the Blue State Coalition on behalf of the latest certified savior of the working men and women, a working-class candidate named Big Bill Flannery, a long-time Boolean Repairman who was running for a seat in the Regional Senate.

The crowd was milling around, shuffling, listening to whatever was being put into their headsets and ignoring both Woody and Big Bill who kept bumping into each other up on the stage. Woody had been dead for at least eighty years but looked good in the sunshine. Big Bill was smiling and waving at the occasional voter who noticed him. Woody had just finished singing "The Jolly Banker" and had planned to sing "The Union Maid," but instead slung his guitar across his back and yanked on Big Bill's sleeve.

"Hey—hey there." Woody watched Big Bill as he snapped his fingers and began a little buck-and-wing shuffle. He was wired as well, Woody guessed, although the wires themselves must be very small. And nothing showed in his ears. It had been like this ever since Woody blew in from wherever it was they had sent him from. He never had figured that part out. "Hey---hey—"

"Wha'?" Big Bill pulled a plug from his ear, from somewhere down deep and showing no sign of itself until he had flipped at it and made it show. And then he turned slowly toward Woody. His eyes were big and wide and his smile showed nearly every tooth.

"Lookit here now, mister—I ain't got no time for all this here mess," and Woody waved a hand out toward the crowd. "You get me?"

"What's the problem, friend?" Big Bill looked genuinely concerned, eyes gentle-looking and nearly sad. "You need something? Some water? Tea?" And Big Bill waved at someone to his left who had noticed he was there.

"Well now—lookit—what kind a gatherin' is this? It sure ain't no union rally. No sir, it ain't." Woody frowned and readjusted the guitar on his back. "What you all meetin' for anyway?"

"I just want to thank you for playing for us, sir. Yes indeed, I do." Big Bill turned his whole attention on Woody. A slight frown of sincerity on his face. "And let me tell you that the brothers and sisters all appreciate it as well." Big Bill was smiling again, arms raised now and waving in the general direction of a group of identically dressed men and women on the outskirts of the crowd who were swaying side to side and holding up signs that said: LOCAL 409 OBAMACARE WORKERS and VOTE BIG BILL and WHICH SIDE ARE YOU ON? and BIG BILL SHARES!

"Lookit—I don't get none of this here. None of it. It don't look right to me. Don't sound right. Don't feel right. It can't be right, see?" And

Woody brought back his guitar, swinging it around from his back and strummed a major G. "You all are goddamn crazy if you ask me. An' I mean that, y'hear?"

"Thank you, sir." Big Bill smiled even more broadly and brought down a massive hand onto Woody's shoulder, patting it gently and then pushing with his fingers, urging him toward the steps of the stage. "Thank you for your help. For your wise words. For caring. We working-stiffs need to stick together, and that's a fact. Yes indeed. And," Big Bill momentarily frowned, trying to remember something, and then he brightened back up. "Ah yes—don't forget to pick up your health voucher as you leave. Good for two free surgeries of your choice."

"Well this here is all bullshit, mister. Straight on. Bullshit." Woody slung the guitar onto his back again and pulled the strap tight against his chest. He thought he heard a train whistle in the near distance and the grind and clatter of a driving wheel. The crowd was losing members, fewer and fewer were milling around, but the folks with signs continued to dance and clap out beyond. Woody shook his head and spat toward the edge of the stage. The train sounds were louder, as if the tracks were close by, maybe on the other side of the stage, behind the big banner that read: THE UNION FOREVER— " Your whole damned union's bullshit too as far as I can tell—why I—"

But Big Bill had nodded to two broad-shouldered policemen who helped Woody off the stage full into an open boxcar door just as Joe Hill jumped in from the other side.

October Games

Apart from photographs the only things left of Cyrus Bloom's father were funny-looking words, Jewish sounds that alone or in
phrases kept turning up over the years on scraps of paper or on the
pages of the moldy books his mother sometimes let him save from
the debris of her spring cleanings. No one in the entire county that he
had ever met had a clear memory of a man who had not waited long
past the birth of his son before buying a one-way railroad ticket to
Chicago and quickly disappearing into the Great Depression and
World War II. Even the few fuzzy photographs (roughly pasted in the
back of a scrapbook he got after his mother's death) gave Cyrus only
a shadowy impression of the man's physical appearance, a wide grin
and hair longish around the temples and ears that seemed to have
been taken from two different bodies and welded on the sides of a
head vaguely shaped like an Idaho potato. His mother had seldom
mentioned him, leaving Cyrus sometimes free to forget the pictures
and the words and create for himself whatever sort of father he had
need of as example or incentive during years of growing up on his
grandmother's farm and attending college and finally opening Ye
Bookery on Main Street in Slackbridge, Georgia, the day John Kennedy died.

It all had become an infrequent game by the time the bookstore
showed a consistent profit, a pale echo of its earlier pattern of personal crisis bringing forth in power and in strength a DADDY OF THE
HOUR, a figure eclipsed only by the needs of yet another patch of
rough road and then the sure and steady reappearance of a grinning,

long-haired savior who always had the time to spare and nowhere else to go. A few such times stood out in memory and he enjoyed replaying them, especially on mid-autumn days in his office behind the cookbook section, with the familiar voices of old customers drifting back and electric heat and the smell of pipe tobacco and scented candles taking away the October chill outside. But today the voices beyond the wall of tinted glass seemed louder than usual, their pitch and rhythm capable of breaking through the scenes that came rolling almost unassisted the moment he had tilted back in the swivel chair and let his boots dangle in the air. He pushed away the voices to let the first one roll—more elaborate than the rest, beginning a day or two after his tenth birthday, a grouping of his father's words serving as herald to a title of his own making. The words: "Look see what we got here—*Makhn fun kinder menschen.*" The setting: A version of the playground at the old grammar school, near the tire swings, September heat giving everything a look of shimmering motion. The children are dancing around him. The title:

THE NAZIS WILL GET YOU IF YOU DON'T WATCH OUT!

> *Cy, Cy, Cy—dirty old Jew-boy Cy—*

"I'm not a Jew. I'm—I'm Baptist!"

> *Cy, Cy, Cy—bust your gut and die!*

"Stop it!"

> *Cy, Cy, Cy—don't get mad and cry!*

"Stop it—stop it or I'll—"

> *What? What will you do?*

"I'll—I'll call my Daddy!"

> *Oooooooo—HE'LL CALL HIS DADDY HE'LL CALL HIS DADDY DADDY DADDY.*

The voices get shriller and shriller, laughter at times choking out the words or running them together.

HE'LL CALL—HIS—DADDY! OH SAVE US!

"Stop it!"

OH SAVE US—SAVE US! DON'T CALL—DADDY DADDY DADDY!

And then the whole scene trembles, horse hooves pounding over hard-packed earth, and HE arrives, a dead-ringer for Johnny Mack Brown with giant gun barrels glinting through the playground haze like stars coming through the middle of wind-driven clouds on a mostly moonlit night. He always reins up in the center of the taunting children, his horse's haunches shifting from the dancing of its hooves right and left in a tight semicircle that sends up dust and bits of candy wrapper and a few lost pages of someone's homework. The children shriek:

WHO IS THAT?

"That's my Daddy!"

NOOO—NOOO—HE DOESN'T LOOK LIKE YOU!

But his voice comes out from the whirling dust and blows away all the children, scattering them, arms and legs all tumbling together toward the gym where Cyrus's favorite teacher and the Principal stand applauding and nodding their heads and smiling at the easy way the kids come back from recess. And then everybody stares out at Cyrus and DADDY and especially at the horse, who rears back and strikes at the air with its hooves and whinnies along with the words of its rider. The children are all huddled together now and quiet.

NO MORE YOU DO THIS TO MY BAPTIST SON!

All applaud and smile at Cyrus and Hannah Roche (the prettiest girl in town) blows him a kiss as the horse stamps and shows its teeth. DADDY takes off his big Texas hat and waves it in the air above his head and turns the horse toward Europe.

AND NOW I'M OFF TO END THE WAR!

And somehow President Roosevelt is there, waving an American flag and holding out a medal for a DADDY who chooses not to notice in the sudden upward surge of the horse's hidden wings. And Cyrus wants to go along, to hold tight to the saddle horn and see the ocean full of ships but the birthday presents and cake HE left are plenty enough and the children's voices make him very proud.

HAPPY BIRTHDAY DEAR CY-RUS,
HAPPY BIRTHDAY TO YOOOOOO!

Someone sounded excited out in the store, toward the magazine racks and the music section, the voice competing with a melody coming in through the newly-installed speakers that squatted high up on each of the four walls like dark birds roosting beside the blunt-nosed security cameras and a line of dangling dust near the ceiling. He flipped on the monitor attached to his desk, clicked on 4 and tried to make out who it was, the screen at first wobbling and rolling before settling down and giving out a slightly tilted version of the shorter aisles near the front door, with three men there close together and talking loud enough for a few stray words to make it all the way back to the office. They seemed a long way off, but cold-tinged in how they made him feel—alone again and not sure of who exactly he thought he was, like always, like it always finally came down around him no matter how hard he tried to step away.

> --selling this—right here—plain sight—
> --ought to—law—this—nigger magazines—right here—here—
> --just like the Jews—always that way—always—always—
> --damn shame—look at it—whole row of them—look—
> --ain't heard last of—be back—back—back—

None of the men looked familiar, but their voices for some reason brought back a heavily marked section from one of his father's books, a passage in which numerous foreign phrases were italicized in print and doubly emphasized by dark underlining and crudely drawn stars; one word in particular had been circled three times, the last time turning into a long line that crossed through the page and pointed to an almost illegible message penciled in the margin.

Grusha......woman-divorced? But when?

He clicked off the monitor and resettled himself in his chair, pushing away the other voices and letting other scenes begin to form, at first episodic and seemingly unconnected, swimming in and out of focus through almost four full decades worth of PERFECT DADDIES ON PARADE. A few of his own titles had changed.

THE FATHER-SON BANQUET—OR—THE SURPRISE GUEST—OR—LATE BUT NOT LOST, MY DAD.

The Red-Clay League Awards Dinner: Cyrus is second-string third baseman for the First Baptist Church Cardinals, winners of the Tri-County Baseball Championship and best uniformed team in the league. What the other guests don't realize, however, is that the man sitting next to him is not his mother's brother, Uncle Buzz, but in real life Cyrus's actual and very famous DADDY dressed in an Uncle Buzz costume so life-like that the tobacco dribble in the beard looks real enough to wipe away. DADDY stays in costume to keep his TRUE IDENTITY hidden until the last second, the moment when the boys line up to cross the gym stage and receive their gold miniature baseballs from the Mayor.

"Hey—hey—look there!" Hannah Roche, the best-built girl in town is the first to notice DADDY stand up and begin to peel off his mask. "Look there at lil' Cy's table!"

The other boys turn and even the Mayor stops talking as DADDY comes free of Uncle Buzz and takes a few steps toward the stage.

Standing at the very end of the line, Cyrus acts like he knew about the surprise all along.

"You mean—*he's* Cy's daddy?"

"Yes—and look at those medals!"

"A hero—nobody could stop *him*! Nazis. Japs. Nobody!"

"And he's real rich, too. Owns a whole town out west somewheres."

"Boy—look at how tall he is!"

"And strong—he played pro-ball, remember?"

"Hey Cy—we didn't know. Why didn't you tell us?"

"But isn't he a Jew?"

"Who cares?"

And the Mayor shakes DADDY'S hand and nudges him toward the microphone and makes the crowd quiet down. Hannah Roche comes up and holds Cy's hand as DADDY begins to speak:

Because of the love you have shown to my only son in my long
absence, I am giving the town of Slackbridge, Georgia, a million
    dollars
to spend equally on candy, toys, and movies for every child in the
    county!

The applause is deafening and Hannah holds Cy's head in her two moist hands and kisses his forehead again and again.

Other titles come quick:

    THE FIRST DATE—OR—NOT WITH THE EPISCOPAL
    PRIEST'S DAUGHTER YOU DON'T, UNLESS...

The house is a brick one, stone actually, and two stories high with stained-glass windows across the front and thick ivy curling around the bottom half of the chimney. Cyrus waits nervously in a small foyer just inside the double-thick front door, a wire-mesh window set into its top panel glowing faintly orange behind his head. Jessica Wheatly (a Hannah Roche body with a softer voice) is just before coming down the spiral staircase to Cyrus's left, dressed and ready to ride with him in the borrowed truck to a football game and dance and all the other things he has been picturing as possibilities in his mind during the five days since she agreed at last to the first part of the whole idea. But her father gets there first, a Reverend Mr. Wheatly, whose white collar and gray shirt seem just about to bust loose from his body and leave his trembling skin exposed to the terrified eyes of his surprise guest. Jessica starts down the stairs but stops quickly on the second landing when she sees her father. The Priest's voice is loud and steady, seeming to break like theatrical thunder just above Cyrus's head, words book-sounding like the way they looked on the pages of the assigned reading in third-period English class.

"And what on God's green earth are *you* doing here?"

"Jessica and me are going to the game, Sir."

"No—no, you most certainly are not, sir. No foreigners!"

"But I'm American."

"Not with *that* face! My daughter is not at home to foreign-looking boys!"

Jessica shrugs her shoulders and starts to go back upstairs to her room.

"But—but, I'm *not* foreign-looking."

And then they hear the sound of many car doors slamming and footsteps outside coming up the curving cobblestone pathway. The front door opens all by itself and DADDY steps in quickly, clerical robes whirling out behind and his mitre tilting, its center tip brushing against the archway. Several hooded figures are gliding in his wake, monks chanting, voices sweetly echoing the words he finally speaks.

"My dear Fr. Wheatly."

DADDY reaches out a hand and pulls Cyrus full into a softness of robes that seem to fill the room with a strengthening scent of incense and sherry.

"M'Lord Archbishop?"

"May I present my son?"

"Why m'Lord, I had no idea!"

"My heir, you know. Wanted to travel. Especially in the American South. Canterbury wasn't to his liking, I'm afraid. Last we heard, he had become a citizen. But his mother dotes on him. She says he wrote her all about your daughter. Is the dear girl perchance at home?"

"Oh of course, m'Lord. The two young people were just about to leave. Please come into the parlor."

And Jessica skips down the stairs and takes Cyrus's hand and in place of his cousin's truck, a shiny convertible sits waiting for the evening to begin.

He tried to place the tune filtering in from the speakers, piano and violin sounding in competition with each other and at times seeming to be racing at top speed to get to the last notes. The monitor looked dusty, like the air in the office, overhead lights and even the desk lamp showing up specks of it that floated or hung suspended or softly touched down to disappear quickly on the surface of bookcases and desk and filing cabinets. He wiped a hand across his eyes. The game was tiring today, with too many scenes left to play and the store nois-es making it hard to step again into the way he wanted things to be.

And soon the store would close and he would drive out toward the county line and a house he never intended to let grow so big and lonely when he finally gave up building scenes and let his Daddy rest.

And the scenes he formed before the coming of the store and house all seem dust-choked today or filled with figures moving with strong lights behind them, faces shadow-caught and features blurred beyond an easy recognition. The Daddy there is known more by his voice, words carefully chosen and growing steadily more subdued the nearer Cyrus came to leaving home. A row of candles flickers just beyond his mother's casket. But the scene will not hold, giving way as he comes near her resting form, cutting back to another night when it is Granny in the box, alone in velvet with a preacher standing near her head and Cyrus trying hard to hear his mother's words.

"You don't need no college." Anger rests just beneath the surface, and something else there too, a sound like fear that pokes and stabs the pauses in between her words. Across the room, the preacher is having trouble keeping Granny in her box. "You need to get saved."

"Stop it, Mrs. Reynolds! Mrs. Bloom, oh Mrs. Bloom! Your mother won't listen!" The preacher holds to Granny's shoulders, the old woman's eyes red-looking and her arms, no longer stroke-wasted, are flailing out like the injured wings of a giant moth, beating rapidly against the padded rim of her bronze-looking box. "Mrs. Reynolds!" But Granny can't talk; her lips are moving but no sound comes out. And then DADDY is there, suddenly stepping out from behind a wall of flowers to get a good grip and help the preacher stuff her back in far enough to shut the lid. DADDY even sits down on the casket-top and pats the sweating preacher on the back and nods out toward the front of the room at the set of matched luggage lined up near the door.

It's time for Cyrus to go off to college but before he can properly say good-by, the fringes of the next scene click slowly into place, shimmering out like summer heat above a black-topped road, his room behind the campus bookstore—the bed, bookcase, night table and chest-of-drawers all popping up like the paper facades in a story book. And DADDY stands above it all, a giant coin-slot mounted in his belly and an infinite supply of pennies there all set to go and seek the answers. The voice sounds foreign, mechanical in its rhythm.

...knows all, sees all, tells all...

And Cyrus slips in penny after penny so the voice won't stop, question and then answer rising litany-like from somewhere in the innards of FORTUNE TELLER DADDY— dressed in wizard's robes and a tall, coned hat, with lips that clank and whir as truths come gliding through.

"Should I go and join the Church?"
Extreme caution should be exercised—your height is 5"9"
"Should I break off my engagement to Polly Martin?"
Stay free of complicating entanglements—your weight is
*   160lbs*
"What should I do?"
A busy life is a good life—your sign is Libra

Then the years click by, fast-forming themselves through scenes of fuzzy-looking busy-ness until Ye Bookery shows clear, its bright red doors come open at the moment Oswald pulls the trigger and sets loose a flood of people come to buy up all the print there is that tells about his victim's life and what he might have been. And, the scenes flash dimmer and dimmer after that with Daddy growing smaller and smaller all the while and taking what became his final leave in haste and free of coin-slots in his belly and the wizard's robes, of medals, Texas hats and flying horses, his last scene simply staged and costumed and with words that carry nothing of their former pitch and power.

Y'see, I've got this train to catch. Chicago, y'know? And well, I got to get going or I'll be late and miss it, y'know what I mean?

He always turns to go, suitcase in hand and head gone shaking as if from a cold wind or the remembered rhythm of a favorite song, and then he stops to stare back at the way his son has made him come, lips briefly forming into words that no one else can hear above the sudden whistled roaring of the train.

Cyrus sat in the chair and checked his watch. In less than an hour the store would close and he would send his people home and lock the doors up front behind them and then leave through the back alley, his new car parked and ready for his own ride home, the day ending like all the others in the more than twenty years since Dallas. But the speakers now squawked, someone changing stations on the master board near the registers, a hymn tune piping out that he had heard as a child and young adult, with people standing all around him in the Baptist meetings where his mother led the choir. The singing sounded muffled in the store, tentative, rising and falling as if on the currents of an inviting, new-born wind not yet strong enough to wipe away the pain it mocked and moved among.

A Deuce on Phoenix Avenue

The foot simply stank. The odor was there right from the first—like rotting flesh with an undertow of kerosene. The old man, Jaspar (he had said to call him 'Jaspar'—with the 'Jas' sounding like 'Jazz') and he had his foot pushed into a murky liquid that nearly filled a medium-sized mop bucket. He was sitting on his side porch. The house was a crumbling two-story on the west end of Phoenix Avenue. It was 1964. Nearly the end of a very hot summer. Later, the young man thought he had smelled the foot from the sidewalk, yards away from where it actually was. He was reading light meters and had to go inside nearly every house and business for it, and this time an old lady had let him in and tried to smile several times but never quite made it work. She was wearing a loose-fitting ruin of a peasant skirt and some kind of fluttery blouse covered with a flowery pattern that seemed all wrong—nothing the same size or color and blotches of what looked like meringues thrown in at uneven intervals around the neck. The meter was near the side porch door, pushed into a dark space mid-wall. The old man was just pulling his foot free of the bucket and letting it slowly down into a rough pile of nearly white towels. A thin stream of blood dripped from his big toe. The smell was nearly gag-level, but the old woman finally made a smile (all her teeth present and shiny and large) and she nodded and almost bashfully rearranged her blouse and skirt. Her voice was low and husky.

"Oh don't let him start talking or he'll talk your head off." She licked her lips and lowered her eyelids. "He's been fussing with that foot all week." And she turned to go, flaring out her skirt (unevenly bunched together in places) as she stepped back into the house.

The old man called out loudly. "Hey there, son—c'mon over here—c'mon an' tell me what you think—c'mon now—"

"Yes sir—but, I've got to get on—"

"Jaspar."

"Sir?"

"Jaspar—you call me, Jaspar—y'hear?"

"Yes sir."

"Now—get on over here an' tell me what you think of this foot."

"Sir?" The young man came closer, meter-book still open. He put his pencil behind his ear.

"Foot—this here foot I'm fixing. What you think?" Several flies were buzzing close to the toes and for just a second the young man thought he saw a number of them dead and floating in the liquid murkiness down in the bucket itself. Blood was oozing out into the towels and the whole foot looked slick and shriveled at the same time. The smell, up close, was enough to nearly push the young man into dry heaves. "I been worrying with it all week—ever since I no-ticed that it weren't right. Bleach an' kerosene, son. Bleach an' kero-sene. Yes sir."

"What?" The young man stepped back, almost reflexively as Jas-par swung his foot up and out of the towels and dangled it over the bucket.

"Bleach an' kerosene—in the bucket—best they is for this here." And he plopped the foot back into the bucket and shifted a bit in his chair. "What you think, son?"

"I—have—have you been to a doctor? That might be—"

"Hell no, son—hell no. Doctors can't help none. Tried to get my kids and grandkids to unnerstand that. Right from the get go I tried to teach 'em what's true. Yessir. No damn doctor's going help with most nothin' but getting you dead quicker. Nosir. No doctor. None can help this here anyways. I seen it plenty times. When I crossed the Pond back in '17? Seen it plenty times. No sir. Bleach an' kerosene. Do it right. How's the meter?"

"Sir?" The foot was now covered up in a reddish-brown soup and each time Jaspar swirled it around, he splashed some down into the towels. They weren't white at all any more.

"Meter? We up or down this month?"

"Oh—about the same—not much of—"

"So what you think?"

"Of the meter? The foot?"

"No—all that nigger mess down in St. Augustine. That nigger King an' all them—"

"I think you need to see a doctor." The young man snapped the meter-book shut and stepped to the side door.

"About the niggers? Why, hell son, that sure ain't going help a bit. No sir, it ain't. No sir."

The old lady stepped back onto the porch and attempted a half-smile and slowly nodded her head. Her eyelids were now painted a deep shade of purple. The foot splashed around in the bucket and the door shut crisply and the young man made it to the sidewalk and headed toward the last meter of the day.

&

The meter was in the warehouse bathroom—up behind the toilet in a curtained box-like addition to the wall. He had to stand on the commode tank to reach it. The place smelled like diarrhea and urine with a too-strong pine scent mixed in. There had been four men on the loading dock when he came in—sitting on peach crates—older men—mostly red-haired and freckled and chewing tobacco. The cement floor was spotted around the large cooking pot they were using for a spittoon. Only the fattest of the four actually spoke, but the others seemed to be in agreement with whatever he said. The young man was finally going home—just a few more feet to the steps and past the peach crates and the rest—but the fattest one had stood up.

"So—you do this job for a living, son?"

"No sir—just for the summer—"

"Summer, huh? You a college boy?"

"Yes sir. I go to—"

"Boy here goes to college—how 'bout that, boys?" And they all had laughed. "Well I bet a young feller like yourself—all educated an' all—bet you seen lots of things out there, right? Doin' your job an' all—right?"

"Sir?" The other men readjusted their chaws almost in a single motion and then spat nearly together and evenly toward the pot. Not a one made it inside. They all were smiling.

"Well like I just said—I bet you seen lots of things out there, huh? Going into all them houses—huh?"

"Sir?" The young man could see the traffic picking up on Phoenix Avenue. Friday. End of day. Everybody going home. Him too. The last day of this job. Back to school next week. Back to freedom.

A Burning of Ducks

"Things—what all you seen on your summer job?" Two of the men laughed, an almost snarling sucking sound that seemed filled with the beginnings of a deep cough.

"I—well—" The Phoenix Avenue bus-stop was a half-block away. He glanced at his watch. Already 5:10. He could hear the bus coming. Just enough time. "Time to go."

"Oh c'mon, son. Tell us something—c'mon—"

"Ok ok—I—I saw lots of dogs. Saw a python once. And a chimp. And a three-legged cat."

"Good God, son—that—that ain't—" The men laughed, a jagged chorus of near-coughs. "No—no, son—no—what 'bout all them women out there? In all them houses? Young man like yourself—all that pussy just—"

"It's—" The young man watched the traffic and felt the time passing much too fast. He saw the bus sputter by. The next one wouldn't come for over an hour. He wanted to get home now. Shower. Drink a cold beer. Get ready for school. "It's mostly old people that I see. Old people." And he moved quickly toward the steps, heading down from the loading dock.

"Well, hell, son—some of that old pussy is the best they is—right, boys—right?"

He could hear the laughter behind him as he made it down the steps and watched the bus pull slowly from the curb and gone.

Down Beside the Crystal Sea

Willy Shaver liked the froggy game the best. The merry-go-round music and the lights. It had one joystick and sometimes got stuck. The screen would get all red then, and the whole box would hum like it was trying to take off and fly through the nearby door. Willy played the froggy game at least two times a week—on days when he was free and could take some pleasure alone. He was a cook at the Prodigal Inn, the largest homeless shelter in Stone Crab Beach, Alabama.

"Whoom—whoom—flippy—jump now! Flippy jump I tell ya—"

He jerked and clicked at the joystick and watched one of the biggest red frogs he had ever seen try to buck his little yellow cowboy into a waiting gator's mouth full of what looked to be too many teeth. It was Willy's day off and nobody but Cap'n Stevens was there in the smoky, semidarkness of the big room. Only Cap'n Stevens, the owner of the place, owner of the Crossroads Funny Gamez.

"Whoom—whoom—flippy—flip—flip—py—now do it—now!"

The red frog burst into flames as his little yellow cowboy fired hard from the hip and made the screen go momentarily blank. Willy waited for the next frog and listened to Cap try to sing along with the radio.

Then what you got?
Now what you done got this time out?
Alone and drunk again—tha's all—

Alone and drunk again—

A big green monster-froggy pushed out quick from a flower near a big tall tower. Willy jerked his cowboy hard to the left and made him shoot five times in a row—zipzipzipzipzip—flames jumping to where the froggy tried to hide, nailing him finally on the last of three big hops. Willy licked his lips. The game was half over and he was ten points higher than the last time out but nowhere near the Crystal Sea.

Cap'n Stevens was through singing but the radio kept it up. Loud. It was hot inside the Funny Gamez. Two ceiling fans stirred up what the big AC in the back room put out. What little cool air there was. Willy shot the next froggy fast, the cowboy nearly hitting a twisted cactus as he jumped up the canyon wall. Willy listened to the music in the box and smiled. He was thinking again. Real slow at first as the little froggies jumped and died. Faster as the cowboy jerked up higher and higher and then began to creep alongside the Crystal Sea. Creeping quick and smooth to where the serious froggies lived. And Willy was thinking the whole time there, harder and clearer right down to the deepest cave of frogs on Level 2. It was hot now and the cowboy seemed to dance on dying frogs, their eyes drifting upward toward the daylight far away—feet and legs and bodies left alone inside the boiling red the cowboy made come down. Willy licked his lips and thought some more and let the cowboy dance. The screen was stuck, the hum much louder than it usually was, his own face somehow out and strong among it all, shadow-streaked in red and helping push his thoughts back home.

He was ten and it was in the summertime. He was sure of that. He remembered the heat on his face. Always the heat. Like now only a little dryer. The heat came first even before the cool feel of smooth stone on his legs and through the thin fabric of his short pants. Cap'n Stevens was singing again. Here. Not back there. Not back home. Willy kept the Cap'n outside his thoughts. Kept him far off. The box was still stuck and humming steady as a frog-dance by the Crystal

Sea. Everything red and boiling out and up around Willy's face. But his thoughts held fast and stayed back home.

There was a wind blowing back then, up from the road, hot and steady and reaching right into the deep shade where he stood at first blinking into the sand the wind stirred free. His grandfather, his mother's father, was inside looking over the live turkeys stuffed into the too-small cages in the dust mote-choked stench and semi-dark of the Dixie Fresh Meats' back room. Willy got outside quick when his grandfather asked for a closer look at a black-speckled bird with a dented beak and a gobble-gobble like a wobbly scream. It didn't sound nothing like the other birds.

Cap'n Stevens was singing loud and all alone. The radio cut off after a strong crackle and pop of static made the Cap'n curse and pound it hard a few times with his good hand. Willy had heard all that before. And he'd heard the song too. His face was smiling now among the boiling red and humming beeps and blips. The machine was taking its time. So he smiled some more and watched the red screen plump up his lips and make them fall away to nothing but a smear on the dirty glass.

Back home that one turkey was loud. It never shut up from the first time Lil' Bob took them into the back room to find the exact right bird. Grampa wanted a turkey. He wanted to cook one and eat it and never mind it wasn't Thanksgiving or Easter or nothing like that. He just wanted to go and get him a turkey live and have Lil' Bob fix it up to cook. Grampa worked for the railroad in Live Oak, Florida, and didn't keep no birds of his own. "I ain't got time for none of that," he'd sometimes say. "I use to but not no more. Too much damn mess in that." He'd hunt birds and deer and such, but never kept nothing live. Not even a dog or a cat. That one bird was a pure mess, gobble-screaming and flapping up a feather-and-dust storm that finally drove

Willy outside into the heat, into the shade and wind and whirling sand that stung his eyes as he climbed onto the back of a stone frog he hadn't noticed was there at all.

The radio came back on in a squealing whine that sounded a little like a dog brought up in pain from a deep sleep. Cap'n was in the back beating on the air-conditioner. It was hotter in the room, the screen still red and not a frog in sight. Willy figured the cowboy would come back first, creeping down beside the Crystal Sea and ready for a frog to show itself. A demon-frog maybe, coming from one of the caves or jumping along the clumps of ruby-reeds the waves rolled in. He watched his own face some more, going big to small, dark red mostly but sometimes a pinkish glow to it that nearly made him disappear.

Back home, there were only two frogs—one on each side of the screen-door—and Willy had picked the one on the right. That frog was a little wider than the other one and had been painted blue, the color deep across its back with drops of dried paint inside its half-opened mouth like bloated teeth. The stone felt good on Willy's legs, cool and smooth and he sat there quiet, staring out toward the road and the little whirlpools of sand that'd jump up quick along the shoulders—watching and listening to that gobble-gobble-scream back behind him in the dark and hot of the killing place.

Cap'n was fiddling with the cash register. Making it beep and beep and beep like it was one of them big trucks backing up to the shelter's loading dock once a month. Groceries coming in. Willy liked supply day the best. The truckers always told good stories and gave him magazines. Big girls in some of them. Big girls. And he'd read the jokes and look at the cartoons once in a while. He'd never been much with girls. Once Grandpa died and the bank took everything, it was the road mostly. Living outdoors and hitching up and down creation until he came here to cook and rest awhile. And bad men were everywhere he went. Beating on him. Tricking him. Cutting him. But no girls to speak of. Just in the magazines. Beep. Beep. Beep. Grampa and Lil' Bob were loud inside the Dixie—laughing and carrying-on and the gobble-gobble-scream was right there with them both, loud for loud and sometimes covering up everything with an almost yodeling screech that made the hair stand up on Willy's arms. And made something else stand up too. Or start to move. Willy could feel the cool stone, feel it like it was alive, had come alive and begun to grow stronger with each and every gobble-gobble that he heard.

"Hey Bob—you figure he'll shut up t'rectly?"

"Well he do like to say his piece, don't he? You sure you want this'n here, Elias? He's mouthy an' old an' I do believe he'll be tough."

"He's fine, Bobby—jus' the thing."

"All right—you got it. All right now—le's jus' see what we can do—"

And the yodel-gobble-scream began mixing itself in with a flap-flap and almost roaring sound at times like some old engine trying to lift something way too big up off the ground. Willy sat deeper on the frog—tightening his bare thighs against the nearly breathing sides and pressing down hard, his eyes shut tight for a little bit and then opened up again to see the sand whirl fast and all around him in a stinging rush against his skin.

"Hold'm , Bobby—hold'im now!"

"I'm Ok—I'm Ok—I'll—I'm—now—"

"He's only nicked there, Bob—watch'm now—he a mean sumbitch. Sure—watch'm--"

"I'm Ok—I'll get—I'll—whew—go—there—there—"

The blue frog seemed to quiver against Willy's legs and up along his crotch and butt, a spasm-like twitch that matched the yodel-gobble-scream and Willy's own breathing in and out among the stinging sand. That turkey was hard to kill. It took a long time to die. Willy sat a long time too on the breathing frog and felt his own belly turn all blue and cold.

"Hold'm, Bobby—hold'm—"

"I'll—I—I'll get'm—now—there—"

"Whew man—whew—lookit at all that—"

"Watch them wings, Elias—watch 'em—"

It felt good riding on a hop of froggy-blue, alone and pushing right on through the dying yodel back inside to hop up high and free away. To the chestnut tree beside the corn field first and then a hop and high-up-hop-and-glide, stone feet spread webbed before and out behind to catch the wind. To catch the sunlight too that sparkled everything below, no yodel-sound there with them but a quiet in the wind all full around and sparkled light until his face felt hot and red just like it looked up on the screen. He rode back there, his thoughts turned free and mixing with the rush of wind like now mixed in with boiling red and with the years gone by since froggy-blue flew-hopped him far from home. He saw so very much then as he flew—his parents dying in a sudden burst of fire out on a mountain road—his Grampa on the day he came to Tennessee and found the place where Willy lived, a county home that smelled like moldy fur—and all the rest was there as well—the days and years since Grampa came: down South and growing toward the turkey afternoon and on beyond all that to mist-filled glimpses of the hard times past the day that Grampa died—a warning there but not quite strong enough to do much good at all. And just before he came back sliding down the sandy wind, a long glide on the sunlight flooding through the trees, he whispered in the place he thought a froggy ear might be, a wish for some way sure to fly away again. But the frog never answered and Grampa was there instead, a slick white paper bag blood-pocked and swinging gently in his hand. And Cap'n now was talking on the phone. The screen was still without a frog. Or cowboy. Or even one thick clump of reeds down by the Crystal Sea.

What Comes Now From the Sea?

At first, Papa Rip had not noticed the two boys as they walked slowly along the beach in the late afternoon sunlight toward his place on the patio. It was his birthday, July 12, 1985, and he had been scanning the ocean, methodically swiveling the tripod-mounted telescope from McCoy's Point to the San Marcos Lighthouse and then back again, his mouth open and saliva dripping down his chin and into the white, wire-like hair on his chest. Each day toward sundown and after his daughter and son-in-law and the two brats had gone shopping or to the club or wherever it was they all scattered to (birthday or no birthday) when he got up from his nap, Papa Rip would carry his battered telescope to the far edge of the patio, aim it at the ocean and try to spot submarines. This afternoon he had gotten an earlier start and had picked up the boys only after the first sweep of the surf and a quick move inland to ferret out any last minute sunbathers. The boys looked bored. Papa Rip sighed and returned to the surf.

He had been living with his daughter for four years, coming to her house in Stone Crab Beach, Florida, right after they signed him out of the VA Hospital in Gainesville and promised his best friend, Monk Elliott, that they would feed him good and treat him right. He sometimes missed Monk and his pet lizards and once had gathered him a pail full and bought a few fifths and took off to go visit. But his daughter's husband had gotten the highway patrol to run him down somewhere near St. Augustine and take away the keys. He never did find the lizards, and he had finished the fifths before the first blue light showed in the rearview mirror. And after that, there had been a few other times with the car and some evenings in the Seacrest City bars until he got sick and had to take naps and give it up. He had been submarine watching part-time for almost a year.

The boys blocked his view of a driftwood formation and he raised up intending to shout them on down the beach when something about their clothes made him stop. They were not dressed for the beach or the weather, wearing what looked to be some kind of uniform, heavy boots and shirts and pants that seemed to have been peppered with glitter to make them flash and sparkle all over like tiny explosions going off in the sunlight. They noticed Papa Rip and stood for a few moments staring up at him as if he were the come-on in a freak show; then they turned and began to walk slowly away toward the nearby pier.

The breeze felt good against his face and bare chest and he kept sweeping the ocean beyond the breakers with his telescope, looking hard for a sign of something big moving beneath the blue-green swells. He hoped the family would take their time and leave him alone until the buoy lights off the Point could be seen and the air smelled of frying fish and boiling shrimp. They hadn't remembered his birthday, but hardly nobody ever did anyway. Monk did. And a few times some nurses had brought in a cake. Stuff like that. It didn't matter that the family forgot. Not really. Of all the places he had lived during all the years of moving in and out of hospitals, he liked it here the best. He sometimes wished he had never begun drifting after the war, had never left that first job at the bank to wander at times so drunk he couldn't make his mouth say his own name or his face feel the touch of his own fingers. His wife had raised their daughter and for some reason had not ever come to hate a man who over the years must have seemed more money-order or paycheck than flesh and blood. And the daughter had taken him in after the last trip south to Miami ended instead outside Daytona Beach behind a speedboat. The young woman he had paid for and her bearded boyfriend had tied him to the boat and dragged him around a small lake until his skin and muscles seemed about to fly off and melt into the muck and black water and leave only his bones to bob and bounce behind. Before the ride, they took all his money and afterwards left him tied to the landward end of a ruined boathouse for some boys to stumble over in the morning and call the troopers. And it was a few weeks later, in the hospital, that he discovered he couldn't even remember what it was he had been trying all those years to find.

The boys were suddenly below him, almost as if they had popped up out of the dirty-looking sand like two periscopes breaking water at the same time. They had identical haircuts and eyes pale blue and seeming to have been pressed into their sockets almost as afterthoughts and told to blink and twitch in the dying sunlight like Christmas tree lights on the verge of going out. Papa Rip didn't want to talk to either one of them.

"What you see in that thing?" The taller one crossed his arms and rested his weight on one leg, head slightly cocked to the side, looking vaguely dog-like in the face of something unexpected or unknown. His friend put one foot on the bottom step of the patio and leaned forward, smiling in a way that made Papa Rip think back to the bearded boyfriend, his voice rough, mingled with the laughter of the woman, and finally come together into an almost growling scream in the first moments of movement through the dark water. Later, the trooper had held Rip's head on his lap and cursed. The boy was frowning. "I said, what you see? Can you hear me?"

"I hear fine. Why don't you boys just—"

"Bet you can see clear to that motel up there." The shorter boy spoke the words down toward his feet and then raised his head and showed the smile again. "Can't you?"

"I'm watching the sea." Papa Rip held tight to the pitted metal of the telescope and tried to press an eye to the lens. But his hands began to shake. For some reason, he found himself wishing that the family would come home.

"Yeah? What's out *there*?"

"Look," Papa Rip raised up slightly in his chair and tried to frown. "Look—why don't you boys just run on home?"

"Home?" The shorter boy swung around the railing and came down on the second step. He stretched his arms above his head and hugged himself before leaning back on one of the support poles.

"This is private property." The sun would be down in about fifteen minutes. Already, long shadows were spreading across the sand, mismatched shafts of dark that made the beach look striped, web-like and delicate. Papa Rip gripped the telescope and watched the taller boy join his friend on the steps. The breeze caused their short hair to jiggle and the sunlight gave their faces a pale golden quality that made the skin seem almost transparent.

"Can we look?" The shorter boy nodded toward the telescope. He wasn't smiling now, his lips slightly apart and showing briefly a row of yellowish teeth before his tongue moved across them. The expression on his face seemed as neutral as that of the doctor at the Gainesville hospital the day the last of the freedom papers got signed. The family had to wait outside and the doctor's office smelled of stale sweat. They had talked about something, the doctor's eyes tired-looking and bloodshot as he tapped at the papers on his desk with a well-chewed pencil; but Papa Rip had lost the flow of it as quickly as memory of what had come before his almost-boat-ride with a girl he thought safe and a man he had barely had time to see. The boys were standing on either side of the telescope looking down at him. He let go and slumped back in the chair.

"Where'd you get this thing. Looks old." The tallest boy ran his hand down the top from front to back lens. "Can we look?"

"I don't let nobody else use it." He glanced toward the Point and tried to find the exact place where the first lights would show. The breeze had stiffened and occasionally carried in it a hint of frying seafood amid the stronger smells of gasoline and exhaust. Behind him, past the house and the stunted grass of the front yard, traffic had begun to pick up, mostly motorcycles and the rebuilt jalopies he sometimes wanted to throw bricks at when they passed in the nighttime and he needed to sleep. The taller boy squatted down and swiveled the telescope toward the north. "Look—why don't you boys just get on out of here before there's trouble?" But even as the words came out, they sounded familiar, used, tired things that hadn't worked with the bearded boyfriend back at that room the girl had rented with Papa Rip's money. His stomach was hurting, cramping in time to the tapping of the taller boy's fingers on the top of the telescope. He blew out his breath, a slight whistle mixing with the sound of the other boy clearing his nose.

"Shit." The word came out slowly, taking two syllables instead of one. The shorter boy moved in closer, jabbing a leg against Papa Rip and leaning down over the back of his friend.

"What you see?"

"The pool—and out back. There's a hole in that fence they got there."

"What you see?"

"Pussy! Man! They ain't got nothin' on!"

"No shit? Lemme see!"

Until then, Papa Rip had not noticed how very young the boys were, pushing and jabbing at each other to look through the telescope, their laughter giggle-like and shrill, making them for a moment seem strangely vulnerable, their eyes briefly reminding him of small dogs left too long in a kennel. But they also had a quality about them that made him think of all the other ones, the dry-land ones who had never known an ocean he himself only now dimly remembered, ones who had not loved it or sailed it but yet somehow managed to make themselves part of a crew he had finally come to notice out there just beyond the hospitals and jails, walking in swaggering groups down the beaches or along the sidewalks or gathering together in knots of sullen mockery in alleyways or in front of burger stands and juke-joints that stretched from coast to coast and border to border, city and town by city and town, until on that last trip south the whole country had begun to seem to him to have been emptied of anyone over the age of eighteen. He now knew that the girl and her bearded friend were in the crew and that these boys were just before signing on with the rest to put themselves to school learning rules less written down or spoken than simply taken in with each breath they drew until even the very dullest of them could swagger and mock without apparent effort of forethought. Watching them take turns with the telescope, he suddenly wanted to push them down and beat them with it and make them see that too much dry land might lead a man to violence and too much looking back made a person blind.

"Hey—it says US NAVY on this thing." The taller boy turned his face toward Papa Rip. "Where'd *you* get it?"

"It was give to me."

"Yeah?" The boy's eyes had widened, becoming indistinctive blobs that twitched and blinked without discernible pattern or rhythm.

Standing up, Papa Rip felt his head go light, like wind mixed with electrical charges were being pumped into it. He tried to stop the feeling by thinking about the family, but not even his daughter's face would raise itself free of the crackle and blow.

"Hey—you sick or somethin'?" The shorter boy stopped swiveling the telescope and rested his hands on its little end. His friend backed up a step and watched half-smiling as Papa Rip stumbled toward the patio railing and leaned his weight on it, his back to the sea and the stiffening breeze fanning his thin hair out in wisps over forehead and temples. "You don't look so good." They both stood in front of the telescope, arms folded across their chests and the nearly gone sunlight making their faces seem to have been divided into equal halves of carefully painted light and dark.

"I'm ok." He thought briefly of the moments just after the bearded boyfriend and the girl had left him tied to the boat house, a feeling of needle-jabs moving through his battered body from head to toes, his lungs seeming to be in competition with his heart, all straining to come through his chest or throat and into the humid air to pour themselves out together on the spongy shore and let it soak up all the memories and the pain. And then his head cleared and he turned toward the ocean with its golden-tinged waves and the blinking lights of freighters moving slowly through the darkening water beyond and for an instant he felt the roll of an almost forgotten deck beneath his feet and a spray coming in that made him blink and rub his face and try to see more in the darkness than the pitch and leap of the bows of the silhouettes of the other ships, seemingly tied all together by invisible wires strung web-like over their rolling portion of the North Atlantic in hopes of keeping whatever moved beneath the surface safely down there blind and ignorant of their passing.

But that had all gone away, forgotten until now even before his first trip to the west coast, left behind in the first hospital along with the medals and letters of commendation and pictures of a wife and daughter who were not as real to him once he returned from sea as his dreams of them had been whenever he had found time out there to sleep. He gripped the banister and sucked in the salty air and strained to make out what it was he hoped to see slowly breaking water out toward the Point, past the puzzled smiles of the boys and the maddeningly forgiving eyes of his daughter, hoping that whatever it was would take him on board and tell him where to look and how far he had yet to sail. The boys were twirling the telescope, making it spin like a propeller on its rusted stand as he heard his daughter's voice from the back door calling out for him in words he couldn't understand in the ocean's darkened spray.

The Devil's in the Details

The night nurse's name was Lakisha. Her mouth was lopsided and her shoes squeaked and she weighed nearly 250 pounds pushed down hard into a too-tight pink hospital uniform. Her face was mostly without expression. Hector Plybon was in for a month at least, for detox and whatever else they decided he needed. They said he had knifed somebody under a bridge on the county line, but he had no memory of that. All he really remembered was being here. In the County Health Center. Again.

This time the Center was nearly full. Only one bed left now. They had handcuffed Hector to the bedrails and stuck him with something that kept him mostly asleep. He watched Lakisha move among the beds, an almost-waddle that made her hips press hard into the pink cloth of the uniform and set everything to rolling and bunching up like some kind of small animal was loose beneath the cloth and trying to find a way out. Everybody was mostly asleep but him. Snoring, whimpering, crying out a name sometimes. Mostly snoring, though, and loud.

He couldn't remember much anymore. He kept trying, of course—trying to bring back stuff he might need if he ever got free. He'd been on the street for three years this time. Slackbridge, Georgia, this time—in and out of the VA at first and then just in and out of jail. And now? Well this one felt different. He jangled the handcuffs and Lakisha waddled toward him, lower teeth pulling on her lower lip and then gone away into a proper head-shake and frown.

"You shush up over there, Hector. You hear?" And she returned to moving slowly among the beds. "Shush now."

"Yeah yeah. Whyn't you come on over here and make me?"

"I'll get Buster do that d'rectly you don't shut up." And then she walked quickly to the far door and disappeared into the deeper dark of the hallway.

Hector listened to the night noises and tried to remember anything of use—anything—long ago to now—something he could hold to or climb up onto—something to bear the growing weight of his own fear. But only shredded things came nearly clear. Again. Only bits and pieces and nothing firm enough to grasp:

-----A woman there. Bonnet on her head. Eyes a pale, pale blue. The woman seemed to be chopping wood. No words. Just chopping at some log that looked worse off than she did.

-----And something from a football game—down in it close and foul and hard—him there, he thought, with the ball in his hands and clear field ahead.

-----Then into the war, he guessed by the look of it: Hueys and jungle green and red, red fire a boil within a smoke so black and thick it seemed to have made the sky forever gone.

-----Then booze mostly but sometimes drugs—all kinds— drifting in and out of nowhere in particular and faces there too—faces all scarred and dead-eyed and lost full deep in whatever dream they lived down in.

-----And the doctors in and out of nearly every flash of light, and nurses, and the hospital stink and now once more all come together with handcuffs and some dude all cut up underneath some bridge they say was home.

No memory of that at all. No way to help the lawyer. No, nothing left but Lakisha's laugh off in the darkness past the first bed by the door.

Hector tried to sleep, and maybe made it this time, dream-caught hard with little left to do but ride it to the end. Satan himself was clear and fire and smoke much hotter and deeper than anything in war. Satan himself and a great big bottle of something mostly red.

"Hector?"

"Do what? Where—where am I?"

"That doesn't matter, Hector. Not at all. Would you like a drink?"

"Drink?"

"Yes." Holding up the bottle. "Best there is, my friend. A drink?"

"I—I—" A glass was suddenly in Hector's free hand, a large glass goblet with gold around the rim. "Drink? But—but, the nurse will—"

"Not to worry. She's not with us anymore. Drink?"

"Well—what is it?" It looked thick in the bottle and the colors seemed to change each time he blinked his eyes.

"Best there is, my friend. Best there is. Drink?" Satan smiled, face pulled into deep wrinkles and ruts across his cheeks and brow. The teeth were uncommonly white. He looked like Richard Nixon.

"I—I—"

"C'mon and try. Nothing to it. See?" and he poured a glass-full and drank it off quickly. His eyes seemed to glow. "Oh my—good good good! Join me?"

"I—well—maybe just one short—"

"Good now—let's get rid of those, though—" and the handcuffs disappeared.

"How—how you do that?"

"Nothing to it—here—just a good taste—a short one, yes?" And he poured the wine into Hector's glass, slowly, a bubbling sound there and a kind of whisper down among it all. Hector looked at it—top down and side to side. He swished it around and sniffed it. It reminded him of something long ago and lost. Something. Somewhere. A feel and a soft voice and a kind of joy out all around. It had been four days since his last drink. He remembered that clearly and all at once. The drugs they gave him did little to keep away the memory of that last bottle. He noticed something in the glass, down in the red, something dancing there and smiling with teeth uncommonly white.

Hector drank it down. All of it. Drank it quickly and then noticed that he was all alone, only Lakisha now returning from the dark, the handcuffs back in place and memory come all in a flash, with groans and moans and pain that stretched down through the years, a life not worth the living and nothing left to drink.

Crossing the Bar

It was nearly closing time, 1:30 A.M., and the snow storm outside showed no sign at all of laying down to rest. Drake Nunn was wiping at the bar, a long curved survivor of the first "Dixie's Best," the saloon opened by his great-great-Grandpap in 1850 and then running on full steam ahead until Prohibition, of course, and then that fire that nearly ended it all in January, 1940. It took a few years for Drake's daddy to get enough money to rebuild, and when he finally did, the new Dixie was much smaller, old-timers said, mostly a one-man operation, but the bar itself, the curved and nicked and deeply polished remnant of the glory days was mostly intact, only a little blackened where the fire had lapped up against it as the roof buckled and split in half and left it (almost miraculously) still ready for steady business—give or take a few sandings and stainings along the way. The new Dixie finally opened in 1945—the year Number Two ended and the boys started coming home—at least the ones that still could—and the mills began to hum in overdrive and the local college began to grow. Pee Dee River City, North Carolina—northwest corner of the state and very near the Tennessee line.

Drake was almost seventy—no wife and kids—and had grown up inside the Dixie the way most folks his age had grown up in the coves and deep woods—and the open road when it come time for it. He now owned the place outright, his father having died over ten years ago, and he had expanded a bit (mostly in the back booth area) but had managed to keep the main room much like what it had always been—Confederate battle flag and portraits and photos of family members and long-time customers behind the bar and to both sides of the giant portrait of Generals Lee and Jackson standing together outside a tent and seeming to be either praying or locked into some very private conversation. The painting was relatively new—dating to the late fifties when Drake's daddy had won it in a poker game down in Winston-Salem. As for the rest, there were deeply comfortable booths and chairs and tables in plentiful supply. And a jukebox with a clear circle of space nearby for dancing. He sold beer (mostly domestic) and wine (all domestic) and had been at it day by day all alone since his daddy died. It was a comfortable living until the mills played out and the college grew right up to his doorstep with major changes all around out past the front door—apartment complexes only a hundred feet away and several layers it seemed of little burger joints and coffee shops and tea rooms and the rest. The new century in particular had started all wrong and never stopped. And then tonight. Worst snow storm in years and another dead college kid with no face left and lying in a pool of blood over by the jukebox.

The place was empty except for two of the dead kid's friends and two old-timers who hadn't been in the Dixie much lately but tonight had seen it all. And the High Sheriff himself calling back to say he'd be along directly. Directly. Drake finished wiping at the bar and sighed. It was always something.

"Hey Drake—hey—" Roscoe Smith's face looked pinched and altogether too red as he shuffled up to the bar and tried to sit on one of the stools—slipping sideways until he grabbed a second one for support. He finally made it and leaned in and shook his head. "My God, Drake—what th'hell? What th'hell was all that anyways? You ever seen them ol' boys before, Drake? You ever seen a damn one a them before?" His eyes were opened wide—the blue a bit fuzzy in the dim light, and the smile more trembly than friendly.

"Naw—maybe that one tall boy—but, naw—in them masks, who can say?" He pushed a dish of peanuts toward Roscoe. "You want 'nother beer? On the house." The two college kids were a few feet distant from the body—backs turned to it and the room. One of them was crying softly.

"I don't want no beer, Drake. I jus' want go home." His eyes remained wide. Roscoe had been a mill-hand for over thirty years—his friend, Jaspar Johnson, the same—until some Chinese company bought it out and shut it down and left town almost all in the same afternoon. Jaspar climbed up on a stool beside Roscoe, his round face full of whiskers and a big scar down the right side that refused to be covered up. They both had been in Vietnam—enlisted together and come home together and went right into the mill. Drake had skipped all that. "You think it was 'cause he was a fag, Drake? That boy over there?" Roscoe's eyes blinked rapidly a few times and settled into a kind of steady stare. "You think that was it?"

"Fag?" Drake chuckled. "You think they's fags, Ros? Really?"

"Yeah. Yeah, I do. Lookit over there—lookit how they's acting. Jus' like fags do. College fags. Yessir. Thing is, though—why them boys only shoot one?"

"Roscoe?" Drake shook his head and winked at Jaspar. "How much time you spend with fags? I mean, since you know how they act and all."

"Shit." Roscoe slipped down off the stool and leaned against the bar. "Shit. I'm goin' home."

"No you ain't." Drake watched the kids begin to hold hands and sob into each other. "Sheriff says to wait. You a witness, Roscoe. You too, Jaspar. Them two over there. Me. Witnesses."

"To what?" Jaspar's voice was low and wavering, something like a wheeze there when he stopped. He rubbed a chapped hand across his mouth and sighed.

"To that over there," Drake said, pushing the words out slowly. The night was almost a total loss anyways—not many come in at all—couple of old-timers—not for long, though. Roscoe and Jaspar come in last, right after midnight. College crowd was pretty thin all along. There had been the usual tension for sure—way early on—like every night since the hard times come and the college kids found the bar. Old timers didn't like nothing that was going on out in the neighborhood and there was less and less of them—but the kids just kept on coming, just wanting to drink, it seemed, and hide out in the shadows a lot—out back in the big booths and along the side walls too. He had quit noticing much but their money years ago. But not tonight. Storm kept most of them away—kids and old-timers both and then in come the masks and shotguns and some long-hair dropped down hard in a burst of fire and smoke and masks gone clean away before Drake could even get it clear what he had seen. The dead kid had no face.

"No kidding now, Drake. Hell, it's jus' us anyways. Jus' us. Why, Drake? Why the fags? When it all start happening?" Roscoe frowned at the very end, on the last word, and sucked in some air, noisily, teeth crooked and a few gaps showing toward the top left.

"What?" Drake was watching the two sobbing kids—one of them was kissing the other's hands.

"Them fags. Didn't use to be like that. Not while you Daddy—" A siren sounded in the distance, suddenly there beyond the front door and windows—muffled at times from a wind come up to rattle the front awnings. Drake figured they were just a half-mile away. Probably two cars. An ambulance as well. Sheriff Martin Spencer and two or three of his pock-faced deputies sure to come in the door directly. And Doc Mutton too, the ME. Directly. Roscoe was still talking."—like what them ol' boys said—that tall one for sure— he said something like 'cornhole,' I think. That was sure in there someplace—right, Jaspar?"

"Yeah. I heard that. Sure. An' 'cocksuckers' too. You hear that, Roscoe? Right before he pulled the triggers. Sawed off. Pretty little thing, though. Barrels looked polished to me. What you say, Drake?'

"What?" The sirens were closer now. Louder and wailing and the kids at the table stopped holding hands and turned toward the door. The nearest kid's cheeks were streaked. Dark lines rolling down and toward his chin. Drake noticed the other one was wearing a kind of silky-looking blouse, with a pearl necklace hanging down in front.

"Th' barrels? Polished?" Jaspar nodded. "Yes?"

"I don't know—I never—" Drake felt as if he was floating a bit, in and out of focus and the words not nearly making any steady sense.

"I mean—lookit what they call this place now, Drake." Turning toward the door, Roscoe began thumping the back of his heels on the bar, down below the brass foot-rail. "The—the Hob—the Hob something, right, Jaspar? Ain't that it? The Hobber or Hobby, right?"

"No." Jaspar coughed and looked down at his hands, resting near the peanut bowl. "It's—it's like—The Harbor." He shook his head and coughed again.

"Yeah that's it. Yeah. The Harbor." Roscoe nodded and smiled.

"What?" Drake wasn't sure he heard the words right, but the Sheriff suddenly came in the front door, stamping snow from his boots, three deputies close behind—the Weaver twins and Moose Baldwin. Doc Mutton came in last, big Russian-looking hat covering his head and two skinny EMTs with a stretcher and various bags slung over their shoulders. The sirens must have been turned off a block away. Drake couldn't remember when they stopped.

"Boys." The Sheriff moved quickly to the body and the two kids, now standing up and seeming to be dancing a funny-looking two-step back and forth a few feet from their fallen friend. The Sheriff glanced down at the body and then shouted over at the bar. "Another one, D-Man? Take a close look, Doc. Boys—see to the witnesses. I'll take D-Man." The Sheriff shook his head slowly. "Drake, my good friend— whew boy—this place's just before becoming a public nuisance, hey?" And he smiled broadly and stamped a few times as he walked quickly to the bar. The two kids were being herded toward the front door and Roscoe and Jaspar toward the back room and the Sheriff wasn't smiling any more. "D-Man, look," and he gently placed his gloves on the bar near the peanut dish; his Stetson was pushed way down on his forehead, giving his too-white face a look like it had been squeezed into place and kept there against both gravity and common sense. He looked lopsided straight on, one eye not quite even with the other and the nose a bit too wide and long. But the returning smile was warming. "Lookit here—this whole thing y'got going just ain't good, y'know? I mean, I'll just guess it's another hate crime, right? That's what I'm going to hear, right? Witnesses. Them two old coots. Them kids over there for sure. Whew boy. Another damn hate crime. All that extra paperwork—my God, D-Man, my God."

"I—I don't know what—" To Drake, the room was too warm suddenly and nothing seemed to stay in its proper place—Roscoe and Jaspar and the two kids and even the dead beginning to move together in a kind of rolling fuzziness that also seemed to raise up booths and jukebox and even the flag-draped and portrait-and-photo-covered wall behind him and jumble it all together into a mix that made no clear sense at all. "I'm not sure what it all—"

"Look," the Sheriff was eyeing the peanuts, "We got rights to consider. Oh yes. And law. Federal and State both. Rights and law both. Yessir. An' I'm sworn to pro-tect them rights and enforce them laws. Yessir I am. And—yessir, I do." He popped a few peanuts into his mouth and chewed quickly and noisily. The room was slowing down a bit. "An' you got every right to be whoever and whatever you choose. Long as you keep it legal." The frown came on slowly with just a slight shake of the head. "Now, look, look, just between me and you—well, I ain't judging—nosir—but—good God, Drake—a damn gay bar right here butted up on what's left of mill-town—peckerwoods everywhere—three Baptist churches just two blocks away—a playground just a half-mile beyond all that. What you expect?"

"Gay bar?" For some reason, Drake glanced almost reflexively behind him at the rebel flag and the rows of portraits and photos of Daddy and family all the way back to Great-great-Grandpap and the soldier boys and the Generals and the rest and then he noticed something else—a feathered boa dangling from the door of the men's bathroom and what looked like a spangled cape draped over one of the back booths—this time distinctive, nothing like the others now rising up from fuzzy memory—all the others he had gathered night by night and thrown away as he cleaned up after hours. Distinctive. Clear like the beads and mascara on the dead's good friends.

"The Harbor. Yessir. That's what they call it—how it's all safe and fun. How everything feels so good. In the pop-ups I've seen—on the damn internet? That's what they all say. That lil' cartoon seal they got? You know the one I mean? Dances on a ball an' says: 'C'mon in to feel the love—slide in smooth to The Harbor for a safe, good time.' Hell, D-Man, you got to know yourself that all that stuff's bound to bounce around out there among the peckerwoods in the wrong damn way. Like a red flag rubbed right into a bull's face." The sheriff shook his head and smacked his lips. The smile was there for just a few seconds. His eyes looked kindly, sleepy and calm.

"This—this is the Dixie—the—" Watching the Sheriff pop more peanuts into his mouth, Drake began to feel sick to his stomach—a rolling ache there that seemed to be gurgling each time he tried to speak. The words were stuck.

"Ok, Drake. Whatever. Calm down now. Whatever. But you got to know that you been shoving the life style a little too hard, that's all. Give it a rest is all I'm saying. Tone it down a notch. Mayor feels the same way."

"The Mayor—but—"

"Lookit, D-Man—this here's a-ready a prime pick-up joint, I hear. Prime. Famous all over th'damn state even. Maybe way beyond that by now. Who knows?" The Sheriff adjusted his hat and his chin seemed to expand and contract with the effort. "An' that part's ok—but, well, it's just that the way it's being sold—like I already said—all them pop-up ads on the internet—I got to tell you (and I ain't no prude) but that seal gets a little—well—too frisky at times and—and you know yourself that kind of stuff's bound to stir up some meanness. Look, why don't you just move all this 'Safe in The Harbor' stuff out to Finch's Corners with the rest of 'em. Makes more sense to do that than to keep on doing what you're doing. Y'know?" He started a smile but let it die quickly.

"What in hell—" Drake tried to find some sign in the Sheriff's face of humor—that a joke was being set up—that something was rising up that everybody (except the dead) would finally be able to join in on. But the Sheriff began to frown.

"Look, D, for all I know this place is doing a real good thing—being medically safe an' all—putting—uh—standards in place like I've been told." He rubbed a hand over his mouth and sighed. "I got friends who tell me things, y'see—how you folks—well—watch out for each other in here—self-police—keep out the bad sort—y'know." And he tried to smile, but only got half-way there. "But it sure as hell ain't physically safe, though, huh?" And he swept out a hand to include the dead. "That one over there's the third one in two months, right?"

"Yeah. Yeah, that's right, but lookit—this—this ain't no gay bar go'dammit—I—I—"

"Right. Sure. Whatever. Hey, look, it's no never mind to me—I got other places to be anyways. But, lissen, who you think it is keeps killing off your paying customers, hey? You ever recognize anybody? 'Cause it's for certain sure none of the rest of them people over there will." The Sheriff sighed. Across the room, Doc kept tugging and poking the dead and writing in a notebook. The EMTs were arm-wrestling at a nearby table.

"The Harbor?" Drake could feel the cold stares from the photos and portraits behind him. "Jesus—my God—how—how'd this all happen? I mean, I never saw—I never did—I—I--"

LANDMARK BUILDING DESTROYED
Leonard Blevins
Pee Dee River Afternoon Sentinel

Early this morning, Dixie's Best, a long-time fixture of downtown Pee Dee River City burned to the ground before the nearest fire station was able to respond. No one was hurt in the fire and owner, Drake Nunn, was not immediately available for comment. A Dixie's Best has been in its present location since the middle of the Nineteenth Century and has recently become a favorite meeting place for students at Pee Dee River Technical University.

The Pee Dee River City Fire Marshall has not ruled out arson, but sources tell the Afternoon Sentinel that the building was minimally insured.

A Little Something for the White Boys

(With Apologies to Kurt Vonnegut)

It was September 1, 2099, Freshman Orientation Day at Obama Polytechnical and Agricultural University (OPAU), the educational pride of Slackbridge, Georgia. It was unusually hot and humid, but most everything else in the outside world was going along splendidly—and everyone who mattered agreed that this was the direct result of Yokimba Obama Jr.'s fourth term as president. That, of course, had been back in the time the Constitution was rewritten and made more relevant to the realities of a downsized, biologically controlled, and severely diverse American population. The Constitution had been streamlined much like the Supreme Court had been during YOJ's second term—the result of the legislative efforts of Speaker of the House of Representatives, Ryman Obama-Morris—a man somehow related to a daughter of the original Obama (while the original was serving—after his presidency—as Governor of Hawaii, having given up beforehand a supply of sperm to the Federal Spermbank substantial enough to insure the production of proper descendants). The Court now had three justices, each one appointed for a period of ten years, but subject to review by a select committee of "Cultural Arbiters," fourteen persons who were in one way or another connected to the original Obama and certified by the Federal Bureau of Internal Integrity (the people who were in charge of all legitimate ancestry searches and their results). By the time of the 2099 OPAU Freshman Orientation, the Obama dynasty had filtered, sputtered, oozed, and splashed out across the United States (like kudzu used to dance along highways and abandoned lots) until it was evident that a family member (either by birth or by adoption or by marriage) was in nearly all positions of authority, secular and religious both, right down to the neighborhood Abortion Specialists (those who maintained the Quick Sux machines on nearly every corner of the major cities, and on what seemed to be every cul-de-sac in the suburbs). Everyone in the know was positive that the best possible world had at last been attained and that this was evident by simply observing how all legiti- mate citizens were healthy and happy and well-fed and working in useful occupations and also were as positively and healthfully diverse as in The Most Honorable Jimmy Carter's "Glorious Dream" back in what was called the "Daybreak"—back among the fragile years way back in the old time, back in the blood-gushing Twentieth Century.

At Freshman Orientation, however, everything already by eight in the morning was showing severe signs of sluggishness all around. The largest freshman class (5000 students) in the history of "Geor- gia's Newest but Fastest Growing" University had been stalled for at least two hours in the antique-looking Jeremiah Wright Auditorium while counselors and advisors and registrar personnel worked to overcome the massive electronic meltdown that had begun at dawn and showed signs of not getting any better despite the near army of specialized tech-help bused in from the nearest satellite campus, the Honorable Jessie Jackson Biotechnical Center near Milledgeville. So far, nothing seemed to be going according to plan. The Jeremiah Wright Auditorium portion of the day-long event was to have taken only an hour (at the very most—a conduit to the rest of the day) and the afternoon in particular (after successful exit from the orientation) was to have been given up to socializing, club-joining, and various other productive activities, all leading up to University Provost Joshua Obama-Jackson-Kennedy's welcoming dinner and the assignment of academic majors. Before the crash, at least various welcoming and informative speeches had been delivered and most of the necessary student information had been collected through the "Cursory Mind Check Ultra" (the newest CMC upgrade which could now mix and match all information stored on each and every entering student by just the wave of a wand down both sides of the head). But then, just before the traditional "March to the Booths" and "Hover Bus Ride" to the Mix-and-Mingle Park—the power had wavered and then sputtered a bit and then simply died. It was a sunshiny day, so at least there was ample light coming in through the numerous windows, stained-glass and each a full ten-feet tall and running the length of the auditorium on two sides and in the very back of the stage. When the power failure was noticed, most of the students began quietly recharging their memory packs and tentatively looking about the room, shyly at first, unaccustomed to being at such close quarters with other human beings, especially in sunlight, even if at second-hand and filtered through various scenes from the life and times of the Original Obama.

Billy Williams and Mark Davis had met by accident, and quickly realized that they were perhaps the only white students on campus. The meeting had occurred in the "Filter Clinic" (step one in the orientation process, a quick brain and body scan to make certain the student had properly passed the various stages in the pre-registration process). There had been no other whites with them so far all morning, and, by the time they were seated on the last row in the auditorium, they were certain that no more were likely to show up, student or administrator (although one of the Campus Policemen looked vaguely Italian). The only whites. Everyone else ranged from deepest black to light chocolate to a kind of brushed charcoal to a grayish mixture to the more conventional yellow shades mixed with a splash of red from time to time. The only whites period. Billy had spoken first, as an apparent administrator in a severely pin-striped robe had waddled by their place on the back row in the auditorium and pushed through the swinging doors with a huff and puff of exhaled air.

"You see his face?"

"Yeah," Mark shook his head and lowly whistled. "Looked like his lips were trying to suck in his nose."

On the semi-darkened stage a tall, thin, gray-skinned guitar player dressed in denim and shoeless was trying to keep the audience
amused. It seemed as though initially he had wanted to sing and play
at the same time but hadn't quite gotten it to work. The tune was familiar, however.

"I know that song," Billy shook his head and wiped at his chin. It
was getting hotter and hotter in the auditorium. "I think I know it anyways. You?"

"Naw. Never heard it before. Well, maybe I have. Dunno. You
think he'll sing something directly? Maybe if he sings something—you
know? Maybe I only know the words. Maybe that's it. Maybe." Mark
wiped a nearly shredded handkerchief across his face and pushed it
back into his shirt pocket.

"I think it's 'the New Time National Anthem.'" Billy's face brightened and he smiled. "Yeah—that's it—'The National Anthem.' Ain't
it? Got to be. Hear the words now—'lift up' and 'wings' and 'sing'—
hear it?"

"Naw. Ain't nobody standing up. See?" He pointed right and left
and center. "Nobody getting up. I think it's just an O-song—hear it?
That real old one they used in the last election? 'Obama-Oprah
something, something'—remember? That real old one?"

"Where you from?" Billy settled back in his seat as the guitar
player began to dance and whirl his guitar over his head. A brass
band could be heard warming up offstage. The auditorium was getting hotter and hotter. Even the giant painting of Jeremiah Wright that
seemed to be floating in air above the main stage looked slick and
glistened, almost sweating in the increasingly steamy air. It smelled
like dead flowers all around. And then, suddenly, the guitar player
was gone, replaced by a tall, thin Asian-looking man who was trying
to get the audience to notice him. At first, it seemed that he was
shouting out a wavering racket of shrill squeals without words, and

then the words began to break free, but at times surrounded by squeaks and with an intonation reminiscent of an excited chihuahua.

"Richmond, Virginia. You?" Mark had to shout a bit to be heard above the thin man's yipping and yapping.

"Montgomery, Alabama." Several students in the next row turned around and glared. One of them held up a finger to his lips and shook his head at Billy in particular.

On stage, the thin man was laughing, and being joined in the laughter by most of his audience. Billy and Mark had missed the joke, but a great many of their new classmates were turning around and staring, nodding, or at least glancing in their direction. The row just ahead now showed only smiling faces, some laughing loudly until the thin man shouted out something like "never mind" which made everyone turn toward the stage and shout back something like "it's all good," and then a brass band came strutting out. The thin man jumped up and down a bit and waved to the cheering, stomping audience and then skipped and jumped his way offstage while throwing handfuls of candy into the first few rows. The band was playing the latest southern states political hit, "All For All, You All." Billy spoke first.

"How you come to be here?" Billy had to almost shout to be heard. The brass band was getting louder and louder, the audience trying to sing along to the rise and fall of horns and drums and a row of something like giant gourds being beaten with short, thick mallets.

"Scholarship—full ride—Kennedy Quota all the way. You?" Mark moved in closer.

"Something like that. Last white male in Lee County. Me."

"No shit? An LWM, huh? How has that worked out?" Mark pulled back in his chair and smiled.

"Very messy mostly." Billy sighed. The band was now trying to play some sort of delta-ultra-rap medley, and most of the audience was shouting out suggestions for the lyrics. "Just me and my Mom. She's on Final White Disability. Full benefits since I turned one." He wiped at his forehead with his hand and coughed. "You here for techno-repatriation? I hear they still hire whites there—agents even. I'm hoping to get into something that'll keep me close to home—for Mom—maybe at that big compound over near Petersburg. Techno-repatriation's real big back home. Especially since the borders got sealed." It was getting quieter in the auditorium. The band had begun to strut offstage and a blast of cold air seemed to be washing over the audience as the stage lit up, and various administrators began to fan out down the aisles. Doors began to open along the sides of the auditorium with signs dropping down from a row of curtained boxes running the length of the room. The power had returned.

"What's going on now?" Mark half stood and tried to look over the heads of the people in the next row. Onstage, a nearly yellow man was waving and using the suddenly revived stage microphone (an old-time version much in keeping with the retro-1990s look of the auditorium). His voice was deep and raspy.

"Look for your door. Look for your door. You are only to go where you are directed by the signs. Look for your door. Your door. The signs will point the way to the proper booth. Look for your door. Hover buses will be waiting. Look for your door."

And the audience was beginning to move. Everyone standing up almost in unison and looking from side to side. Reading the signs. And then moving quickly toward the one made just for them. Billy and Mark were soon alone in the back of the auditorium. No sign seemed to fit.

"Where do we go now?" Billy sat back down and rubbed his neck.

"Got me. But, what's that down there toward the exit? See it—that sign down there—can you read it?"

A Burning of Ducks

"I see it ok—yeah—but—I can't make it out—the one past the Pacific Rim Coeds? Down near Southwest TexMex? That one?"

"Yeah. I see "White" on it. You see it?"

"Wait a minute—I think that's the janitor's closet. I saw it coming in. Said 'Janitor' on it somewhere, I think."

"Nothing else left, though."

The auditorium was now empty. Everyone had exited through one of the side doors, beneath an appropriate sign, moved on into the rest of the day.

"Check it out then?"

"Sure. Yeah. Check it out."

The sign was larger than the other signs, the ones marked as Native-American Highest Plains or Crossover Aleut or Latino Upper Central or Viet-Chinese or Compton-Brownish—a sign that was coarser than the others, not shiny or even mounted all that securely over the very last door past the stage steps. "Whites Only" and a glass door handle battered and gouged. The air was nearly suffocating as Billy and Mark pushed through and found themselves face-to-face with a giant smiling clown face and at least fifty older male students holding up smaller versions and all pointing and laughing and whooping and finally turning around and dropping their pants. And many farted, almost in unison, a squeaking bellowing rush of noise that mixed in curiously well with a final humming of a tune that Billy and Mark later decided actually was the New Time National Anthem. And then they left. Nothing there but an empty parking-lot and a battered hover-van and the only other white they had seen all day.

"Hey there, boys—hey—" He was walking toward them from the left, from the opposite direction of the humming students. He was a tall man, dressed in the uniform of a janitor-third-class. "Ain't seen one of them in a long time—surprise, huh boys? Catch you, did they?" Billy spoke first.

"What th'hell was all that?"

"Whoa now, son—whoa—nothing to get riled about—just the 'Whites-Only Welcome'. They do it ever once an' awhile. They call it something, too. What was it? Oh man, sometimes I can't even remember what day it is—but hey don't tell nobody that, hear? They'd have me in one of them Senior Sleepy Tanks faster'n you could say Michele Obama. Right?"

"But," Billy's face felt hot, and his breathing was shallow. Mark seemed not able to speak at all, "but—what th'hell they—"

"Let it go, son. Just let it go. You passed. No violence. Nothing but big eyes and gulping a few times. You passed. Leave it be. An' c'mon, I'll take you down to where you supposed to be. Ok? C'mon—get on in the van there. Ok? You ready, I think. Ready. Plenty of good times coming. Yes sir, they is."

Billy and Mark slowly walked to the hover-van. Mark still unable to speak, just a few coughing gurgling sounds, and Billy shaking his head and muttering "shit" every so often. The van was cluttered. They cleared two seats—passenger right. Up front next to the janitor. Behind them in the van, piled neatly one on the other, were at least fifty white hoods with robes there too, and a cross wrapped tightly and thickly in burlap and cotton. The janitor smiled and made sure the boys had their seat belts safely secured.

Alma Mater

Billy Puffin's name came right before Ben Punder and right after Sara O'Hara on the roster. They never socialized or really even spoke much to each other at all in the various classes they had taken together over their four years at Pee Dee River Technical University (PDRTU—"Where Tech Says It All!"). This present class was Billy's final course, a techno-humanities survey taught by a visiting professor and centering on the Chicago Uber-Obamalites— especially on the Professor's favorite: Phrenezia Bonifa Olusu—a Nigerian-American author who had written a series of novellas (illustrated by Chick Moretta) somehow involving a character named Riley Sullivan who wanted to join the circus but never did. The visiting professor's name was Dr. Randy Beluga and he didn't like reading student prose.

"I don't want to read none of it!" He had said this to the class the first day. Adding: "So don't write any." And further adding: "You read Olusu. Writing proves nothing. Writing is passé. No writing at all, you got it? No writing at all. None. And grading? I'm sure you all want to know about grades. Yes? Well, I'll do the grading on how seriously you seem to appreciate what you read. Got it?" And he had smiled a big smile, teeth showing and then he winked several times (which left his eyelids fluttering).

Billy, Ben, and Sara talked that day in the Student Lounge after the class finally let out (ten minutes past time). The course was required and it was too late to drop and add. Ben had spoken first, sipping his coffee slowly from a big, school-issue plastic cup. "He's nuts." And he sipped some more at his coffee and winced.

"That doesn't help." Sara pulled briefly on a striped straw stuck down at an angle into what looked like a ginger ale and brushed back a stray lock of hair (decadently shaded a kind of plumb red with drizzles of blue spots mixed in). "That doesn't help us—appreciate—it—it doesn't help…"

"He's nuts." Ben again.

"I don't get it." Billy this time. "None of it. That lecture—it—it—"

"What lecture?" Ben and Sara together.

"That stuff on Chicago," Billy arched his eyebrows and then frowned. "All that stuff about Chicago and Oprah and Obama and Olusu and Sullivan somebody."

"I never heard that," Ben and Sara again. The Helio-Century Tower chimed outside in the Quad and the three headed off in different directions.

Billy walked in the nearby woods before returning to his apartment. He thought about many things as he walked, but mostly about his future—the job he had been promised and the way his father smiled each time he mentioned it. Running the family electronics business—all of it. Coast to coast. In the woods, there was a wind blowing and the trees were swaying some, with their leaves bottomsides-up and silvery. Billy never noticed. He stopped by a wooden bench, sat down, and decided to order a pizza. Giant extra cheese with pineapple. Sent to the apartment. The phone clicked shut, and he dropped it in his shirt pocket. The phone was new. From his father—a new model that Billy was supposed to try out and report on. Or something. He stood up and began to walk again. The apartment was about five minutes away. The semester looked like it would be misery even with just the one course. Professor Beluga seemed to Billy more bad dream than flesh and blood, something he had not seen coming when he planned the semester back in the summer. The course itself was usually taught by Professor Bullwine, an ancient blowhard whose lecture notes were yellowed and whose eyesight was so bad he never even knew what was happening beyond the first row of the lecture hall. Billy had chosen carefully and was all set for a nothing course, a course not taken until all the real courses were finished and on the transcript. But Bullwine had broken his hip or something and was out for the year. The sun was setting up ahead, in between the Library and the Campus Police Station. His Dad had promised him a BMW convertible for graduation; Billy had even dreamed about it. But all he could see now was Beluga winking and fluttering his eyelids and showing his teeth. The sunset was quickly over. It would be a long night.

Back in the apartment, between bites of pizza and on his third beer, Billy tried to listen to the recording he had made of the first class. But, even with the new phone, the quality was poor and at first only a few disjointed sentences had come through.

"...brilliant...Olusu...Oprah knew best..."

"Obama...down in Chicago...protypical..."

"Who doesn't like...my own opinion...a Lexus..."

"Yes...and much more...but a Lexus...no shit..." Nothing made sense, but then nothing had made sense during the entire class. The Lexus part most of all. He, Professor Beluga, had emphasized the Lexus over and over at the end of the class. Lexus. On the recording, on one of the clearer places, he had said: "To Riley Sullivan, the Lexus was the symbolic essence of America and America's zeitgeist—pre-Obama. Yes, a Lexus—no shit! An Obamalite epiphanous realization of encroaching impotence. But who knew exactly. Right?"

Billy finally gave it up and decided to set up an appointment with Professor Beluga.

The office was a large one—three massive windows and book-shelves (floor to ceiling everywhere else) and not a single book on any of them. All empty. Not even a plant. Computer screens were glowing dully on various tables and on the Professor's massive desk, and the Professor himself peered over the top of a funny-looking screen that was trying to hum some almost familiar tune. He seemed to be looking at some spot directly behind Billy's head.

"Who are you?" The Professor seemed edgy, head jerking about as he spoke. "Didn't you read the sign?"

"Sign?" Billy shook his head. "There was no sign."

"Yes, yes there was, is, a sign." The Professor arched his eye-brows and began to tap on the top of his desk with his very long fin-gernails. Billy noticed that every other nail was painted green. "There was too a sign! On the wall outside?"

"Then I didn't see it." Billy was beginning to regret deciding to come here at all.

"Can't you read?" The Professor smiled and licked his lips with what looked to be a very purple and very long tongue. "You can read, yes? I said: read!"

"I heard—yes, I can read. There was no sign." Billy wondered why he hadn't gone to lunch instead. The conversation was remind-ing him of the class itself—the lecture—the discussion—the whatev-er."

"The sign clearly said: DO NOT ENTER—or words to that effect. Is not this Tuesday?" The Professor's eyes widened and then nar-rowed and then widened again.

"Tuesday?"

"Yes—is it not Tuesday?"

"No—it's Wednesday."

"Oh—Wednesday then is it?" The Professor made a clucking sound in his throat like a startled chicken might make. "Wednesday. Then the sign clearly states:

NO ADMITTANCE EXCEPT AUTHORIZED HUMANITIES PER-SONNEL. Are you Humanities-authorized?"

"I—no—well, I'm a student in your..."

"Then begone! Go! Go! Now! Not authorized!" The Professor was frowning and making an almost snarling noise as he half-stood and pointed almost frantically toward the door, fingers, green nails and all, rising and dipping in the air. "Now!"

"But—but, I need to discuss..."

"Go go go—now!" And he rose up with—taken from somewhere under the desk most likely—a short feather-duster. He then moved unsteadily around the desk shaking the duster at Billy who by now was backing up quickly into the hallway. "You have your A! Only fifteen more to go! I'll remember you. See me after class tomorrow! Perfect Olusu diction. Perfectly appreciated. Neo-Obamalite texture around the edges. Well done, young man, well done! But you must go now—go on go on!" The feather-duster continued to sway out before the professor, an up-and-down movement that caused a few loose feathers to flutter out and float in the air. The door shut quickly and loudly and a sizable cardboard sign bobbed a few times and fell to the floor:

ALL DELIVERIES IN THE REAR.

&

The Helio-Century Tower chimed outside. Billy was suddenly hungry. A good lunch would help, he thought. A good lunch and then a nap. A long nap. That would help. He'd feel better then. Able to wake up and go finish out his senior year. And get that BMW and start that job with his Dad. Coast to Coast.

License to Kill

The wait had already made him thirsty. And then hungry. And then a mixture of the two that got his stomach to growling in a layered kind of way—soft to loud and deep to shallow and back again to soft. Ripley Carver was alone in the outer office, the Federal Options Secondary Field Unit—Southern Division. He needed to speak to a Marletta Brown, Third Assistant to the U.S. Piscatorial's local Division Chief of County Operations, Gustav O'Reilley. Ripley was reconsidering his decision to come here at all. His cousin, Buster, was supposed to come with him but dropped out at the last minute, looking a little pale as he did so sitting in a battered rocking chair about four hours ago. Buster was the best one in the family too. Four championships in the old days. Way back. Tops in six states. But today, he looked bad and just sat on the porch, his skin as white as the belly of a deep river catfish. Buster's voice was raspy and soft sounding.

"Naw—ain't going down there now." And he had tried to spit but thought better of it. "Naw. Ain't my way no how."

And Ripley was beginning to think it wasn't his way neither, starting to wish he was back home in Hawkins Knob, fixing to hike down to Roaring River. The office had been full when he first arrived, and most had been called right away, but no one had come back. For four hours now. Not a one had walked back through the doors marked A and B with flowers and what looked to be bees painted on the wall above them. Ripley was beginning to consider leaving altogether when he heard what might be his name being called crisply through a speaker hidden somewhere near the doors. This had taken too long, much too long. And the what might be his name had begun to sound even more wrong the closer to the doors he came.

Senor Raply Carved. Senor Raply Carved. Entrad por la puerta B. Senor Raply Carved...

He pushed through the door and entered a corridor. A fully armed guard motioned for him to follow and Ripley did, right to a well-lighted cubicle which butted up against a window, momentarily shut but its shade slowly rising as Ripley sat down, a computer screen seeming to pop up from the counter. The woman was cheery-faced, bright-eyed and smiling broadly. She tapped on a hidden keyboard and nodded toward him.

"Señor Carved? ¿Cómo es usted, señor? Senor Carved? That's you, yes? Eso es usted ¿sí?"

"No, ma'am."

"Beg pardon—pido perdón," almost in one breath. She looked genuinely confused. "Are you not Señor Rapely Carved?"

"No, ma'am. No seen-your—no rape-ly—no car-ved. No ma'am."

"I—oh—I see," shuffling some papers, "I see—then you must be Mr. Ripley Carver, yes? Route 5? Box 1222?"

"Yes'm. That's me." Ripley noticed that it was dark behind the woman, back into what must be a general office of some kind. Dark, but lively. Movement there like shadows drifting across the valley back home, down from the high ground where he lived into what was left of Roaring River, a rippling of the dark as it moved across rock and short grass and the flowers in the early spring, giving everything a look like nighttime flecked with bobbing spots of day. He wished he was out on the river, anchored at his favorite spot, down below the Carson Bluffs in a little place not touched much by the run of the river and the Army Corps of Engineers.

"But this shows you owe money to the Department of Interior Integrity. Two fines and a half-day broken pass." She bit on her lower lip with two front teeth that seemed flecked with gold. "Owed since last year, it seems. Since 2068."

"Ma'am?" It was hard to understand her the longer she spoke; her words were slurred together (at least to his ears they were) and she was squinting at the computer screen.

"Two fines and a half-day broken pass. Didn't you receive word about all this? It says the notification was emailed two weeks ago. To rcarved76@motorrock.com, yes? Your address?" She smiled over at him and tapped something into the computer.

"No ma'am."

"What?" The smile began to die a little around the corners of her mouth and her eyes seemed to be turning into slits as she frowned and pushed back a lock of hair that strayed down onto her forehead.

"I ain't got no address like that. I don't got no computer, y'see, and, well…"

"No computer? Not even a palm-pad-mini?"

"No ma'am. I ain't." Ripley noticed that she was tapping something into the computer and seemed to be humming to herself. He didn't recognize the tune at all. "Y'see, I just want the one thing—the two-year permit, and just for the one place."

"Roaring River, yes?" She brightened a bit and the smile revived and the eyes opened wider than they had been before. They were dark brown. "You're overdue on that, Mr. Carver—by two months, I see. Right?"

"Sounds about right. Yes ma'am." Ripley decided that he wouldn't never come back here no more if he could just get himself free of all this today. He was the only one still coming in. Nobody else in the family was. Nobody else on the Knob was. Nobody at the sawmill was. Nobody. Just him and right then he couldn't figure out why. It hadn't been like this ten years ago. Then it was all done down at Martin's Hardware—like always—with Pug Martin filling out the papers and taking up the money. And then the Army come in and the river got fixed (something about dredging it so's it would get more water down quicker to the city folks) and buildings went up all up and down the valley. And Pug lost the business. And signs went up telling everybody where to go and a few had gone—Buster and Ripley every so often and sometimes together for the past few years, but most everybody else just ignored the whole thing and kept on like nothing was different. And now Buster didn't look well. Not well at all. "I just don't see the need, Ma'am."

"What?" She made a little clucking-choking sound in her throat, her face shifting into what seemed to be a mass of wrinkles as she turned from the computer to face Ripley full on. "What did you say?"

"Can I get my papers now, Ma'am?" Ripley was beginning to feel a little sick. Maybe what Buster had was catching.

"Um—I—I think you need to be reminded of the seriousness of this procedure, Mr. Carver. This is no game, sir? This is the government."

"Yes ma'am." Ripley thought briefly of his favorite spot on the river, the bluffs up above, trees along it close together and making the water down below look deep and nearly solid black from the shade. The boat was waiting on him. But this day was nearly done.

"Well then—I think we can proceed. The only thing new that you need to submit would be the signed, notarized Form-P4 from your attorney?"

"Ma'am?" Her words were beginning to blur into a buzzing sound much like tree-frogs make in the summer nighttime heat.

"Form-P4—the explanation of the Life-Scale and its applicability to leisure activities? We sent out a notice of this about a year ago. Did you not receive the notice?" She was humming again as she tapped absent-mindedly on the side of the computer.

"No ma'am. No I never did get nothing like that." And the river was surely slipping into darkness the longer this took, daylight gone and him too tired to do much of anything at night. The woman was shaking her head and frowning.

"Well there is nothing I can do without that form. I'm sorry, Mr. Carver. You go see your attorney and try again. And get her-slash-him to explain to you the complexity of what you are asking to be licensed to do. We take killing very seriously, Mr. Carver. That's why the new form. To let you know exactly what you are doing when you do it. The biological impact. The specific steps from life to death and beyond. Fishing is serious to us. Very serious." And as the big guard suddenly appeared just behind Ripley's chair, she smiled broadly and nodded a few times as if in step with some tune only she could hear.

In a few hours, the river would be in total darkness, the night wind a moan and clack among the tall pines and the white-woods up above, and Ripley Carver moving with the big guard far away from all of it and with no legal way to set his hook.

What Would Jesus Do?

I'm not sure who to blame. The police were no help. And even the next-door neighbors didn't seem to know what made things turn out like they did. I don't think it was the house—no matter all the talk of jinxes and the like—not the house itself—the way it *was* at least—the Tudor-Spanish front, two-storied with the roof a gentle drop and slide down from the chimney to the sun-room and garage. Not the latticed windows surely—little ones and bigger by the doors. And not the backside porticoes, gazebo, and the flowers everywhere. No it's not the house itself or the grounds or what happened would definitely have happened everywhere in Briar Bluffs. The houses here look pretty much the same, you see, and mine, Hedgecoth Manor (what the little sign says on the lawn out front—HEDGECOTH there for me, for Barton and my wife, Helene—no children yet—"no children likely now to come, thank God," is closer to the truth for we, Helene and I, no longer even speak of such a thing now that the latter forties are upon us both)—my house, at any rate, is near about the Conlon's twin except for where the chimney sits and shutters for the windows on the second floor. It's not the house or it would show up every-where just like I said. And it hasn't shown up anywhere but there (five times now)—the Conlon house—Jim Conlon's place for ten full years or more until that prowler business sent him south to rest. His wife and boys moved with that young policeman out to Fisher's Point (into a trailer park I'm told) and Jim himself went off for five to ten down in that psychiatric jail near Starke. And that was sad enough but now—well, what it was was no fault of the house. We were never really close but Jim had always seemed a little strange and what he finally showed himself to be could just as well have happened out in Fisher's Point as here—a prowling thief with stolen goods (my lawn chairs there among the rest) locked in his storage-shed and garage—a heavy drinking man (I heard) who always shouted at his kids and beat up some old woman from the rest-home in the Prescott Woods. No, it's not the house but something else, a something else that boiled up one more time a day ago, a something else I'm starting to believe might be here close at hand, passed on and waiting, ready set to come again.

It's quiet here in what I call my shop. A typical north Florida autumn day. The day after Thanksgiving and quiet everywhere and more so past the yellow tape that stretches all around the Conlon house. I've only worked with wood a few months, maybe more, more I guess—but, not a year. Not that long yet. It only seems that way when I'm alone. A doll house now—Victorian or maybe Georgian if another gable cracks. My wife is gone (for good I think—for her own good and mine and for the safety of her soul I'm told as well) and I've got supper at a simmer on the stove—lamb stew and smelling now just right. A rich smell mixed with pine each time my jigsaw makes a cut, its sound there like a friend and steady, clean and true and just like something with me all my life. It's like that *now*, of course, but saws were not all that important on those evenings at the first when I walked past the Conlon house (no longer *Conlon's* house I know since Jim went south), my thoughts I guess fixed mostly on the last three owners in and out almost before I knew their names—an Adams and a Smith I think, the first a suicide and next one caught embezzling from his bank, and one more then, yes, a Bryant, bigamist and land-fraud there in all the papers for a month—until the Benningtons moved in at Eastertime. And since I like to walk, long ones every day (five miles sometimes at a crack) and Conlon's place is where I turn for home, I met the newest owner not long after he moved in, a springtime evening all filled up with the scent of wisteria blooming and the scattered hum of bees. Jesus Bennington. He said he owned a chain of hardware stores.

"Best inventory in the southeast too, Bub. An' nobody can't beat our prices. You need a chainsaw or something? You come to *me*!"

Saws. There from the first time that we finally talked. But I had never even thought the word those weeks that I had passed by whine and sputter-pop-and-crack of daily changes in the Conlon yard—to trees and hedges first and moving slowly toward the bushy shrubs against the house. I guess I noticed all the shapes he made but not the saws themselves. In fact, I seemed to notice everything but what now is the biggest thing of all. The saws. Long and short, red and green and blue. The saws and Jesus Bennington come closer month to month to what he finally did. The dollhouse will have to wait. I need a drink.

I try to keep a bottle in my toolbox. Scotch. The best. So I can sit behind my boat and drink in peace. Helene doesn't drink. I have some cigars here too. She doesn't smoke either. And doesn't like the boat. Or even coming in the shop. I come here every chance I get. I own two newsstands and an interest in three malls and working in the shop helps rest me some. And so does scotch and fishing when I make the time. Helene's a born-again in some church with a funny name. We seldom talk and when her friends are here I walk or drink or I smoke and drink or (now especially) work the wood (the jigsaw's fairly new—a Bennington Elf-light Special—with the newest saws in a box unopened to one side). I used to only drink and smoke out here or tinker with my cars or maybe wax the boat (I've only had it in the water twice). But Jesus Bennington had changed all that. One scent-ed springtime evening when my house was full of Christians and my scotch down close to gone. We talked as he was shaping up the tall-est boxwood, something like a mini-chainsaw popping in his hands and smoothing out what looked to be a camel's head.

"You mean you ain't *never* worked with wood? Never?"

"No—no, I mostly just—"

A Burning of Ducks

"Lissen, Bub—woodworking is *the* thing. Working it"—he had turned off the saw and lowered its blade, little teeth then glinting in the dying sunlight flat side in between us as he spoke—"like *this* stuff right here— making it *do* something—*be* something—making it do what *you* want it to. Yeah. Fixing it up—see? It wasn't much of nothing before *I* started in. See? How about *that*?"

"Interesting—it really is but I—"

"An' the beauty of it is it don't cost much. No—sir. F'instance— here— how much you figure this thing right here'd run you retail?" He had lifted up the saw and nodded at me, eyes wide and surprise-wrinkles bunching out across his forehead. "Huh? Retail now. How much?"

"I wouldn't know—I've never really priced—"

"C'mon—guess. Ballpark it—g'wan—give it a try—huh? Huh?"

"A hundred dollars?"

"Hundred dol—a *hundred*? Did you say a *hundred*?"

"Yes but I—"

"That's your guess—a hundred?"

"Well I—well yes—but I don't—"

"Man alive—whew boy—hundred dollars—no—sir! No—sir you ain't even close—forty. Huh? Hello? Forty I said—forty clean."

"Forty?"

"Right. An' lissen—I got all kinds a saws. Astros, Bendeckers, Whomble-Pyrex, Firebirds, Stellars, Bush-Mans, Centaur-Combos. You name it. Indoor, outdoor—jig, chain—diesel, gas, electric—even computerized. No fooling! Every damned kind you ever heard of— and not one over a hundred dollars neither. That's our gimmick y'see—Cut-Rite Hardware. I own 'em— fifteen stores—four states. What you think a that, Bub? Huh?"

"I—"

"Right right. Hey—you look like indoor t'me. Right? You an indoor kind a guy?"

"I like to—"

"Well that's fine—yes—sir—you got a garage, we got th'saws. Work some wood for Godssake. You look like you need *something*— right? Right?"

He had nodded toward me a few times with his head and let the saw blade almost touch my walking sweats—the new metallic blue ones Helene bought on sale. "Dressed like that—yes—*sir* you need something. You jog or what? You a runner? Like all them old codgers I see huffing and puffing around here every day? You one a *them*?"

"No—no I just walk—it's something to—"

"Shoot fire—work wood! Get you a Fiber-Lux Woodshop Set— thirty-nine-ninety-nine—on sale this week—Elf-Light Santa's Helper Special—we run it every spring and fall. Set of extra blades thrown in for free too—and cherry mix—start with cherry—we got kits. Make you some Chris'mas orn'ments—mangers maybe—the lil' ones— th'indoor kind folks put up on the mantle or under their trees—you can make a pile on them things y'know? An' Bub—we got all kinds a kits—huh?" And he had started up the little saw and raised the camel's ears.

I bought a jigsaw set next day. I'm not sure why even now. Perhaps it was the prayer-group gathered when I got back home, the fourteen ladies and the preacher-boys my wife let in on Tuesday nights. Or maybe it was Jesus with his little saw and joy at play about his face and leafy camel humps and ears awhirl among the darkness where I hid and drank and waited out the praying and the singing in my house. I do know the garage looked empty, even the boat and two cars not enough to make it full, a whole back wall was there bare and lonely as I sipped a scotch and smoked my last cigar. So that perhaps was what had sent me to his store (the Cut-Rite in the Centre Mall): the bare and lonely wall in need of all the things on sale by Jesus and his men, his young men dressed in Santa suits with full white beards on every one and section after section stuffed with saws.

"No—Mr. Bennington isn't here today. He's working at Number Three, I think. In Jacksonville. May *I* help you? Are you looking for a particular saw?" And I had bought a Fiber-Lux Supreme with extra blades and manger kits enough to last me through the summer into fall. My wife had crossed herself a few times as I set it up at home.

"My sweet Lord deliver us—what *have* you done?"

"It's a woodshop set—a Fiber-Lux Supreme—"

"And exactly what are you planning to do with *that*?"

"Work with it—build things—like mangers—I'm going to build Christmas mangers."

"Mangers. Creches? *Here*? In the garage?"

"Yes—I'm going to turn this wall area into a shop—I've ordered a bench—and other things—they should be here this afternoon, I think."

"Sweet Mother of God send us help!"

"Why are you doing that—that—"

"What?"

"Crossing yourself. You're not a Catholic, are you?"

"No—we're borrowing gestures—ancient gestures—to help us pray. Pastor Bob had a vision—he saw Jesus and heard a special word: Gestures."

"Gestures."

"Yes. The Lord wants universal gestures—to help His Body on earth. Before He comes again."

"Pastor Bob crosses himself too, does he?"

"Oh yes. Yes. We all do. The word was for us all. Jesus spoke through Pastor Bob but the word was for the whole church. He told us what to do."

"Well Jesus told *me* to buy a saw—yesterday. We had a long talk about it and he said—"

"Barton! Blasphemers shall be—"

"No—really—Jesus—that's his name—Jesus Bennington—"

"Jesus? No—no it must be Hay-soos—not Jesus—Hay-soos—"

"Well *he* said Jesus—Jesus Bennington—he lives on Pine Tree. The Conlon house."

"Then—then they sold it again? Those people *bought* it?"

"Yeah—and this time I think it'll stick. He looks sturdy. He's in hardware. I haven't met his wife." And he had really said that—*Jesus*—several times emphatic and with teeth all white and thick and looking strong just like the blade whirring at the camel's neck—*Jesus*:

"Jesus Bennington—and you?"

"Barton. Barton Hedgecoth. I live on Willow Court. Just over there."

"Then we're neighbors, eh? Fellow mortgage-slaves—right?"

"Well yes—yes I guess we are. Welcome to—"

"And it's Jesus. OK? Gee-zus. My mother was a wetback, not my dad—huh? Hello? That's a joke, Brandon—a joke."

"Yes—Barton—it's Barton."

"Come again?"

"My name—Barton."

"Ain't that what I said?"

"No—you said—"

"Well OK Barton—Barton it is then. Barton. And I'm Jesus, got it? Jesus H. Bennington. Me father was from London an' me mother from San Juan. Another joke, Brandon—family joke. They're dead now."

"Beg pardon?"

"My parents. Dead. You married, B?"

"Yes—yes I am."

"Me too. Though I don't get to take advantage of it a whole lot. All them stores, y'know? Gotta watch 'em close or they screw up. But I'm solid married all th'same, Bub—ain't no doubt about it. No—*sir*. Maria. No fooling. That's her name. Maria. I was in the navy. Met her in Tampa. Ybor City. She hates saws." He had winked and moved on to the camel's humps and tail, the haunches coming clear with one quick swipe of whine and pop-pop, saw-teeth blurred in leaves and bits of wood.

I hadn't really planned to buy a saw but all those cars in our front drive, the Christians in my house all clapping-shout and hallelujah-howl had made me really look at where I went to hide away—the boat that barely got a chance to sail and cars I'd tuned up twice a month for years and lonely wall and, well, I've already told what happened next. My wife, of course, hadn't been there.

"Why did you buy all this—this—*stuff*?"

"I already told you. To build mangers. I might sell them or something. Flea markets or some place. I don't know. A hobby. Yes. It's going to be a hobby."

"Cutting things?"

"Building—the cutting comes first, yes—but then comes the building. And painting—"

"Is he that little man who's ruining the Conlon yard? Is that who caused all this? That—black-haired little man? The one everybody's talking about? Is—is *that* who it is?"

"Yes. Jesus. Jesus H. Bennington."

"Oh Barton—it's—it's horrible there—the side-yard hedges look like kangaroos—he--"

"That's Jesus—yes. I'm not sure why he's cutting them that way—he never said. Did you notice the camel?"

"Oh Barton—oh my—"

"We never really talked about why. The kangaroos. And camel. And the rest. He never mentioned that. But his wife hates saws, you see, and I guess she won't let him have a shop like I'm doing here so he works outdoors in—"

"It *must* be *Hay-soos*, Barton—that must be the pronunciation. He looks Mexican."

"Well he's not. His father's from London. That is—he *was* from London. You see, his parents are both dead. Now the mother, I think,

was from San Juan. I think that's what he said. San Juan. Puerto Ri-
co, I'm guessing, not Mexi…"

"It's just horrid what he's doing—what he's already done. I heard
from Madge Purlear—they live behind the Conlon's, you know—the
next lot behind the Conlon house? Well Madge says he's even ruined
the grape vines— that arbor that Katie Lynn Conlon was so proud of?
It's ruined now—all cut up—"

"What does it look like?"

"Cut up, I said. Madge has a Conservation Club petition started—
to the Community Life Commission about the yard and the arbor—
how everything is ruined and—"

"Is it like the hedges?"

"What?"

"The arbor. Is it kangaroos? Or camels?"

"No—I—I don't know what it is—Madge said it's—it's frightening."

"Frightening?"

"Like a monster lying down—a *male* monster."

"What do you mean—*male* monster?"

"You know—it—it has one—sticking out—"

"One?"

"Lord save us now!" She had crossed herself three times, kissing
her thumb between them quick and loud, a smacking sound like
some lost bird afraid. The bench had come soon after and I guided it
to just the spot I had in mind back when I waited out the Christians in
my house. Right up against the sad and lonely wall.

"Barton—why? Why are you doing this?"

"It looked like fun—sawing things—I don't know. Jesus looked like *he* was having a lot of fun and it just made me want to have some too. His wife hates saws. Have *you* seen her?"

"No—but we—we *are* going visiting Thursday night. Evangel Squad. Did you know there are ten unchurched households right here in the Bluffs?"

"No I didn't."

"Yes—Pastor Bob commissioned a county-wide survey. Ten households was our number of unchurched. And a few lapsed luke-warms. So we're visiting on Thursday nights—a Unity Blitz—"

"Blitz?"

"Yes—a five-month sweep door-to-door. Baptists, Methodists, Episcopals, a few charismatic Catholics—I think they're still coming—Assemblies of God observers. Our fellowship is sponsor this month so we're working the Bluffs. Oh—oh and a Jew."

"A Jew?"

"Yes. Mordecai Boyle. Pastor Bob found him. A doctoral student at the University. Anthropology, I think. He's just the cutest thing—and very interested in our work."

"And you're all going together?'

"Yes."

"Well just remember she hates saws."

"What?"

"Jesus's wife, Maria—she hates saws. I know that much about her. So you might want to talk about something else. Tell everybody to keep away from saws."

"I don't think we'll spend our—"

"Now with Jesus himself that might be a problem. He loves them. Maybe you'd better just try to see them separately. Yes. That's probably the best way to go at it."

"*I'm* hoping *he's* not at home at all. It's wrong, I know," and she had crossed herself and genuflected as she kissed her thumb, "but I *hate* the mess he's making in that yard."

The dollhouse roof is crooked—somehow—tilting too far forward like a hat brim low across the eyes—the upper windows nearly too far back to see. Jesus wasn't there to greet Helene's Evangels and the wife had kept them standing on the porch. And Jesus wasn't there much through the summer months at all, a few times early on and nothing in July, the clipping that he'd done now closer to the house itself, the little trees turned into dogs and cats and one big rose bush looking like a fish. By then I'd left off doing mangers, fifty of them stacked from floor to ceiling near the boat and not a single sale no matter what I tried to charge. And one day late in August, Jesus showed up in his yard again, in bright red swimming trunks and see-through shirt and standing with a full-sized chainsaw in his hand.

"Barclay!"

"Barton."

"Right—sorry—where've you been, Barton?"

"I—I've been right here in the Bluffs all—"

"How're the mangers going?"

"I—uh—not well—I mean I haven't sold—"

"Then give it up. Try dollhouses. Victorian. We have kits. Give up the mangers and go to dollhouses."

"But what—what am I supposed to do with all the mangers I've—"

"Chris'mas is coming, Barton."

"What?" He had put his free hand on my shoulder, chainsaw in the other one, blade tip resting on the close-cut grass, on the lawn the Conlons sodded in that spring before their bad times came.

"Chris'mas—" and the fingers squeezed a few times gently on my shoulder and then left. "It's coming."

"But—but this is August."

"Barton—look at the house. What do you see?"

"Brick—wood—it looks a lot like my—"

"No—look again—*really* look—"

"Shrubbery—I don't know the names—wait—there's a shrimp-plant—and some kind of juniper—I think that's what it's called—and that bushy stuff I'm never sure of but it's expensive—at least its first owner, Jim Conlon, said he spent a lot of money to put it in—"

"That his name? Conlon?"

"Yes. The first owner. Jim Conlon. His wife did most of the planting, though—Jim wasn't very—"

"So all you see is shrubbery?"

"Yes."

"Well *I* don't, Barton. No—*sir*. I see Chris'mas. Yes—*sir* I do! All across the front. Chris'mas. I see lights and Santas—I see reindeer—and a rotating tree in front—with—with *mangers* on it—all lit up—rotating and blinking. Can you spare me some mangers, Barton? Do you have some mangers for my tree?"

"Yes! Yes—I have fifty of—"

"Good good good. Now those shrubs will have to go, Barton. To make room for the lights and the rest of it. And maybe a section of the roof—there—where the chimney meets it—see? For the rein-deer—so they can fly!"

"I—I'm not sure that's a very good—"

"Now don't worry none about Maria. She'll be fine. I'll cut all that across the front—it needs to be level to the ground, I think. I'll come for the mangers in November, Barton. You go to dollhouses. You'll never regret it. There's something about a dollhouse. I don't know. Something. And a star. Barton! We'll need a star. Yes. A moving star. Great big! You'll love it, Barton. I know you will." He had cranked the chainsaw then and headed for the side-yard where the holly bushes stood, half-cut and bulging in some vague and leaning ostrich shapes along the boxwood waving hands and kangaroos already there. I bought the dollhouse kit and hid out from the Christians and my wife the best I could and worked and waited until Jesus came to take the mangers to his tree.

It was a Thursday when he finally came. Cool and damp and just a week before Thanksgiving Day. My wife was baking heart-healthy cookies for the homeless and my saw was whining loud and sweet with wood dust blowing everywhere. My first and only dollhouse wasn't shaping up too well at all, but I was having too much fun to quit. I had thought of Jesus as I ripped along another line, half-dreaming of the Conlon house in flashing lights and reindeer on the roof, with Jesus there to throw the switches or to dip out cups of egg-nog on the lawn. And there he was inside the shop, in suit and tie and looking almost bashful as he waved and came around the boat. The saw shrieked into silence and I pushed my goggles up above my eyes. His eyes had seemed about to close in sleep, dark circles un-derneath and just a flicker of a twitch across his cheeks.

"Maria hates it, Barlow."

"Barton."

"No she means it, I think. Just like in Macon. And Waycross. And Valdosta. And all the others. I never even tried nothing in Jacksonville no matter what she says. But it's always the same thing, try or not. Always. Won't let me touch nothing up along the house. 'Leave the damned house alone,' she said. Same old thing, y'know? But shoot—this time I was so sure. I mean I was extra special careful all the way—step at a time—everything prepped just right. No surprises and plenty of time set aside for getting used to it. Shoot, you can testify to that yourself. There wasn't nothing rushed. Nothing. Right? You saw what I did, Barlow—you saw it all. Right?"

"Barton."

"Hey—now don't worry—I'll still take the mangers. No—no, I want them. I'll send a man over later today. We'll talk price later. I'd do it myself but I got business in Atlanta. That the dollhouse there? That it?"

"Yes—what there is of it. I've had to start and stop. I keep breaking—"

"Looks real good, Barclay. Real good."

"Barton—my name is—"

"Just make sure the front door's wide enough. Don't ever fudge on a front door."

"What?"

"Front doors. Mine's too narrow for the candles."

"Candles?"

"Now the choirboys'll maybe look OK but the candles won't without I widen the front door—needs a backdrop there. Th'candles need something solid behind 'em. A part of the house itself, not some phony plywood thing. So you got room in between an' it won't look like you're trying to keep nobody out. So your guests won't have to squeeze in sideways or something. So nothing'll get knocked over every time you open up the door. Make your doors wide, Barton. OK?"

But I had never thought about the doors again until the police came. A week later. Yesterday. Thanksgiving afternoon as I was working off the meal Helene had cooked before she went to join the Third-World Fast and Reparation Vigil at her church. The dollhouse had begun to look like hell and so I let it go and sipped a scotch or two and sat back in the shadows wondering how I'd ever get it right. And wondering too how far along the yard was now, Jesus's yard all cluttered up with boards and ladders, tarps and piles of rope the last time I walked by, a day or so before. The place then looking like he'd somehow changed Maria's mind, had finally gotten past whatever it had been that held her back so long, had made her ready now to see the many things he saw: The blinking lights and manger-tree, the giant star and leaping reindeer on the roof. And doors full wide enough to keep the candles safe and let the neighbors through. Anyway—it was warm in the shop, lazy and smelling good and I had noticed that the dollhouse doors were hung all wrong when the policeman's face came clear, back past the boat and calling something like my name.

"Mr. Hedgecoth? Mr. Barclay Hedgecoth?"

"What? I—uh—what?" I sounded a little drunk, I know. In memory, I sound that way every time I think about it hard, my voice a husky low one with the words come slow and thick. Closing in on drunk. Just like I'm getting now. Not sloppy yet. Not dangerous. But closing in on both. Close and closer with each sip I take.

"Are you Barclay Hedgecoth?"

"I—I'm Barton—"

"Do you know a Mr. Je-sus Bing'ton—33 Pine Tree Landing?"

"Why—yes—yes I do—" I got up quick, that much I remember clearly, quick and just a touch afraid. And I had shuffled through the sawdust and the woodchips there half-hoping it was nothing but a friend of Jesus, like the one who carried off the mangers just last week, another friend come now to take the dollhouse to some orphans maybe and to tell me it was time to work on weather vanes. But the sweating cop had never made a move like that at all.

"Will you come with me, please?"

"What? I—I can't just—"

"He wants to see *you*. He won't talk to nobody else. Will you please come with me?"

"I—well—yes." And I had walked on toward the squad car with my legs like rubber and a something in my stomach boiling through the overdone of Helene's food and tasting rusty when I tried to swallow hard and keep it down.

"What—what's this all about, Officer? What's the—"

"You'll see. Do you mind me asking you a few questions?'

"Uh—no—no that's OK."

"We've been questioning everybody. You know how it is."

"Yes—no—I guess I—"

"A'ready done the clostest neighbors a course. Always best to start with them. An' we'll get his employees directly. Everybody. Y'know?"

"I'm not sure I—"

"How long you known this Je-sus Bing'ton?"

"I—not long—months I guess—we're—"

"He ever seem—well—diff'rent?"

"Different?"

"Yeah. Strange. He seem strange?"

"No."

"How about th'Missus?"

"His wife?"

"Yeah. How about *her*? She seem OK to you. Y'know—normal?"

"I—I never met his wife."

Helene was outside in the yard when I got back, four hours later, everything all quiet at the Bennington's by then but my house packed with born-agains in burlap robes. And Pastor Bob himself had even come in close to squint and look all pained and sad.

"We've heard all about it, Brother Bart. Sister Helene asked us in to pray."

"She did?"

"Yes and praise God but we know how very hard it is to lose so dear a friend." I had started in to tell him, straight-out and quick that it wasn't anything like what he seemed to think it was, that Jesus wasn't what you'd call a friend at all, not close or anything like that. Not like someone from your days at school or from your club or back when you played sports—a team-mate yelling 'Way to go' or 'Nice catch Bart-o-boy' or 'Heyyy'. I wanted to say that he was more a hobby, like the jigsaw in my shop and woodchips curling deep upon the floor. A hobby that had somehow broken full apart and then got glued together long enough to carry off and maybe mend for real. But it was hard to say the things I thought just then, the cops and born-agains and pictures in my mind of what I'd seen and heard all whirling fast together on my lawn. And Helene popped up next to Pastor Bob, her face streaked dark from ashes and her tears.

"It—it could have been *us*, Pastor—oh my God—all cut up like that—oh my god—"

"There there, Sister Helene—there there. We're with you now— we're praying hard and thanking God that you—that you know His only Son—"

"Is the Fast and Vigil over then?"

And *that* was what I finally said. My voice turned high and cracking like a child's. A nothing sound among the rasp of burlap and the moan of prayers, the clap of hands and shouts of "Glory to the King!" All lost and gone before I took another breath. Not coming close enough to even touch the hem of what they seemed to think. I guess I should have tried to make the truth come out, to force them every one to hear, to paint in words the horror at the Benningtons's, of Jesus in his psycho-jacket tight and eyes so deeply dark they seemed on fire. But I was tired and stomach-sick with coming through the scenes of twisted wood, the front doors gone and where they'd been now wide enough to let in trucks, and holes above it on the roof like some great beast had landed there and stomped and kicked and tried to claw the chimney down, and ripped-up floors and ceilings torn away, the sad and splintered beds and chairs and tables like polished rafts upon a sea of wreckage everywhere right to the place where Jesus sat, against the rough stone of a battered wall with dust and trailing smoke and smell of burning like a blanket thrown round about him soft and thick. I should have tried to tell it straight but nothing else came out and what was left inside me now seems like a dying echo of the growling sounds he made.

Barrrrrrrr Barrrrrr Barrrrrrrrrrr

A red-faced sergeant shook his head and tried to smile. "He just now started doin' *that*. But he *was* callin' for *you*, Mr. Hatecut."

"What? What—where's his wife?"

"A'ready gone. An' buddies we like to never got that chainsaw away from *her*. Thank God she run out of gas is all I got to say. They a'ready took her out. To th'Adler Clinic, I reckon. That's about the closest nut farm anyways. He's next."

"But—but what happened?"

"We was hoping you might tell *us*."

But there was nothing I could say—to them, to Helene and the born-agains, and most of all to Jesus by the time I saw it all and bent down near to where he sat: *BARRRR BARRRRR BARRRRR* And eyes that seemed to burn into my own, and back behind us both out toward the shredded nothings in the yard—no boards or ladders, tarp or rope—the hedges, arbor, trees and shrubs gone too, cut down and level with the ripped-up lawn. And bits of colored manger-wood a flash and sparkle in the sun alone. *BARRRRR BARRRR BARRRRRR* So I had asked the cops to take me home.

"There there, Sister Helene—you're safe in the arms of Yeshua— safe in the loving arms of the Lord—" And Pastor Bob had kissed my wife and oh so gentle on her lips and (what came next so clear it's still there when I shut my eyes) gave just a little pat-pat to the place I'm sure her bottom hid beneath her burlap robe. But no one seemed to notice the delivery man but me. He looked and sounded a lot like Chico Marx.

"'Scuse a me, Meester—hey!"

"Yes?"

"Is ju a Meester a Hatch-a-cothy? Hatch-a Hatch-a—is dis a ju house?"

"Yes—yes—I—look this isn't a good—"

"Den I gotta ju order—on a da truck—see? But ju gotta sign a here—jes? By dat hex—see? Ju sign now. Ho-kay?"

"But—but I haven't ordered—"

"Sure a sure—ju gotta top-a-da-line. Best dey is f'sure. Hey? Ju gonna sure like a dese boy—Ass-a-tro Cy-a-clone a Whiz—whole damn line a boy I tell a ju—chain-a-saw heaven—whew—bring on a down dere, boys! Whew. Ju gotta cook-out, Meester Hatch? Beeg a party hey?"

The other men were dressed in Santa suits, the big box clanking as they got it down, as tall as Pastor Bob and swaying on the dolly as it came, a bump and clank of Cut-Rite cardboard holding maybe fifteen saws inside. And on the very top a purple sticker flapping by, just two words written there: a jagged DOORS and slender JESUS—paper rippling in the golden light—in joyous Christmas crinkle and in sizzle sound—like tiny wings aflutter near a flame.

The Last Night

The Body

It was late summer in 1954 when the body was found partially rolled up in ripped newspaper near the entrance to the only Negro cemetery in two counties—the Golden Rest Awhile (no gate there and no walls but plenty of tall grass and sunken gravesites). The body was shredded and alive with maggots when it was found. Deputy Mike Rominger saw it first—newspaper flapping in a hot wind blowing in from the north—the body face down in the weeds and gravel and packed sand off County Road 19. The body was later identified as Abigail Osteen who had disappeared a week before while coming home from work. She had been a maid for two white families in the Southgate Arms subdivision on the opposite side of town from where she lived. She lived in Lincolntown, near the rail yard and a good hour or more from the cemetery. She had called her children to say she would be late. The transfer bus driver had remembered her getting off at her usual stop, near Lincolntown Road, and then nothing. Her children had come to the Sheriff's office and filled out a missing person's report, but the deputy on duty had lost it somehow before it made it to anyone's official notice. The body made it official, but just barely. It was unusually hot and the flies, crows, and buzzards had done their job.

"Another nigger killed," Deputy Rominger had radioed to the Dispatcher back in town—Cowford, Florida. "Damn mess out here. Send the truck. "

And they did.

Abbie in the Morning

The house had many windows. A proper cracker-shack but no longer lived in by whites. Not very long ago, with others of its kind, it had been part of a white working class neighborhood just across the main Seaboard rail yard, on the rim of the fast-growing Negro section of the city and the piney woods beyond. Not that anyone said so, but more than one city father thought of it as an additional buffer that protected downtown Cowford and the better neighborhoods from being pushed into the mess of negro businesses and jumbled and mostly tumble-down shacks called collectively "Lincolntown. " But, a few years past, the last whites had moved out (something that had been going on for years as wages increased and housing opened up nearer the center of the city and along the river and in the suburbs to the north) and soon only the Seaboard rail yard and a half-century of law marked the clear and necessary division between black and white. Lincolntown, it seemed, had spread out as far as it could go.

Abigail Osteen lived in this particular house, newly settled in, a maid sixty-years-old with three mostly grown children and a sometimes husband, Julius, who worked as a mechanic up north for a trucking company. He sent checks south and sometimes came himself, but for the most part it was Abigail who attended to the daily doings of the family. Before moving here, they had lived a half-mile away in a shack that was owned by some landlady who lived up north. The place was nearly falling down and when the new houses came open (after the last of the whites had left), she was first in line. With help from one of her white families, she was able to sign a lease and move in. She worked as a general maid, washing and ironing and sometimes cooking for white families on the second or third rung of the social ladder, the young attorneys and salesmen and bankers and a few school teachers as well. But, where once it had been five families, it was now only two and she rode the bus Monday through Friday, transferring downtown and coming off finally at a place very near the subdivision entrance. Her last day had been no different from all the others since they had moved into the new house. Her children said that. Neighbors too. Nothing seemed different. Except that she never returned.

"Mama never went no place but home after work." Carmen, Abbie's daughter, had told the deputy downtown. "She ain't never not come home."

Across the Tracks

Beckham ("Beck ") Blanton was fifty-five-years old and a rail yard mechanic and carpenter since he was ten. He now lived by the railroad tracks on the northeast side of Cowford with a clear view of Lincolntown. His family once lived where the niggers had come. His daddy never lived to see it. Not even the beginnings of it. And that was a good thing. But Beck did, moving with the rest on past the rail yard as soon as he could, not going as far as the suburbs or near the river or the city parks, but settling in where he worked, into one of the identically shaped and painted Seaboard shacks the line kept for its full-time rail yard crew. The shacks stretched in a mostly straight line for almost a mile down the tracks, on an east to west line, and on the front porches was a clear view of the nigger mess just a stone's throw away. Beck saw that mess every day. Watched it grow. Watched it send out its own each morning to ride on those buses the city let cross the tracks. Beck drank every afternoon at Connie's Bar with his friends. They liked the Delmore Brothers. And Hank Williams. And they all were in the Exalted Knights of the White Camelia, Gordon Division. Since they were teenagers. Since forever. But nothing felt the same any more. Nothing felt right to none of them. Most felt that something was just not right since the War. Both Wars. Beck had served. And most of the boys had too. In Number Two or Korea or both. And they had come home to good pay and jumping good times, but even the wives and kids just weren't the same. And across the tracks most of all. The niggers seemed on edge or something. Uppity. Not often but enough to notice. And the boys didn't like what they were beginning to see.

"Damn jig didn't even step aside t'other day, I heard—didn't even make a move to get off the sidewalk. Right downtown." Red Jones had said that last night at Connie's. After two beers. Sitting at the bar.

"Downtown?" Beck had shook his head and took a long pull on his cigar. "Where downtown?"

"Down near the park, I heard tell. Down past the courthouse anyways. Somewheres. " Red motioned to Connie for another beer. "Hell, it don't matter where. I been hearing shit like that for a month now. Niggers not tipping their hats. Niggers pushing in here and there. Y'know? You hear any of that? "

"I did." Connie set down the beer in a circle of wet near Red's elbow. "Mark says he heard of some nigger down in Gainesville asking for a sandwich at the drugstore counter. No shit. Sat his fat black ass down and asked for a go'damn sandwich." Connie shook his head and wiped at the bar with a red cloth. "He thinks it's all that damned Su-preme Court shit—y'know all that shit's been in th' papers? "

"Yeah. I read about all that. Word's out about it too. Big article in this month's *Rebel Thunder*. You see that? "

"Yessir I did." Connie shook his head and dropped the cloth down out of sight.

"And—somebody says them Lincolntown niggers are planning something. You hear any of that?" Red took a sip of his beer and ran his left hand over his mouth. "Bosley told me about it."

"I did hear something last week." Beck was beginning to relax; the third beer doing its job, and his thoughts now beginning to race and tumble over each other. "Something. Going to buy up land across the tracks somewhere? Was that it? Anybody hear that? Big niggers from up north getting up the money to buy up land down here." Beck felt good now. Relaxed. Thoughts free to do whatever they wanted to do. No longer having to tumble around with his mostly dried-up wife and big-eyed kids who didn't seem to know when it was morning. Free to spend his money however he wanted it spent and no damned body there to tell him to stop. He felt good. "Niggers up north doing this. Some damned tap-dancers or singers or something. Going to buy up land down here and put in nigger towns everywhere. Yes sir. What you think of that?" And Beck thought just briefly of the shacks across the rail yard where he had been born and grown up in and now all filled with niggers and who knows what other kind of trash. "Think we ought to put up with shit like that?" And the words came out in a near-growl, deep and rasping and making everbody at the bar turn and look. Beck felt good.

"Hell no, Beck—hell no." Red spoke up but the rest had come in closer, Connie himself leaning in a bit, and at least six of the boys shuffled in, carrying their beers to the bar. "Hell no. Niggers up north, you say?"

Preparations

-i-

Abbie had talked to Julius on the phone for what would be the last time. It was the night before she went missing. They had discussed the recent move into the new/old house and how he was planning to find work down closer to home. She had told him about the loss of several of her white families and how the ones she had were nothing like what they used to be when she had first started out. He had told her that he loved her and she had told him the same. And then the children had talked with their father and Abbie had come on at the last to say good night. It had been Abbie and Carmen, her daughter, who stayed up awhile to drink a cup of tea and talk. Carmen later told the police that nothing had seemed out of the ordinary.

"Mama was going to work in the morning same as always. We talked about that. And about school. And about how she wanted my two brothers to do more around the place while she was gone. Stuff like that. "

And then they had gone to bed. About eleven o'clock. Hot in the house and tree frogs making a racket outside. And Carmen dreamed about a boy in her class. Simon. And how they had run off north and got good jobs and were happy. Mama had cried out one time in the night, she said. Had cried out "No! " and then went quiet. And nothing more until she left the next day. Like always. Up and gone away. But this time never coming back.

-ii-

Beck Blanton had called the special meeting. In the evening in the back room of Wilde's Hardware with all the boys present. Beck was in a foul mood, having polished off nearly a six-pack of Jax Beer back home before leaving and had nearly run over his own dog backing out of the driveway. He had called the meeting a few hours before and the boys present were the very core of the White Camelias, the best there was and solid all the way. Mark Stevens, Randy Rambeaux, Billy Brolin, and Eddie O'Rourke. All four were proven true. Solid. Last of the St. Johns County crew that had taken out the nigger church over in Springfield and stopped them union boys from organizing in Lincolntown last year. Some sort of carpenter's union, he remembered, or maybe just a jumbled up something with yankee niggers in the middle of it all. Something. Anyways, he had led the charge there and got a personal call from Harland Mahoney (leader of the Florida United Klan) himself about how good it was to see white boys who wasn't afraid of getting their hands a little dirty. Beck was sick and tired of the damn niggers across the tracks. Sick and tired of them taking over everything his daddy and his daddy's daddy had built up. Coming closer and closer to crossing the tracks and then who knows what. The meeting was necessary. Long overdue.

"So we all agreed? Get one tonight. Warn 'em all. Won't be hard. Plenty a them comin' home at all hours. Drunk and just lookin' to grab somebody's wife or daughter—right?"

"You right there, Beck. Yessir." Randy Rambeaux took off his hat and rubbed his right hand through his hair. "Yessir. You said it right. Make 'em back up a lil', yeah, back up an' maybe get on back up north where they belong."

"Right." Beck looked at the others and smiled. "Rest a you all in this here?"

"Tonight?" Mark Stevens finished off his beer and tossed the bottle into the trash can near the door, rattling it in with a clank among the others. "Right? You did say tonight?"

"Yes sir I did." Beck noticed something about the others. Not Randy. Randy was in. Straight in. But Mark and Billy and Eddie looked a little shaky. Like they was getting sick or something. Not straight in no more. "Yes sir—tonight. We grab one and see where it goes. Some damn black bitch's sure to be comin' in late from this side of town. Yes sir. Every damn night." And he had remembered sitting on his porch and watching the headlights and flashlights and for all he knew damned candles crossing the tracks every night, in the dark of it moving from his side of things on into Lincolntown, carrying no telling what with them and settling in to come out first light and do it all over again. Back and forth. Back and forth. And it had to stop. "Whose with me on this here?"

"I'm there, buddy—yes sir I am." Randy stood up and stretched. "Le's go right now far as I care. I think they need to know what's the right of all this. Keep 'em down with their own damn kind—or on back up to New York or wherever in hell they all come from. That damn Lincolntown ain't no natural nothing far as I can see. Set up by damn yankee nigger-lovers I hear tell." Randy reached for another beer.

'Who else?" Beck looked at the rest, but he didn't need to hear them say nothing. He could tell they were not in. He could see it in their eyes. "No body?"

"I got to go to my wife's family's dinner tonight, Beck." Mark got up and moved toward the door.

And Billy: "My God, man, I need more warning'n that, Beck. My boy's in some play at school tonight."

And Eddie: "I been called in to work early, Beck. Can't be out on no ride. I really need the money."

"Jesus God, boys—Jesus H. Christ a-mighty God—you just goin' let them damn niggers keep on till they living in your front yard? Jesus. Well—go on then—go on." And Beck spat to one side, hitting the corner of a peach crate as the door closed leaving Randy and him alone in the room. Outside, they could hear the whistle of the 7:30 as it began its last turn toward the rail yard.

The Meeting

-i-

Abbie was late finishing up at the Mahoney's weekly card night. Later than usual but not too late to make the last bus. She had telephoned her children about the change in schedule. Carmen had answered the phone and told the police later that, no, her mother had not sounded any different than she always sounded, and, no, there was not loud music in the background. Abbie had caught the last bus to Lincolntown and was let out at her usual stop (the bus driver barely remembered her at all, but did recall the stop and that one person had left by the back side door). And then nothing. No sight, no sound, nothing of Abbie until she turned up at the Golden Rest Awhile.

-ii-

Beck and Randy had waited at the tracks for an hour. After driving around for three hours, they had finally gotten some burgers and some beer and parked in the deep shadows near a bus stop. Just over the tracks and out of sight of the road. Nobody much had showed themselves worthy of attention so far. A few boys and a couple of busted-down-looking uncles outside of some crowded juke joint up near the piney woods. But, nothing clear so far. Nothing solid. Nothing easy. And so they got the burgers and waited.

"Maybe this ain't th'night, Beck." Randy pulled at his Jax Beer in the mostly wet paper bag and flipped a nearly gone cigarette out into the darkness to one side. "Damn coons seem to be indoors. Too damn late now."

"Yeah. Maybe. But something's got to be done, y'know? Can't wait no longer." And Beck swallowed some beer and glanced out toward where his house was—out in the blackness slightly to his left, out across the tracks and down the little road that linked all the company houses. He felt a pain in his belly. Deep down in there like some kind of something sharp and prickly was growing each time he breathed in and out, his face hot and sweat dripping down when he moved his head even a little bit. "Can't wait no longer. Damn spades'll be across the tracks t'reckly. You just wait and see if I ain't right." And he swallowed some more beer and sighed. It was almost too hot to breathe.

"What's that?" Randy pointed to a speck of light that seemed to be growing bigger, coming from the left of the car, out on the road about a few hundred yards away. "What's coming?" Randy threw out his beer and leaned forward, hands grasping the metal of the dashboard and face close to the glass of the windshield. And then he settled back in the seat. "Damn bus, right? Ain't that a damn bus, Beck?"

"Yeah."

The bus had stopped a few feet away from the car. But Abbie had not seen anything but the darkness and the beaten down sand of the pathway leading home. And soon she was dead and saw nothing at all.

Sentinels

The patrol car was parked in the free space between the main tracks. In the middle of the rail yard. Two officers were in the car and there were three more cars on both sides of them. Stretched out along the rail yard, the cars were pointed in both directions. Toward Cowford. And toward Lincolntown. Nobody knew what was coming. What was being planned. It was easier in the daytime. All the officers agreed that it was. Easier to see what might be crossing the tracks and easier to intervene if nothing looked right. But not at night. At night it was mostly blackness on both sides of the tracks. With the occasional scream and the occasional gunshot. And people watching night by night. Waiting. Like it was the last night for everybody. And maybe it was.

The Barmaid and the Orangeman

It was late October in St. Albans, Vermont. 1978. An early snow had come and gone and left great lumps of itself along the streets and on the sidewalks. Most businesses had closed early. It was Saturday, and the downtown was mostly deserted. Only O'Brien's Irish Pub still showed life, but only just a little bit. Daisy Morton and Kitty Donovan were alone at the ornately carved and curved bar, sitting together on stools at closing time. Daisy was the barmaid, working at O'Brien's now for five years, and Kitty had been tending bar for at least ten. Tonight, they had at first been talking about all that "Boston shit" and how the coloreds were messing everything up. Daisy had heard all about it from a cousin of hers who lived in Southie and she was afraid it might show up other places, even in St. Albans (although as Kitty reminded her, there were only twenty coloreds in the whole county). But it was upsetting all the same, Daisy had thought, and she had decided that nothing was like it used to be, with coloreds every night in the news for years now and even showing up in her dreams and leaving her no place to hide. And then Kitty told Daisy that Johnny Conner was a terrorist, a member of some Ulster orange brigade or something. Kitty whispered the news while the last of the usual drunks were singing their way toward the front door.

"He's even wanted or something."

"Wanted?" Daisy felt a knot begin to form in her stomach. The whole evening had been a bust—few customers, no real tip money, the colored mess down in Boston (always there, it seemed), and now

Johnny a terrorist. She just wanted to go home; she wanted to take a shower and then turn off all the lights in her room, and bundle herself into the quilts. It had been a miserable night and nothing showed any signs of coming along to make it better.

"Yeah—an' he's wanted by somebody or other—something like that. Lenny told me. Friday, I think—yesterday. For a bombing—somewhere back home."

"Ireland?"

"Yeah. Years ago. Blew up something. A bridge. Or a house. Schoolbus. Or—oh I don't know what. Just that he did it, Lenny says." Kitty rubbed her eyes and sighed.

Two of the more persistent drunks were trying to sing "Galway Bay" just inside the door. Lenny Burke, the owner, was pushing them firmly toward the outside. Lenny was tall and muscular in a long-distance runner kind of way. With bright red hair and a smile that highlighted his big front teeth. He had taken over the bar from his father five years earlier and had even settled into taking care of problems like his father and grandfather had done before him, helping find jobs and emergency help for the Irish community in a three-county circuit. He never had held a public office, but they all came to him anyway, the politicians both local and state, the desperate ones and the powerful both. The Irish Catholic vote was still important in his part of Vermont and Lenny knew how to turn it out election after election. Always safe. Always together. As steady on as in his father's or his grandfather's time. Across the room, he finally succeeded in getting rid of the drunks and waved to the two girls at the bar.

"Going out back for a while. Get on the cleanup."

The girls looked at each other and sighed. Kitty Donovan was the older of the two, in her fifties, with three grown children who had scattered from Franklin County as soon as they turned eighteen. Three sons. Two in the Army and one in the Merchant Marines. The husband had died in a thresher accident.

"You sure, Kitty?" Daisy Morton was thirty and single, deeply Catholic and deeply shocked at the news about Johnny Conner. It took away the coloreds real fast.

"Yeah. Lenny was drunk when he told me, but he knows about such. Lenny knows. He's—ah—connected. Believe me, he knows."

"I can't believe it." Daisy was sweeping under the booths. She still couldn't take it in. Johnny was real sweet and lived with his sister. But for some reason it did seem romantic the more she thought about it all—Johnny with a gun in his hand or a sword, with flags flying out behind him and strong music playing as he and his lads marched off to face something or do something not at all clear but surely grand. And Johnny was good-looking too. Thick, red hair and green eyes and a smile that made her feel all fluttery inside. Made her think about having kids, too. About babies. In the earliest dreams, somehow Johnny was always there in her room all peaceful-like and rocking a red-haired little baby girl who smiled and cooed and came easy to her breasts. Their own little baby girl. But he lived with his sister and Daisy lived with her aunt, so nothing much had happened besides a few sweaty fumblings in the backseat of her old Buick. And she had known all along that he was a Protestant. That was the hardest to take in.

"The Rising of the Moon" suddenly boomed out from the jukebox. Lenny had done it as he passed by and waved again and headed for his office. He would eventually deposit the day's money in the First Republic's night box, but he would stay in his office in the meantime downing shots of whiskey until he got done whatever it was he needed to do every night after closing. By the time he left the pub, the girls would have been long gone.

"He'll be sloshed soon," said Kitty.

"Why does Lenny do that?" Every night the same. There was no good reason for hiding back there in the office but he did it anyway. Until they had gone home. Daisy left off sweeping and began to wipe down the bar. She tried thinking of Johnny as he first was but all that would come clear were those flags (now tattered and ripped beyond repair) and the music (an almost devil shriek and moan) and the way he grinned (a jagged one like a rough-carved pumpkin at Halloween) and how he waved his lads to follow now behind him on a road to somewhere blood-soaked and all filled up with pain. Blocking out forever the baby girl being rocked, the baby girl nuzzling and sucking at Daisy's nipples in the moonlight with a soft music coming in from beyond an open window in a long and pleasant summer's night. She knew now that Johnny would always be changed in her mind. Always. Before he had been just sweet and handsome and fun to hold to in the darkness of the Buick. Before he had been a maybe husband and father. But now it was all different. It was harder to see him as he had been. Before the flags and music and guns had come. Before the blood and pain, the tears of mothers crying for sons no longer coming home. The stories of the centuries being sung and told and made a part of her own growing up, a part of who she really was and always would be. Crowding out what she thought she knew. Making it hard to see him as she had first seen him. She knew other things about him, but even they were beginning to crumble and go away. Just a few things left. He went to church every Sunday. New Scotland Presbyterian. He was a youth counselor (ever since he moved from Ireland two years ago). The kids all loved him. Daisy went to St. Malachi's. They had met at a Church League baseball game last year. Johnny was a coach and Daisy worked concession for St. Mal's. She guessed she loved Johnny right from the first. She thought she did. But it was all different now. Kitty's story was changing everything. Leaving nowhere safe to hide.

"Lenny says he can't come in here, y'know?" Kitty straightened out a table near the restrooms, and began to stack the chairs on it. She shook her head and suddenly bent down to pick up something beside a table leg. "Look at this now. A fiver! That'll help sure as hell, right?" She snapped the bill twice and pushed it down the front of her blouse. "Nosir—Lenny says don't let him in if he tries."

"But, he never comes in here," said Daisy. She wanted to go home and try to forget about all this. "The Rising of the Moon" was replaced by "Roddy McCorley."

"Good thing too. Lenny says nobody wants his orange ass in here." Kitty laughed and moved quickly to the bar and a half-empty bottle of vodka. Glancing toward Lenny's office, she poured herself a shot and tossed it back. "Ah yes. Good good good."

"How does Lenny know?" Daisy was feeling a bit sick to her stomach.

"Know what?"

"The bombing stuff. Johnny."

"Oh he knows stuff." She poured another shot and held the glass between her palms. "Lots of stuff. He knows, believe me."

"But Johnny's a minister."

"Well so's that—what's his name? That bastard in Ulster—oh—pasle—palse—Paisley—Ian Paisley or whatever in hell his name is. Don't mean nothing that he's a minister. And that other orange prick—the one who's always in the papers—y'know the one—beard and a lot of teeth in the pictures—right?"

"I don't know." Daisy tried to see Johnny sneaking in a bomb to blow up something but all that would come clear to her mind like a grainy film bumping and shivering along were the lads and Johnny and some fine music and everybody cheering as it all went marching by. Everything was confused.

"Never mind." Kitty sipped at the shot at first and then finished it quick. "And, hell, what do you care anyway?" She coughed and wiped a hand over her mouth. "Whew boy—good good good." And then she looked straight at Daisy. "Oh—I see how it is. I see—" Her laugh was something between a cough and a gargle.

"You see what?" Daisy's stomach continued to hurt and she felt cold although the heat had been turned up so Lenny could work in short sleeves to show off his new tattoos. She suddenly felt a need to go to church and pray. She could almost see the face of Father Reilly if she told him about all this. About the backseat of the Buick and most especially about the bombings and the children that maybe had died. And Johnny a Protestant too. She'd have to tell that the most of all.

"You and Johnny, eh? Wow. You and Johnny. Jesus, Mary, and Joseph, does your Aunt know?"

"I don't know what you're talking about." Daisy's stomach began to feel like it was somehow flipping and rolling back and forth.

"Oh I think you do. Hell, girl, I think you love him, don't you? That piece of Protestant shit. That baby-killing scum. You love him! My God! Why not a Boston nigger then? Why not that?" And Kitty shook her head and gathered the few glasses left on the bar.

"What?" Daisy could see Johnny now clearly a bomber and a bomber whose face was black. A leering grin on his thick-lipped face. Flattened ape-like nose with nostrils flared and hair like wool and him all crouched and waiting in the darkness to carry off a little girl. A red-haired little girl. Maybe like that daughter Daisy wanted someday for her own. Johnny leering in a Southie alley as dark and black as his face, with shiny teeth and bulging eyes that seemed to glow. And hands reaching out like claws to rip the child away. It was all clear to her now. The jukebox was playing "The Foggy, Foggy Dew" and she watched as Lenny saluted the two women from the door of his office. He had never done that before, but it suddenly felt good to see him there. Tall and white and comforting. Making Johnny run away. Making her feel safe among her own kind.

The Rocky Road to Justice

The Reverend Royall Silas Myers was late for the press conference. After two sizable tractor-trailers had somehow collided and sucked in three or four compact cars, he found himself solidly stuck on the Jesse Jackson bypass on the Arlington side of the St. Johns River. In a Jacksonville Metro Cab; in the backseat and alone, he was cursing under his breath and hoping the driver, a Middle-Eastern-looking cabbie, didn't hear. He checked his phone and saw that he would be late perhaps by as much as an hour. Ruining everything he had worked for the past seven months—since the terrible tragedy in Ailey, Georgia. The murder of little Cornelius by a depraved racist. Reverend Myers was supposed to open the final session of the Anti-Racism United Front's annual convention—the most important meeting of the year—attended this year by some thirty thousand delegates, to be covered by every television network of any substance and untold numbers of bloggers and whoever else could reach the general public. The ARUF was meeting this year in the coliseum of the M.L. King Vacation Complex, a mock coquina-faceted series of castle-like structures that sprawled down in the piney woods south/southwest of the Jacksonville business and government district. It would take at least two hours to get there now, he guessed, which might make him miss the session altogether. He cursed lowly again and fidgeted in his seat.

Watching a painfully thin police officer run by the cab blowing a whistle and shaking a nightstick at a group of rubber-neckers who had gathered to gawk on the right shoulder of the expressway, Reverend Myers thought back to the beginning of it all—back before the murder of little Cornelius—back into his own life, a shimmer and a shiver of things he usually kept well hidden and protected and never ever shared with anyone. He had been born into an affluent life in northern California. He was an only child, and his father had been a judge, his mother a psychiatrist, and they both had died young and left him a sizable estate. He himself had felt something like a religious calling early in life and had bounced around several denominational seminaries before finally graduating from Yale University with a degree in Theology and no particular interest in settling down. This was about the same time the Struggle had begun in earnest in the South, something he followed with keen interest back home in California while he tended to his now massive real-estate holdings and other financial investments. He particularly enjoyed watching Dr. King and Dr. Ralph Abernathy and had several times traveled back east to try to meet them in person. Once he had spotted Dr. King in a train depot outside New York City and had followed after him as he made his way toward the exit. That time, he had even pushed through the reporters and the milling crowd to walk alongside Dr. King until finally, losing his nerve, he had very loudly blurted out: "Morning! Do you have the time?" Dr. King looked a bit puzzled, but had finally said: "What?"—and then disappeared into a crush of cameras and hangers-on and baggage carriers. This had been in 1967, and later, in 1968, Reverend Myers had been in Memphis on *the* day. In town to visit an apartment complex he owned, he had gone to the Motel to maybe visit Dr. King but again lost his nerve, and, sitting in a rental car nearby, he had witnessed the assassination, ducking down and hiding for at least thirty minutes before he carefully walked across the street and slowly mingled himself in with the sobbing, screaming crowd down below the balcony. He had been interviewed and photographed and eventually accepted into the confidences of the remaining leaders of the movement (expect for Dr. Abernathy who had called him a "hustler") and from that moment on began to emerge as a "Civil Rights Leader" who, in his own press releases and his motivational speaker advertisements, had "walked and talked with Dr. King" and "had been there when he died." The "Reverend" he added himself, a nod to his degree from Yale, and over the years he had become a favorite consultant to the media.

He had founded the ARUF (with the help of an order of Episcopal nuns, the New York State Yoga Instructors Association, the Arts Council of Compton, California, and massive amounts of cash from various guilt-ridden celebrities and university professors) in the early 1970s and used it as his own personal platform for righting all racial wrongs that came to his attention. In this he was assisted by a staff of volunteers housed in property he owned in Chicago and helped as well by the Reverend Jesse Brownstone, a sometime follower of Dr. King who had figured big in racial matters ever since the murder, and Mr. Buster Stonebridge, supposedly a former bodyguard of Malcolm X.

But sitting in the cab on the wrong side of the St. Johns River, it all was becoming more and more ephemeral, far away and maybe on the verge of collapse. After nearly a decade of mediocre progress, ARUF mostly on the fringes of celebrity, today was to make all the difference. Today was to be a massive push back into the center of the national spotlight. Having total control of the little Cornelius murder—just a few weeks old—having the family on board with his crusade to find justice for an African-American boy murdered in cold blood by a vicious white racist in a corner of the South well-known for its viciousness was so far resoundingly successful in arousing the loyal to a near-frenzy of protest and donations. He was supposed to introduce the family to ARUF's general membership—and ask for approval of a massive allocation of funds to help bring the story to the whole world and finance the best legal advice possible to see to it that the murderer was convicted and, if possible, executed (even if state laws had to be changed).

Until this morning, everything seemed to be going well. The rehearsal last night, while a bit rough around the edges, seemed finally to point toward success. The family and he had met near Jacksonville Beach, at The Right and Abiding Word in a Weary Land AME-Zion 4th Street Church. Everything seemed to be in place. But then the phone call had come just as Reverend Myers was settling into the cab.

"We can't do it, Reverend." The voice was that of Lazer Simmelwise, grandfather of the slain lamb and the spokesperson (so far) for the family itself.

"What—what did you say?" The Reverend had nearly swallowed the breath mint he had carefully positioned in the back of his mouth (for longer-lasting protection—in case of a need to come in close and stay awhile).

"We just cannot do it. We prayed on it and decided. It ain't Christian to do it." The man's voice had sounded somewhat echoic, as if everything he was saying was being said twice, but gently so—the second rendering mostly a whisper. But the what he was saying was very clear.

"But—but—last night we went over everything and you all were ready to—to knock that racist back where he needs to—"

"We just don't feel that way no more, Reverend—but, thank you for all the prayers an'—"

"Where are you?"

"What?"

"Where are you? Now? Where?"

"Why—back in Ailey."

"What?"

"Ailey. We took the bus. Thanks though for the plane ride and the hotel, but—"

"You're back home? In Georgia? But—but you were supposed to be ready for the Conference—all the news networks are—" The private jet had cost a small fortune and the family had been put up at the most expensive hotel in Duval County. The expenditure would have to be hidden somehow through the next audit. "You're back home?"

"Yes sir, we are. We can't do it, Reverend. We just won't do it."

"But—" And he had heard the line go dead and then the wrecks and the traffic jam had come and the cursing and a feeling of hopelessness like he hadn't felt since the days when nobody had paid him any attention at all—back when he had tried to march with Dr. King.

Watching some wreckers push up against the two tractor-trailers, Reverend Myers called Buster Stonebridge. Although his mind was racing with ideas, one big thing needed doing first. Quickly and completely. Maybe something could be saved.

"Make it special, y'know? Real special. The whole media cover this time. All the way."

"Where they gone?"

"Ailey—back home to Georgia. They've already suffered enough, so make it special."

"What happened?"

"Changed their minds. But we need to forgive and then help. Forgive and help. Like that time in Detroit. Ok?"

"Real special-like. I got it."

"And don't call me for a while."

And the Reverend Myers had settled back in his rented seat and thought of the rehearsal and back before that to the crime itself and about many other things as well. His way to here had been long and multi-faceted indeed. But he knew the way beyond all this. Knew it well. Shutting his eyes, he could almost see the family down around the pulpit. Last night when the previously stamping, yelling, shouting, singing crowd had gone and the church was empty except for them, himself, and Jesse and Buster. Now he could see that there were warning signs aplenty that this time the agreed-upon story would not hold—like the only other time—the girl in Detroit who changed every-thing the closer to trial it came. And then she died and gave up three full months of headline news and money rolling in.

"So you all will come in after I announce you. After I tell what that racist devil did to your baby boy, Cornelius."

"Cesar."

"Pardon?"

"Cesar. His name was Cesar—Cesar Rayshawn."

"Cesar?" Reverend Myers had looked over to Jesse, puzzled at how he had gotten the name wrong, but Jesse and Buster were not paying attention.

"Yeah. His Momma liked how it sounded." The old man had been dressed in a yellowish seersucker suit and had a white stubble of a beard. He was tall and lean with hands like the farmer that he was.

"Well then—Cesar. You will all come in after I tell what that white racist murderer did to your baby boy, Cesar Shawn."

"Rayshawn. Rayshawn. His middle name is Rayshawn. His Granny picked it."

"Ok—Cesar Rayshawn. After I give the facts to the Convention, you all will come out and say a few words about how miserable it is to be proud black people in rural Georgia and how the racist devils are always ready to beat you down or worse—just like they did to Sammy Devon."

"Cesar Rayshawn." The old man's voice was patient, tired-sounding, rough and low. "His name was Cesar Rayshawn. And—" He had looked up at the empty seats of the Church and over at the family who had begun to stir nervously the more the two had talked.

"Yes—yes—sorry—I'm just—just so outraged by it all that I can't keep my thoughts from—"

"An' I don't know about all this." The old man had shook his head and smacked his lips. "The accident and all?" He waved toward the empty seats as if he were including everything from where he stood all the way back home. "I mean, we ain't got to talk about it much, but—"

"What? Accident?"

"Well—yeah—an' what about that Phillips boy being drunk when it all happened? He was drunk, wadn't he? Drunk. Hell, they all was, I heard. In that damn juke-joint over in Mt. Vernon. Drunk. An'—an' Cesar did cut off that boy's ear. Marcus, my other boy, saw it all." He had wiped a rough hand across his mouth and his eyes had filled with tears. "But—Cesar's gone and his Momma's near dead. And—yeah—well—"

"Good. Yes. I think you agree that somebody's got to pay!" The Reverend's voice had been louder than he had intended, and Jesse had jumped a bit, breaking off his whispered conversation with Buster. Buster had moved in closer to Reverend Myers. "We got to have justice here, Mr. Williams. Justice. There can be no hope of forgiveness without justice."

"Collins."

"Collins?"

"Yeah. My name is Collins. Cesar Rayshawn was a Williams, I think. And Marcus is a Billings. I'm sure about that." And a flicker of a smile had almost formed on the old man's face.

"Well now look, Mr. Collins—look—you do want justice for little Cesar, don't you?"

"I do. But—"

"No buts in justice, Mr. Collins—no buts—" And the Reverend had thought about all the missed opportunities, all the times that just hadn't worked out the way he thought they would, stretching from St. Augustine (in 1964 when, still new at the trade, he had managed to avoid anything more dangerous than running out of gas on the way down—in northern Georgia—which gave him time to think and to decide to serve the Cause better back home in California) all the way to just last month in Winston-Salem, North Carolina (where a solid report of an African-American second grader being terrorized by the flying of a Confederate flag had proven to be caused by a family of British visitors flying the Union Jack at a picnic) . But this one looked to be the one big one for sure. The biggest chance of all. "No buts in justice. That racist killed your baby in cold-blood and needs to pay. And those are the hard, cold facts of it, yes sir."

"Oh my baby boy—oh—" Cesar's mother had fainted and the rest had clustered around her. Mr. Collins, however, had bowed his head and sighed.

"Mr. Collins, Mr. Collins," the Reverend had used his best "consoling voice," the one he saved for those times when he was stuck offering condolences to someone he didn't know.

"Will you help me strike a blow against racism tomorrow, Mr. Collins? Will you come with me and stand up for your murdered boy?" Cesar's mother was still on the floor, and several of the younger men in the family were with her, kneeling around her, and murmuring something about "killing" and "back home" but nothing clear enough to really make any sense.

"I—I'm not—yes." He looked over at the boys and the wilted mother. "Yes, we will try." And he had shook his head and walked away from the family, up the side aisle and toward the restrooms.

But next day, today, Conference day—the phone call had come instead and the Reverend was left with nothing much at all.

The traffic was moving again. He called Jesse and told him to cancel the press conference and the special address to the final session. He told him to say that he would try to get there as soon as he freed himself from the accident—that he'd been involved in an accident. He told him to tell them that he was ok, but might not make the session at all, that he was busy helping other survivors. He saw a TV news mobile unit pull up just behind, and he got out to go say a few words about the horror that he was almost a part of. Of the horror he was helping to set right. He tapped on his phone as he walked, and glanced down at a random headline on the screen: **African-American Boy Taunted by Classmates Commits Suicide.** Noting the city and the time-frame, he smiled and waved a friendly hand at the newswoman setting up just over by an empty school-bus in the shade.

A Burning of Ducks

Robert Tillworth thought the young man who had come to visit him in the place they kept telling him was his home was nice enough, but, for some reason, troubling. The room was nice also, with a row of tall windows that looked out onto a deeply green lawn that bordered a smallish lake. The lake seemed to be filled with lily-pads with a clear spot in its very middle. Robert liked the room and liked especially to see the occasional duck that flew in to feed and swim. The young man had shown him something when he first sat down—in the chair opposite—the only two at the big table—the table that was Robert's favorite. The rest of the room was empty—empty of people, that is, Robert suddenly thought—only the furniture, the ping-pong tables and the rest were still there—and the young man, of course. The young man had shown him a badge and a picture of himself behind some smudged plastic. The young man spoke softly and at times seemed familiar. Somehow.

"So you were in St. Augustine, Florida, in the summer of 1964, Mr. Tillworth? Is that correct?" He was tapping on a tablet-looking something that beeped sometimes and seemed also to purr. His eyes were dark brown, and his skin near black, and he seemed to be surprised all the time—wrinkles on his forehead rising up each time he spoke. "Is that right?"

"The ducks don't fly here much no more. I used to see lots of ducks. Back when I first come here. Back then." But he couldn't remember when that was. Not anymore. Everything gone or going away. Some things clear, though. Way back. "Yeah I was there. I was born there, I think. Yeah. And the ducks were all here, I think. Lots of ducks. Y'know?"

And Robert smiled, remembering the ducks.

"Do you remember Marcus Bolles, Mr. Tillworth?" The young man's eyes seemed kindly, eyelids heavy-looking and drooping as the tapping stopped.

"What?" Something was heavy inside, in his head, something not right in there, deep in a darkness he could almost taste as he blinked his eyes and tried to swallow. Something was trying to come clear, free of ducks and lake and the young man's deep brown eyes. But the young man was talking again.

"St. Augustine, Florida? Marcus Bolles?" And the tapping began again for a few seconds—and then stopped. "Do you remember him?"

"Them ducks used to fly in here all the time. All the time." But the heaviness, the darkness was killing off the ducks, one by one just as he tried to remember when he first came here. His son's face came clear. And his daughter's. A long time ago. Surely. He looked at his hands. They were wrinkled. When had that happened? Fear was rising up. In his belly. Like it always used to do. Back somewhere. Marcus? He saw a face, a black face. Marcus. And the ducks too. Flying around Marcus. Flying everywhere. Pretty ducks. The heaviness and the darkness kept growing. Marcus. There too. Among the ducks, flying with them. His face black and his eyes seeming to glow. He was trying to talk. Maybe.

> —*Lord God a-Mighty, Mistah Till'orth. My God my sweet Jesus why you doin' this to me—why?*

The words were flying with the ducks. And his son. The duck's son. And his daughter. The duck's daughter. Surely. And the lake felt good. The water soft. The lily-pads slick and slimy green. Marcus was dead. Long dead. Ripped apart a long, long time ago. "The ducks know Marcus. The ducks know. Marcus was an uppity nigger. The ducks fly everywhere. Everywhere."

"What did you say, Mr. Tillworth? 'Uppity nigger'? Did you say that?" The young man tapped faster and faster. "Did you?"

"What?" He never knew no Marcus. Except for that one. The ducks were loud and getting louder. Ducks everywhere. Flying. Covering the lake. Covering Marcus. He never knew him. Not really. "Uppity nigger. Uppity, mouthy nigger." And the ducks were now out in the room. All around the young man. Quack quacking. Quack quacking. Quack. The pretty ducks. That Marcus was no damn good. And the boys had got him good. Cut him and hung him and burned him. "We got him good, boys—got him good."

"Mr. Tillworth—are you saying that you killed Mr. Bolles? Are you saying that?" The tapping got faster and faster. And some kind of other thing was there on the table. Standing up. A little thing with a blinking red light. He couldn't remember seeing it before.

"What?" The ducks were carrying Marcus away. Flying him back where he belonged. Back to his place. Back in his place. Back there with the ducks. "You staying for lunch, or what?" He thought the young man would enjoy the lunch. Salisbury steak day. Tapioca pudding day. He seemed like a nice young man. Maybe he was hungry. Robert was. Real hungry.

"Mr. Tillworth? Sir?" The young man had stopped tapping and was staring hard at Robert. The ducks were quacking loudly. "Mr. Tillworth?" He shook his head and closed the tablet.

"Do you like tapioca pudding?" Robert could see it in its little red bowl. The ducks didn't like pudding. Maybe Marcus did. Who knows? The young man was leaving. Ducks everywhere. Marcus too. Going with him. Leaving Robert alone. Alone. Marcus free and burning in the swamp. Burning all alone. Without a single duck.

Lunchtime!

Acknowledgments

The acknowledgments in my previous book of short fiction pretty much used up the people near and far who needed to be immediately thanked. Of course, I am sure that some were left out, but I want them to know that I am grateful for their help nevertheless and will make up for my forgetfulness in future books.

As for this book, I would like once more to note that I remain in debt to Chris Brincefield for his excellent editing services. The stories owe much to his careful eye and most especially to his patience. My wife, Kathleen, needs special mention as a most talented editor and sensitive reader and someone who deserves an award for slogging through all these stories numerous times without losing her sense of humor. Other people: a sixth-grader named Highsmith of Arlington, Florida, for saving me back in the third grade from a mob intent on inflicting much pain and injury for some reason I now cannot remember (all I can clearly remember—apart from Highsmith's heroic and timely actions— was being dragged by my heels down Chaseville Road from the Arlington Elementary School to a place not far from the post office. Ah, those golden days of carefree youth!). I also want to thank Father John F. Lima for his careful attention to my religious upbringing and his refusal to give up on me when I began to roam and ramble. Thanks to my Brother R. Wayne Fortuna for his encouragement and willingness to read, comment and most especially listen (no small matter and something sorely needed during the process of gathering together this collection). For his wife, Debbie, a class act who only gets classier with each passing year. For Carolyn Fortuna whose superb talents as illustrator are amply displayed in this, her second, cover. Lastly, I want to thank the good people of Duval County, Florida—Family, Friends, and Foes—who gave me and continue to give me more than they will ever know—and to them this book is dedicated.

About James L. Fortuna, Jr.

James Fortuna, Jr., a seventy-one-year-old still fleet enough of foot to avoid becoming a passenger on "time's winged chariot" or a more than occasional landing pad for flies, currently teaches English and Holocaust Studies at a community college filled with enough characters (himself included) to keep a satirist in business for at least ten more years. He has worked at various other jobs and has had various other experiences in various places over the course of a lifetime that incudes being thrown out of a pretty decent university's creative writing program, becoming homeless after a civil rights disagreement with an unnamed college in the Shallow (as opposed to the Deep) South, being hugged by Lyndon B. Johnson, becoming tangled in the Alabama state flag in Governor George Wallace's office, and trying to establish a homeless shelter on a not very welcoming New Age commune. He also plays at the five-string banjo and is living in nearly perfect peace with a wife who approaches sainthood by the simple fact of putting up with more nonsense than any human being should ever be subjected to. And he apparently is reckless enough to end a sentence now and then with a preposition.